HE LAY QUIETLY
BESIDE HER

As Luke stared up at the ceiling, he gradually became aware of the mural covering the whole expanse above their heads, a strange and lonely vista of a pockmarked, gray, rocky landscape.

"That's the surface of the moon?" he asked, pointing upward.

Jessie laughed self-consciously. "Yes. The moon got me through the worst times. There's no gravity there. It comforted me that there was still someplace where I could dance, and if dancing wasn't impossible for me, then nothing was. I used to look up and go to sleep, moon-dancing."

"Oh, Jess," Luke whispered, enfolding her in his arms so hard that he startled her. "Jessie, I love you. I have since I first saw you. And if I could, I would draw down the moon and dance with you in my arms—tonight and always."

ABOUT THE AUTHOR

Vancouver writer Bobby Hutchinson became
interested in the lives of the "differently abled"
while posing for a Harlequin publicity picture.
Bobby was struck at the time by a studio portrait
she saw of a woman in a wheelchair, surrounded
by her children and husband. An introduction was
arranged, and Bobby and the stranger became fast
friends as they worked together on a book about
childbirth and handicapped women. Inspired by
their friendship, Bobby decided to write her third
Superromance about this very special group.

Books by Bobby Hutchinson

HARLEQUIN SUPERROMANCE
166–SHELTERING BRIDGES
229–MEETING PLACE

HARLEQUIN AMERICAN ROMANCE
147–WHEREVER YOU GO
173–WELCOME THE MORNING

Bobby Hutchinson

DRAW DOWN THE MOON

Harlequin Books

TORONTO • NEW YORK • LONDON
AMSTERDAM • PARIS • SYDNEY • HAMBURG
STOCKHOLM • ATHENS • TOKYO • MILAN

Published March 1987

First printing January 1987

ISBN 0-373-70253-1

Printed in Canada

Dedicated to my friends on wheels,
Judy Norbury, Brenda Glaubitz and Lori Bremner,
for sharing their experiences with me.
Thank you to my favorite radio announcer,
Casey White.

CHAPTER ONE

THE UNIVERSE WAS limited to the sounds of his Adidas runners hitting hard pavement, the echo of tortured breathing rattling in lungs that ached and burned and the vacant spreading numbness that had crept over his body and mind at the twenty-fifth mile.

Luke Chadwick thought in one-word images, primitive words.

Hurt.

Run.

The term marathon no longer mattered. At mile twenty-two Luke had experienced the nemesis of long-distance runners, the invisible devastating wall where the body's supplies of energy are gone, when each step is an agony of mind over matter, where the mind played tricks on the body.

Stop, it prompted.

Why? it demanded.

It was indicative of Luke's physical strength and mental stubbornness that he continued to run at all after the wall's violent onslaught of muscle cramps, disorientation and nausea.

Now, finally, he was at the bottom of the hill leading to the finish line, the final quarter mile. It was all uphill, where the wide, crowd-lined street led to the triumphant red-and-white banner, the merciful end of three hours and twenty-two minutes and the token presentation of a monogrammed T-shirt to the triumphant runner.

Run, Luke.

Finish what you started.

Finish, put one foot after the other.

The pavement angled up at an impossible grade, and his calf muscles sent agonizing cramps into his buttocks beneath the brief red nylon shorts. He concentrated on his feet, head down.

Luke was halfway up the hill.

"Lookin' good," some liar in the crowd encouraged.

"Nearly there," another optimist yelled.

Luke glanced up, and then he saw the wheelchair.

It was a few yards ahead of him, also halfway up the killer slope. For the first time in what seemed like hours, his attention was captured by something outside the pain in his own body.

The woman in the chair had a bright blue ribbon tied jauntily around a thick white-blond braid hanging low on her slender neck. Luke agonizingly increased his speed a fraction, drawing closer to the armless vehicle. The woman's delicate profile took shape, and horror and an overwhelming pity penetrated the dulled edges of Luke's mind.

She groaned aloud with each revolution her arms made turning the wheels of her chair. Her body was trembling violently, her face a fiery, sweating red mask, features contorted into an inhuman grimace as she fought the incline. Her slender arms were long, and her upper biceps flexed in startling outline as her gloved hands wrestled with the wheels. She wore a shiny, electric-blue runner's singlet, and her long spare legs were defiantly bare in matching shorts. Her ankles were strapped together to hold them securely on the footrest.

Incongruously, she had blue Adidas runners on her narrow feet, the same brand Luke was wearing. Hers, however, were pristinely unmarked, aligned side by side in decorative irony as her arms propelled her.

The hurting, sobbing, low sounds she made tore lesions in Luke's soul. She seemed so female, so vulnerable, with her pretty blue ribbon.

He forgot why he was forcing himself up the hill, pushing the limits of human endurance. The bystanders and their cheers became only a buzzing annoyance, as if they were far away. He forgot the marathon, the months of training, the few yards he had left to cover in order to accomplish what he'd worked toward for so long. His actions were instinctive. He did what any strong, compassionate man with full use of his limbs would do when confronted with a disabled woman in acute distress.

Luke Chadwick grasped the back of Jessie Langstrom-Smith's wheelchair, and with the last shreds of reserved energy, he pushed her up what remained of the hill, thereby disqualifying them both from the Vancouver International Marathon. Less than a hundred yards remained of a grueling twenty-six mile, three-hundred-and-eighty-five-yard endurance feat.

WORDS, AND THEIR MYRIAD USES, were part of Jessie's profession, yet for the first time in years, she found herself speechless. The force that propelled her from behind and drove her up and over the crest of the hill also carried her past the banner gaily proclaiming Finish Line.

Numbly she registered the astonished horror and then the pity on the faces of the authorities.

"Sorry, lady, it's not your fault, but rules are rules."

"Disqualified."

Still, Jessie found it impossible to fully comprehend what had happened to her. Her chair slowed, stopped. She tipped her head back to gaze up at the panting man in the brief red running shorts who'd just destroyed the dreams of an entire year.

His hair was thick and black, wet with sweat, curly. There were traces of gray at his temples, a few lines on his forehead. He looked older than her—perhaps—a young forty?

His deep-set eyes were a startling shade of almost turquoise blue below his red headband. His broad chest heaved with the effort of recovering his breath.

Jessie gaped up at him, oblivious to the sympathetic remarks of the crowd or the officials, unable to gather her wits enough to even rage. She heard herself ask, "Why?" and her voice was husky, mildly curious.

"Why?" she repeated reasonably. "Why did you do it? We were both nearly at the finish line."

He shook his head, frowning in embarrassed confusion, but before he could answer, Cy descended upon him like an aging, angry mastiff, striding protectively to the side of Jessie's chair.

Cy was her friend, and he was outraged by what had just occurred. He was panting from his climb up the hill, and his worn jeans had a clumsy patch below one knee. His blue flannel shirt was obviously for comfort, not fashion. The brown cardigan that topped the outfit had seen better days. Dr. Cyrus Grant held firmly to the belief that clothes didn't make the man.

Cy's voice erupted in rumbling fury. "How could you do such a thing? You ruined her race!"

Jessie knew he'd been waiting anxiously for her at the bottom of the hill. She'd heard his familiar voice cheering her on in ecstatic triumph as she used her will to propel the chair and herself those last few impossible yards.

"Nearly there, Jess..."

Nearly...there...almost...home...

She'd been using the words like a mantra with each revolution, dredging up reserves of sheer nerve to compensate for the lack of strength in her shivering arms.

Nearly there...

"We oughta have you arrested, you bloody idiot." Cy's anger was reaching formidable proportions.

She'd known she could make it. For the first time she'd been positive she would actually make it to the finish line, back there on the hill.

Before—she broke off the thought and focused her vision on the man standing silently, enduring Cy's ranting with impassive stoicism.

"You need a mental examination." Jessie's housemate was berating the much younger man. "Damned if I don't feel like punching you in the snot, you cretin!"

Cyrus's rumbling, threatening tone forced her attention back to the scene erupting just above her head. At sixty-one, Cyrus Grant was just too mature to engage in fistfights over her. Jessie tugged at his old brown sweater to distract him, and finally, with a last humph of disgust at the stranger, he gave her his attention.

"Cy, I'm cold. I want to go home."

It was the truth. The cool May air was full of moisture, the gray sky, which had threatened rain all that endless morning, began to spit on cue.

Jessie shivered, and her aging knight hurriedly tucked a flannelette blanket warmly around her.

"Let's go," she insisted again.

What was there left to do except go home? Nothing could change what had happened. Time never reversed itself for if onlys. Jessie had learned that lesson unforgettably well in her thirty-two years of living.

Cy stepped behind her chair to wheel her away.

Suddenly Jessie found herself staring into crystal-blue eyes, the sides of her chair caught and held by muscular bare arms. The stranger was crouching in front of her, his eyes level with hers.

"I want you to know I'm sorry, and I do apologize. It won't correct what I've done..."

The words were rumbling and intense, directed only to her despite Cy's snort of derision and his furious orders from behind her. "Damned right it won't. Now get out of the way."

"Wait a minute, Cy." Jessie glanced down at the brawny arms on either side of her body. Rain was mixing with sweat, and the thick black hair on his forearms was flattened into curly whorls. He was smoothly muscled, extremely big and macho-looking and roughly handsome. Arched black brows punctuated the deep-set blue eyes, and anxious lines fanned out from their edges as he frowned at her. His mouth was wide, narrow lipped beneath a trim black mustache. A deep cleft divided his strong chin, and for one mad moment Jessie considered putting the tip of her baby finger lightly into the crevice, just to see if it would fit.

Low blood sugar, she told herself with disgust. That's what was making her crazy. She should scream creative oaths at this maniac, unleash the frustration and anger she ought to feel at what he'd done to her race. Instead, here she was admiring the dimple in his chin.

"I'm sorry," he went on, and she had to admire his dignity, crouching there in full view of a curious and hostile audience, making his apologies as if she and he were entirely alone in the world. Race officials and onlookers were staring openly.

"My name is Luke Chadwick. I'll make this up to you somehow."

With those words Jessie quite suddenly reached the end of her patience. With a quick turn of her wheels, she backed the chair, nearly running over Cy.

"Forget it, mister. There's not a thing I need or want from you except a promise that you'll stay out of my way from now on." Her words were tough, but weariness and disappointment made them less effective than she'd intended.

Cy maneuvered her deftly through the crowd, making a path to her silver van, which was parked on a side street. For once she didn't object to his help as he activated the lift and placed her chair in position. As the mechanism slowly elevated her into the van's interior, she glanced over the heads of the dispersing crowd and saw Luke Chadwick, standing a short distance away, staring intently at her. Then her chair was inside, and Cyrus slammed the sliding doors behind her.

5156 MIKE KILO.

Luke swiftly memorized the license plate number of the silver van as it pulled into traffic. He still had friends on the force, even though he'd been out for eight years now. Rod was on traffic detail. He'd run the number through the computer for her name and address.

Finding her again would be no problem at all. The problem was going to be living with himself, knowing he'd destroyed her dream. A wheelchair runner, he reflected dismally. If he was going to flip out and wreck somebody's race, why the hell did it have to be a woman with the face of an angel and a broken body?

Nice going, Luke.

The old guy with her was right. You need psychiatric help. Again. Just like when you had to leave the force.

Self-disgust welled up in him, and the soul-deep weariness he thought he'd overcome long ago dogged him like a hangover all the way back to the race area where he'd left his sports bag.

A sardonic half smile twisted his mouth as he again recalled the feisty old man with the mane of faded ginger hair. His other suggestion was more Luke's own style of handling matters. "I should punch you right in the snot," he'd threatened.

Luke almost wished he had. Even a broken nose would be easier to bear than this overwhelming sense of shame and humiliation. Why, why, had he done such a stupid thing?

He saw his twin sister, Lorna, and her husband, Denny, hurrying his way with all three of his small nephews in tow, and he groaned aloud. Now he'd have to explain to them how he'd managed to get disqualified from the marathon.

"Unca Luke, show us your T-shirt, show us your marathon shirt you got, Uncle Luke." Robbie, the three-year-old baby of the family, locked his arms around his uncle's bare knees. The other two boys each grabbed an arm and hopped up and down in frenzied excitement.

"Did you win, Uncle Luke? Daddy said you wouldn't win, but you did, didn't you?"

Luke gripped the small, trusting hands, feeling rotten at having to puncture their confidence in him.

For a day that had begun with a bang—the starter's gun—at the crack of dawn—this one was threatening to end with a whimper.

"Well, jock, how'd ya do? Was it worth giving up cigarettes for?" Denny demanded exuberantly, and Luke slowly drew in a weary breath and released it before he began to try to explain how, and what, he'd done.

JESSIE HAD a blissfully hot bath, a peanut butter-and-banana sandwich washed down with a quart of milk and then she slept for the remainder of the afternoon.

For the first time in years, she dreamed she was dancing again.

The music filled her, urging response, and she felt the rock-hard ballerina's muscles in her thighs and calves pull and flex as she twirled, flirting playfully with her lithely attractive partner, sliding away with tiny, mincing steps as he reached for her, counting the bars, plotting the exact moment, the soaring instant in the musical score, when she would allow his powerful arms to catch her in midleap, anticipating the way her body would soar, weightless, as he lifted her effortlessly in the elaborate pattern of the ballet.

She rose, en pointe, like a bird about to take flight, legs tensing for the combination...

The telephone shrilled and shrilled again. Dazedly she awakened, unsure which world was real.

Like a thunderous weight, the heavy realization of herself and her limitations descended, and she felt the wrenching pain of comprehension twist inside her.

She was no longer Jessica Langstrom-Smith, prima ballerina.

It had been years since she'd dreamed of her other self, years since this instant of waking awareness made her clench her fists and long to return to the dream.

Why now?

She grasped the phone from the bedside table and held the receiver to her ear.

"Hello?" Her waking voice was gravelly, and she cleared her throat and said again, "Hello?"

"Jessica, we've just walked in the door, how was the marathon, dear? What was your time? You finished under the four-hour limit, of course? I wish we could have been there, but this trip was planned for months—"

Before Jessie could respond to her mother's rapid-fire questions, her father's quiet voice interceded.

"I'm on the extension, Chandra," he said to his wife. "Are you all right, Jess? No strained muscles or anything?"

Jessie's mouth twisted into a rueful grin. How like her father to worry about how she was while her mother concentrated only on performance, success, competition. To Chandra, it wasn't at all how you played the game. It was whether or not you won.

Jessie chose to answer her father first.

"I'm a bit stiff, but yes, Dad, I'm fine. However..." Might as well get the bad news over with, she thought. Succinctly Jessie outlined the disastrous ending of her marathon, shutting her eyes tightly and biting her lip as her mother exploded with predictable horror and outrage. And disappointment in her daughter, of course.

"There wasn't anything I could do about it, Mother," Jessie finally managed to insert. "Yes, he told me his name. It was Chadwick, Luke Chadwick. No, I didn't ask for ID because I never want to see him again."

"Arthur," Chandra challenged her husband, "there simply must be something you can do about this." It took numerous and detailed assurances from him that what had happened wasn't a matter the courts would consider a suable offense. Finally, Chandra subsided enough for Jessie's father to ask gently, "D'you want us to come over and take you out somewhere for dinner, cheer you up a bit, Jess?"

Before she could answer, Jessie heard her mother say in an exasperated voice, "Arthur, you know we're expected at the Richardson's."

Hastily Jessie got her father off the hook. "Cy's cooking for me tonight. Thanks, anyhow. Have a good time at your dinner."

She sank back into her pillows after she'd finally hung up the receiver, staring blankly up at the mural of the moon she'd had papered to the ceiling of her bedroom. The silvery, pockmarked surface was endearingly familiar to her, the vista of planets and stars in an endless velvet sky comforting in its vastness.

"The more things change, the more they stay the same," she muttered wearily up at it.

Her mother went on being disappointed in her, her father went on loving her. Jessie believed she'd long ago come to terms mentally and emotionally with the situation, but at times—like right now—Chandra still managed to make her feel ineffectual, guilty, inadequate, a failure in her role as daughter to a beautiful, accomplished woman and much less than successful as a thirty-two-year-old adult.

"Hey, in there." The thump on the door and Cy's cheery bass tones interrupted her bleak reverie.

"Dinner's nearly ready. How about moving your bones out here, woman? I'm starving."

Thank God for eccentric housemates. Cyrus Grant had rented the self-contained upstairs apartment only a week after Jessie had bought the house five years ago. He'd told her after they became friends that his childless marriage had ended years before and that one day shortly thereafter he'd suddenly realized he'd never done any of the things he'd always dreamed of doing.

"I turned the practice over to a younger man, sold the house I'd been a slave to for years and went off to live in India for a while. I got tired of the crowds there, however, and decided to come back here until I decided what to do next."

He was still deciding, and their friendship had flourished from the beginning.

"Coming, Cy. Hold your horses," she called, using one of his favorite expressions. With an ease and grace resulting from years of practice, she transferred from the bed to her chair, hurried into the adjoining bathroom and began her feminine grooming ritual, giving extra attention to the faint traces of blush and touches of eye and lip color she used on the unusually pale and slightly drawn countenance in the mirror. She was absolutely determined that the dinner celebration they'd planned so optimistically would be a cheerful occasion.

Wakes were determinedly cheerful, weren't they?

"Smells like pizza," she commented appreciatively as she rolled into the bright open area of her kitchen-living room. It was decorated with gay posters and white wicker furniture strewn with rainbow-shaded cushions.

Cy had an oversize towel tucked into the front of his comfortably sagging jeans, and he was using another towel to precariously rescue huge rounds of bake-it-yourself pizza from the low wall oven. On the central work island—custom-built like everything on this level of the house so that it exactly suited Jessie in her chair—was a glass bowl and salad fixings, and Jessie wheeled over to finish chopping the onion and celery.

Cy glanced over at her, noting her resolute smile and purposefully uptilted chin.

"Of course it smells like pizza. You oughta be damned grateful I bought it instead of trying to make it from scratch."

Jessie's smile became more natural as she silently reviewed a few of Cy's past culinary disasters.

"And don't play the martyr with me, either," he ordered sternly, dumping the pizza abruptly on the island and blowing on his burned fingers. "Don't try pretending that race today doesn't matter. I've been around while you trained for this idiotic performance, listened to you moan about sore arms and early-morning runs and inconsiderate cars and Gatorade. Go ahead and get it all out of your sys-

tem. Hell, I'm used to your rotten artistic temperament, remember? So feel free to rant and rave and gnash your teeth
in style. Anybody would after what happened on that hill.''

Cyrus beetled his heavy ginger eyebrows at her in a per-
ceptive glare. ''That your mother on the phone just then?''

Jessie shot the chair across the floor, stopping it with a
flourish inches from the table, thumping the completed
salad down on the yellow cloth. There was no fooling old
friends, after all.

''Yup, that was Mother, all right. She wants our hero, Mr.
Chadwick, sued for everything he owns, then drawn and
quartered and hung out to dry on her lampposts at a convenient time. Preferably after her dinner engagement this
evening.''

Cy gave a rumbling snort of acknowledgment. He knew
Chandra well.

''For the first time since meeting the lady, I have to agree
with her. Apart from that, how're you feeling, Jess?''

''Stiff. Sore. Hungry. Mad. I thought you said dinner was
ready.''

Throughout the simple, hearty meal that followed, they
kept the conversation light and general, touching on a play
Cy had attended at the university theater the week before
and a new science fiction novel Jessie had recently read.

The round butcher-block table was set in an alcove of the
kitchen that had been a sun-room at some stage in the old
house's evolution, Jessie guessed. Three walls were half
glass, overlooking the large but sadly neglected back garden. Rain pattered dismally on the windows through the
late-afternoon grayness, but inside, the soft light and Jessie's flowering plant pots on the low windowsills made the
room seem cozy and welcoming.

Cy opened a bottle of fine white wine, and Jessie sipped
appreciatively.

"Were you going to waste—" she hesitated and hastily checked the label "—Château Gourgizad on me regardless, or is this a sop to my injured ego?"

"I'd planned on hootch, to tell the truth," Cy admitted teasingly. He raised his glass in a toast. "Here's to next year, girl. Although I hope you come to your senses before then and take up knitting or something equally productive. Too much exercise just has to be bad for your health, I'd say." Cy pretended to denounce exercise, although he rode a ten-speed bike all over the city. "There'll be another marathon next year."

Next year. Would she find the resources in herself to go through the months of training necessary to try the marathon again? It was doubtful, Jessie decided, sipping her wine thoughtfully. Training was fine when it was a job, as ballet had been, but as a leisure activity, marathoning ate up too much of her time, demanded too much energy in a life already full to the brim.

"What made you decide to take on such a damn fool venture in the first place?" Cy demanded curiously, sliding another slice of pepperoni pizza free of its aluminum backing before he devoured half of it in one huge bite. "I don't think you ever really explained it to me, Jessie."

"It was the wind, I think," she said thoughtfully, toying with her own slice. "Wanting to feel the wind in my face, that sensation of moving through the air quickly, under my own steam, creating it, controlling it. I got hooked on running track, and even though you'd never know it, I'm compulsive. And a tiny bit competitive. So I naturally went from one mile to five miles to twenty."

Cy gave her a look and shook his head. "I always said it's a good thing you never took up drinking," he commented dryly, and Jessie laughed, the first time that day.

Cy. He was her friend, and as he did with a dozen or so other young women, he often played the part of her therapist.

During the past four months he'd devoted countless hours to helping her develop the exercise routines necessary for increasing her upper body strength and her stamina, enough to make those twenty-six miles she'd faced today a physical possibility.

"How come you never asked me before why I wanted to? You grumbled and grizzled a lot about fanatical nonsense, but you never questioned me about the marathon."

Without his help she might never have attempted the race. Although he'd never admit it, she knew Cy's disappointment today was just as intense as her own.

"It made you happy, Jess," he said simply. "I figure if something's making you happy, don't mess with whys and wherefores."

They had pecan ice cream with chocolate sauce for dessert, a favorite of Jessie's. She motioned to the quantities of pizza left over.

"There's enough of this left for an army, and I go back to work tomorrow afternoon, so there'll be nobody around to eat it. Take it upstairs with you and have it for breakfast," Jessie urged. "I've heard you hungry university students will eat anything."

Cy shuddered. "Not all of us have stomachs made of cast iron," he said sternly. "Thanks, anyhow, but I'll stick with bran flakes and an orange."

"Isn't your semester nearly over?"

Cy nodded. "I'm trying to get signed on to help crew on a boat heading for Australia next fall. This academic life is great, but I don't want to get stagnant. Besides, my education is fairly well-rounded by now. I've done photography,

Eastern religion, Canadian history and introduction to computers. Among other things," he mused thoughtfully.

"Maybe you ought to stay in Vancouver and take kung fu," Jessie suggested tartly. "Didn't I hear you threaten to punch that guy in the nose today? Honestly, Cy. He looked pretty tough to me."

He'd looked more than just tough. Luke Chadwick had an air of physical competence about him, as if he used his muscularly compact body for more than just running marathons. For some reason Jessie remembered his hands best. They were large, wide hands, long fingered, with tendons and veins showing prominently across the backs. Stained and weather-beaten. Nails trimmed short. His were a workingman's hands, she decided. For a moment the image of Luke's hands on her chair, his blue gaze drilling into her, flashed into her mind, and she shivered. The man had an intense physical presence, a nebulous air about him that was hard to define but difficult to dismiss.

Cy was studying her with an intent, troubled expression.

Damn. She'd done exactly what she'd vowed to avoid at this dinner—raise the subject of infamous Luke Chadwick again.

"It was a rotten break, Jess," Cy stated quietly. "You had the thing beaten. At least you know you can do it now, you've gained confidence in your physical ability. That's something."

It was, a big something. Still . . .

"I wanted the damn T-shirt and the certificate that said I did it," she proclaimed passionately, smashing a fist down on the sturdy tabletop. "I almost tipped over half a dozen times, transferring from sidewalks to paved roads, and some of the potholes were so deep I thought the wheel on my chair was a goner. The wind in the park nearly froze my face. I cramped. . . ."

Jessie's voice trailed off, and her fist unclenched. Like so much else in life, the marathon experience was intensely personal. She'd pitted herself against time and distance, and that experience was hers forever. Luke Chadwick's inexplicable actions didn't alter that in the slightest.

She looked across at him and shrugged dismissively. "You always say nothing happens in life without a reason, but I sure don't see much sense in this one." In a determined effort at lightness, she added, "Now, delicate as I am, do I still have to do dishes just because you cooked? Baking store-bought pizza isn't the same as concocting a meal from scratch, you know."

"I cooked, you clean," Cy declared autocratically. "The rule was your idea in the beginning, after all." He poured them each a cup of coffee.

"You going to do a program on marathons, Jess?"

She'd planned to do exactly that during the optimistic weeks of training. Her radio show was constantly hungry for new subjects, and Cy often helped her with ideas.

"I was, Cy," she admitted. "Now I'm not so sure. It's going to be tough enough explaining what happened to all the people at the station without including a listening audience, as well. Besides, I've lost my enthusiasm."

Cy got up and plunked his coffee mug on the counter.

"If I know you, you'll have your enthusiasm back with interest by tomorrow morning. You're just physically drained today, Jess. Matter of fact, I don't feel so spry myself, and I've got reading to do for tomorrow's psych class. Jokes aside, you want me to help here before I go up?"

"God forbid dishes should interfere with Freud. Besides, you must be due for some phone calls. It's a whole hour since one of your harem dialed your number. Isn't it tiring having all these women chasing you? Who's the new one that came to the door the other day—Maryanne somebody?''

"Maryanne, yes, well, she's madly in love with her husband, but they fight a lot, and then she comes to me for advice. Strictly platonic, Jess."

At first the steady stream of female visitors and callers had alarmed and puzzled Jessie. Just exactly what was her aging tenant up to? she wondered. But as she'd gotten to know him, Jessie had realized that Cy attracted women of all ages, and although he loved to pretend otherwise, the reason wasn't sexual. It was simply because he listened to them, with an insatiable but sincere interest in their lives and problems, and then did his imaginative best to help in any way he could.

Just as he did with her.

With a roguish grin he said, "It's my body. They can't resist me. I'm off, then, before you have a chance to change your mind about the dishes. Night, Jess. Sleep well."

She heard his footsteps climbing the wide stairs, the soft closing of the door at the top that effectively separated his living area from her own.

She glanced at the winding stairs leading to the upper level and lifted an eyebrow sardonically. Those stairs and her chair were what effectively separated the living areas when it came right down to it.

She began clearing up.

She really didn't mind doing it at all, she mused, but of course she'd never admit that to Cy. There was a deep feminine satisfaction in putting her own kitchen to rights and a fierce pride in being able to do it all from a wheelchair.

The telephone rang again as she was rinsing off the cookie sheets Cy had used under the pizza, and she groaned aloud. It was probably one of the other announcers from the station, wondering how her race had gone. How many times

today would she be forced to go over the ignominious ending of that damn marathon?

But she relaxed as soon as she recognized the caller's
cheery voice.

"Kathleen. Oh, I'm so glad it's you," she exclaimed, and
this time it was cathartic to pour out the woeful saga of the
day. The spritely redhead on the other end of the line was the
only person Jessie knew who would fully understand all the
facets of the day's frustration because Kathleen, too, was in
a wheelchair. She also happened to be Jessie's closest
woman friend.

A smile lingered on Jessie's features as she slowly hung up
the receiver ten minutes later. Trust Kathleen to put the
whole thing into perspective.

"Next time," her friend had instructed succinctly, "pack
a can of Mace to use on misguided heroes."

For the next half hour Jessie glided quietly and smoothly
around her gleaming kitchen, hands deftly performing the
necessary chores. It seemed that wherever her random
thoughts began, they ended by stubbornly returning to a
black-haired, blue-eyed man saying, "Look, I'm sorry. I'll
make it up to you."

Finally, Jessie slammed the door shut on the dishwasher
with much more force than necessary.

"Just exactly how are you going to go about that, Mr.
Chadwick?" she demanded of the empty kitchen.

CHAPTER TWO

WHAT COULD HE DO to apologize to her?

Luke asked himself the question repeatedly over the next several days, and whenever he wasn't asking himself, it seemed Denny was doing it for him.

"Found out yet who she is, Luke?"

They were having a coffee break, perched on bundles of concrete tile soon to become a winding driveway leading up to an imposing mansion in Shaugnessey—the latest in a lucky string of lucrative contracts their company had captured over the past months in this elite area of Vancouver.

"Yup." Luke poured muddy coffee into his thermos cup and squinted up at the sun, knowing his reticence was driving Denny nuts.

"Jeez, Luke. Don't pull that strong silent act on me. This is your partner, your brother-in-law here, the father of your nephews, for cripes' sake. So talk."

Luke watched longingly as Denny tipped a cigarette out of a crumpled package, lit up and inhaled long and slowly, an expectant look on his appealingly homely face. Giving up smoking had been his original reason for starting to run, and apart from great calf muscles, where had running gotten him?

"Why couldn't Lorna have fallen for the strong silent type?" Luke mourned, inhaling the secondhand blast of Denny's smoke greedily and wondering, as he always did at 10:00 a.m. over coffee, if good lungs were worth the sacrifice. Certainly that ill-fated marathon had been reason enough to give up exercise and return to smoking.

"Strong, I am," Denny was saying modestly. "But silent, I ain't. Us Wops never are, that's why we're such great lovers. So make with the words, Luke. Who was she, what did this Rod guy find out about her? Surely those fancy computers the RCMP use these days are good for something?"

"Rod checked the RO." Denny's puzzled expression cleared when Luke explained, "Registered owner, through the motor vehicle department. Surname, Langstrom-Smith, hyphenated. Given one, Jessica, given two, Marie. Address, 3990 West 6th Avenue."

"Married?" Denny took another deep pull on his cigarette.

"Dunno. The RO report doesn't go into detail." Luke remembered the older man with his hand possessively on her shoulder. Father? Husband?

Not husband, something told him. There'd been an innocence about her.

"People like her wouldn't be married, I don't suppose," Denny commented thoughtfully. "Unless they were already married before it happened, of course. But afterward, hell, spending your life in a wheelchair, what chance would you have for something like marriage? It's tough enough when you're both normal. Not that you'd know anything about it," he ribbed. "Seems to me you've become a dedicated bachelor these last coupla years." He tossed the remainder of his coffee into the shrubbery. "Guess if a guy goes past a certain age, it gets harder to take the leap. Me, now, I like bein' married, having a wife and kids and a mortgage." He stretched and stood up.

"C'mon, let's get back to work, this lawyer's probably got us on some kind of time-and-motion study. You know what these wealthy guys are like. So what're you gonna do about it, Luke? Gonna go see this Jessica Marie Langstrom-Smith?''

LUKE DREW UP in front of 3990 West 6th at eight that evening. His throat was dry, and he slowly unclenched the hand gripping the steering wheel like a lifeline.

He was scared, no question about it. But if he wanted a good night's sleep ever again, he knew he'd better get on with this. He'd been awake this morning before 4:00 a.m. with her image still vivid from dreams.

The sidewalk was wide, with no steps up to the red painted door. For the wheelchair, of course, Luke realized.

He buzzed the doorbell and waited. Nothing. He buzzed again, longer this time. Nobody home.

He was about to retreat, feeling both let down and immensely relieved, when the old man who'd snarled "I should punch you in the snot" strode briskly up behind him, pushing a ten-speed bicycle. He wore old khaki shorts, and his legs were still well shaped and muscular, Luke noticed.

"You're lucky she's not home," he greeted Luke dourly. "She's liable to meet you at the door with a shotgun. What are you doing here, anyway?" he demanded suspiciously, beetling his heavy eyebrows and narrowing his eyes. "How'd you find out her address? I'm warning you, mister, I don't take kindly to anybody who'd do what you did to Jessie. I'd suggest you clear out of here before I call the cops and tell them I caught you trying to break and enter the house."

His bulldog expression and his protectiveness endeared him to Luke despite the threat. He was a wonderfully feisty old guy.

Wordlessly Luke extracted his wallet from the hip pocket of his clean jeans and drew out a white card with a green border, carefully heat sealed inside tough plastic. Skeptically the old man took it.

The RCMP coat of arms was displayed prominently at the top, the majestic crown over the buffalo head. He read, "This is to certify that Luke Chadwick has retired and is a life member of all RCMP sergeant's messes."

Luke held out a second card, his photo driver's license ID this time. Cy thawed slightly at the introduction.

"Retired member of the force, huh? A nephew of mine is a constable, stationed in Yellowknife. Kinda young to be retired, aren't you? How old are you, anyway?"

"Thirty-eight." Luke carefully kept his voice and expression neutral. This geezer was nobody's fool. "I wanted to go into business with my brother-in-law, landscape gardening, so I got out some years back. What's your nephew's name? One of the guys I know is sergeant up in Yellowknife, big guy named Norman Claire."

A little more of the older man's animosity faded. "Yeah, that's him, all right. Heard Kenny mention the name last Christmas. He's my sister's kid, Kenneth Turner." The faded blue eyes assessed Luke. "Maybe you better come upstairs. I need a beer, and you need to explain a few things. Like why the hell an ex-sergeant would pull a stunt like that one you pulled last Sunday. And why you're hanging around now looking for Jess." He turned his back and strode around the side of the house, seeming sure that Luke would follow. Leaning his bike against the house, he led the way up a winding outside staircase, unlocked the door and muttered testily, "Come in, come in," when Luke hesitated in the tiny entrance hall.

The apartment was homey and comfortable, with a definite bachelor flavor. There were dishes stacked in the sink, and a bicycle wheel and spokes were spread across newspaper in the middle of the combination kitchen-living room.

Books were strewn everywhere, spilling out of rough brick-and-board shelves and filling the room like colorful ornaments. Several closed doors led off the main room, and wide windows afforded a view out over the rooftops to the ocean. They were thrown wide open, and the sea-scented air wafted through the room.

Luke walked over and gazed out.

"Wish my apartment had this," he admired. "I'm down in the West End, living in a closet, and instead of the ocean, I get a view of an alley. You're a fortunate man, Mr...?"

The ploy didn't fool the older man, but it worked anyhow.

"Cyrus Grant. And my ex-wife was about the only one who called me Cyrus all the time. She and I finally decided we'd never get along, so we divided years ago. She was a hard woman, that's why I prefer Cy. D'you want a beer? I make it myself."

They were seated on the fuzzy blue sofa sipping foam-topped mugs of dark ale when Cy demanded simply, "Okay, now explain."

Luke met the other man's astute eyes and held his gaze. "Grabbing the wheelchair and pushing it up the hill? I can't explain what made me do that. I've tried, but I can't. No excuses, except that I was pretty light-headed. That was the first marathon I'd ever attempted, and it's going to be the last, believe me." Luke felt the flush of humiliation all over again, and he caught Cy studying his expression carefully, as if searching for more than what the words implied. It suddenly made Luke unreasonably angry. Did Cy think he was lying? What right did the guy have to give him the third degree, anyway?

"Are you related to her?" Luke suddenly demanded belligerently.

Cy slowly moved his head from one side to the other.
"Nope. She's my landlady, technically." He paused a second and added softly, "As well as one of my best friends
and the only woman I'd marry if I was thirty years younger. If she'd have me, that is. Which she wouldn't."

Cy's admission surprised Luke, and the flash of his anger disappeared. Curiosity took its place.

"Why do you figure she wouldn't?" Denny's harsh assessment of women in wheelchairs came back to Luke.

Cy gave a snort and took a long pull at his mug before he
answered. "Jessie's not the marrying kind. I've watched her
turn down far more promising prospects than I ever was."
He caught the fleeting look of disbelief on Luke's face, and
he smiled and shook his head.

"So you only saw her chair, did you? It's like that at first.
But after ten minutes with Jessie, you forget all about the
chair and only see the woman." He stopped abruptly.
"What did you want with her today, anyhow? There's not
much point in going back over the whole disaster, is there?"

Luke was tempted to say it was none of Cy's damn business, but he suspected that would get him hurried out the
door and down the steps. Hesitantly, feeling like an absolute fool, he ventured, "I wanted to find out if there was
anything she needed doing, if there was some way I could
make a concrete apology to her."

"More for your sake than hers, right? You need forgiving, is that it?"

Damn the old man. Luke was uncomfortable enough
without amateur psychology, and his reasons were his own.
He'd had enough. He set his mug on the stained low table
and got stiffly to his feet. Cy lifted a hand and lazily waved
him back down again, but Luke's expression was stony.

"Sit down, Luke," Cy said placatingly. "Sorry. I retired
from medicine some years back, and my hobby's taking

courses at the university. One of them is an introduction to
clinical psych. We didn't seem to pay as much attention to
the workings of the mind in my day." He gestured at the
half-filled mug on the table. "Another was a course in
brewing. Personally, I think it was the more successful of the
two, don't you? Certainly makes for better friends, anyway."

The admission brought a reluctant grin to Luke's face,
and he sank back down onto the sofa. Cy glanced at his
watch, reached over and flicked a switch on a small radio,
and soft music filled the air. Then a woman's rich, warm
voice announced, "Evening, everyone. This is 'Night Shift'
from CKCQ, and I'm Jessie Langstrom-Smith, here to
spend the evening hours with you. From nine to one, we'll
listen to music, talk to friends and wind our way pleasantly
into darkness. My lines are open, if you care to call with requests or want to chat. The number is 555-7333."

Luke sat frozen, his beer glass halfway to his lips, his eyes
on the small radio, as if by staring he could see through it,
see the face and features that had inexplicably haunted him,
waking and sleeping, since the first moment he'd seen her on
that infamous hill.

Jessie. Her voice made the fine hairs rise on his arms, and
he wished she'd say something else.

Anything at all.

"Good voice, hasn't she?" Cy remarked proudly. "She's
been doing 'Night Shift' for six months now. Got a real
good following, too. Before that she used to get the suicide
shift, from one to five in the morning. Even picked up fans
on that one, weird as they were. She had to fight hard to get
this show, but she won. The station manager's one of the
Old Guard, not too sure radio's anyplace for women. Jessie had to do a better job than anybody else even to get a
spot in the middle of the night. But she won him over, fi-

nally." He gave Luke a significant nod. "Jessie usually does win. She's a fighter. Had to be."

Luke found his voice again. Music drifted from the radio, and he cleared his throat. "A radio announcer. Somehow I didn't, well . . ."

"Didn't what?" Cy sounded peeved. "Didn't think people in wheelchairs had glamorous jobs? Y'know, for an ex-cop, there's big gaps in your education. Just like there were in mine, and I was a doctor."

Luke was only half listening to Cy. Jessie was taking a call now on the air, from a young, shy-sounding woman who requested a song for her husband.

"He works at night, cleaning offices," the woman explained. She added that she listened to Jessie's show regularly, adding ingenuously, "as long as there isn't anything good on TV."

Jessie was gracious, amusing, sympathetic, and the woman related easily to her. Strong, yet easygoing.

Professional.

Something more? Luke swallowed. Jessie's voice was definitely the most sensual female voice he'd ever listened to. It purred. The timbre was both soothing and somehow exhilarating at once, silk-edged, throaty. It was a voice that made him want to close his eyes and dream of holding the woman behind the voice. . . .

He snapped to attention.

"She's pretty independent about everything," Cy was saying. "There's not much she can't do herself. Keeps the house spotless and she's a fine cook, not that a man ever dares compliment those talents anymore." He gave Luke a measuring look.

"The back garden could sure use a mowing, though, if you're dead serious about doing something practical for her, that is. I used to do it, but last summer I hurt my back. She was talking about hiring a boy, but she wants some of it left wild. Wild, huh! It looks like a bloody jungle out there. I'd show you, but it's getting too dark to see."

Cy drained his glass. "Another?" he queried, but Luke was getting to his feet. He held a hand out, and Cy stood up and gripped it firmly.

"Thanks," Luke said quietly. "I appreciate your help."

"You believe in Karma, young man?" Cy demanded suddenly.

"Karma?" Luke frowned. Maybe Cy didn't hold his booze too well.

"Destiny. Kismet. The belief that every action an individual takes will have a consequence according to laws that are universal and unchangeable," Cy explained impatiently.

"Never gave it too much thought," Luke temporized.

"Neither did I when I was your age. Often think I should have, though," Cy stated. He raised an eyebrow. "It could mean this meeting with Jessie was part of your Karma."

"It could also mean I should give up running and just stick to handball," Luke said wryly, and they shared an amused look before Cy saw Luke out, waving once from the top of the stairs.

Luke took a look at the garden on his way past. It was pretty much like Cy said—a jungle.

He turned the ignition key on inside the car, and before he started the motor, he impatiently dialed the radio to Jessie's program and turned up the volume. Her voice had an addictive quality.

Almost of its own volition, the car headed through the night for the stretch of beach called Spanish Banks, a long, narrow strip of sandy beachfront facing, across the inlet, the mountains of the North Shore and encompassing the bejeweled view of downtown Vancouver. Tonight the parking lots were nearly deserted. It was still early in the season, too cool at night for beach parties. A few cars held lovers admiring the view and each other, and Luke thoughtfully doused his lights before he pulled into the lot and stopped.

He slumped back against the seat, looking out at the spectacle of buildings and lights floating in the millpond stillness of the inlet, letting his eyes slowly lift beyond the water to trace the path of traffic up the faraway roads on the mountains of the North Shore. The pinpricks of car headlights looked like fireflies from that distance.

He listened to Jessie.

Soon he did more than listen.

He relaxed and absorbed the texture and the essence of her voice, her infrequent velvet laughter, her inflections. They permeated the pores of his soul, like a soothing unguent rubbed on muscles he hadn't realized were aching with strain.

The sound of her voice gave him the most curious sensation of utter peace.

THREE MORNINGS LATER Jessie was dragged from the depths of concentrated sleep by the sound of male voices in her backyard.

She determinedly ignored them at first, trying to slip back into the wonderful floating state she'd been in before they started. But persistently they continued until she woke enough to peer blearily at her wristwatch.

"Six-thirty?" she mumbled in disbelief.

She held her watch still closer to her nose, carefully confirming the hour.

"Six-thirty." She became more aware and more awake as the voices went on and on, coming in the open window, scraps of puzzling words without meaning.

"...raised...four by fours...maybe...fountain?"

" . . . shrubbery . . . root feeding . . . pruned . . ."

Fully awake and thoroughly puzzled, Jessie grabbed the pink terry robe at the foot of the bed and wrapped herself in it, plopping into her chair and shoving the stubborn curly tangles of her long hair out of her sleep-filled eyes.

Another moment and she was staring incredulously out her bedroom window at two men perched high in the old apple tree with short saws in their gloved hands. Even as she watched, a huge limb sighed, cracked and crashed to the earth. The saws bit deeply into still more limbs, and she frantically opened the window wider, leaning until she almost toppled out of her chair and hollering as loud as she could, "What do you think you're *doing*? Come down out of there, at once."

The sawing stopped, and they obediently began to clamber, one after the other, down the short aluminum ladder propped against the trunk. The first man held the ladder for the second to descend. They turned toward the window, and Jessie suddenly clamped a hand over her mouth in horrified recognition.

"Luke Chadwick," she whispered. There was no mistaking him. He strode through the underbrush like a warrior, and Jessie could only stare helplessly as he came nearer and still nearer the window where she waited.

"My hair, good grief, and my nightgown . . ."

Those instinctive and purely feminine concerns swiftly faded as he gazed in the window and grinned cockily at her, his teeth white and strong against the tan of his face, his black hair with its peppering of gray curling in an unruly mass down over his open collar. His face was narrower than she remembered, lean and strongly featured, and the blue of his eyes vied for color with the patch of morning sky she could see over his left shoulder.

"Morning, Jessie," he said casually, as if he'd wished her good morning every day of his life. "You don't mind if I call you Jessie, do you?"

"How ... what ... where ..." she stuttered, and then she demanded, "What are you doing here? Are you some kind of lunatic, going around wrecking marathons and cutting down trees?" *And calling me Jessie in that intimate, sexy voice? How did you find me again? How do you know my name?*

Unperturbed, he said cheerfully, "Don't know if you caught my name the other day. It's—"

"I know your damn name," Jessie spat. "I'm not liable to forget it." That admission, for some obscure reason, made her blush. She reached up and touched her wildly disarranged hair, shoving it back over her shoulders, glaring at Luke as his eyes flicked swiftly down to her breasts and then away. Reflexively she drew the pink robe tighter around her body.

"You have five minutes to get out of my yard, or so help me ..." she began.

"Now just stay calm, lady, and we'll explain, okay?" The second man, whom Jessie had hardly glanced at thus far, stepped beside Luke and grinned placatingly. He was rather short and stocky, with hair as black as Luke's and just as curly. His dark-brown eyes dipped down at the outer corners like those of a sad-eyed spaniel, and his mouth was too wide for his face. He had an appealing, bad-little-boy quality about him.

"All we want to do here is give this poor yard of yours a little face-lift, see, prune the trees and do some weeding for you, cut the grass, like that. We're landscape gardeners. Maybe I have a card on me." He started searching through his pockets without taking his eyes off Jessie. "Anyway, I figured some guy here said to go ahead. Isn't that what you told me?'' His grin disappeared instantly when he turned an accusing eye on Luke, who had the grace to look slightly abashed as he took up the story.

"Actually, Jessie, the truth is I came over a few days ago, but you weren't home, and I talked to your friend Cy. He dropped a hint about the grass needing cutting. Told me all about his bad back. It's the least I can do after... Well, anyway, as Denny here says, gardening is our business. And my back is just fine." The teasing note disappeared as he asked, "You will let us finish, won't you? That apple tree is going to die if it's not pruned—it's a shame because it's a thin-skinned McIntosh—and the damson plum tree will start bearing fruit again if it's cut back, all those suckers trimmed."

His old blue shirt was open at the collar, and dark curls showed dangerously in the V at his chest. His blue jeans were streaked with dirt, comfortably loose, riding low on his narrow hips. Jessie felt suddenly prickly and uncomfortable looking at him standing there. She couldn't help remembering the strong, long muscles in his body, bared by his running strip.

"Cy?" she heard herself repeating stupidly. "Cy said the grass... Cy has a bad back?" It was news to her. "Well, damn him, I saw him just last night, and he didn't say a word about meeting you or talking to you." She felt vaguely betrayed and not a little furious with Cy.

"This is my brother-in-law, Denny Mason. Den, this is Jessie Langstrom-Smith." Luke introduced them, just as if they were at some polite garden party.

Denny inclined his head politely and finally found the card he'd been frantically digging for in his pants pockets. He stepped closer, leaning over the overgrown flower bed at his feet, and handed it through the window.

Green Thumb Gardeners it announced. Professional Service with the Dutch Touch.

"You're Dutch?" She aimed the question at Denny, but Luke answered.

"Nope. I'm Canadian, and Denny is as well, except for some latent traces of Italian in each of us. He'd ordered the cards before I joined the business, and I can't get it through his thick skull that it's fraudulent to say that."

Was she actually having this insane conversation at an uncivilized hour with these two escapees from the loony bin?

"I think I need some coffee," she muttered weakly, and Luke immediately strode away, returning in seconds with a huge silver thermos.

"We'll buy," he said magnanimously, "as long as you bring your own cup. Why not come outside and join us," he coaxed. "The morning's fine."

Jessie started to giggle. She couldn't help it—the whole scene was so audacious. She had an infectious giggle, and Luke grinned back at her, taking note of the rosy, rumpled way she looked, the outrageous length of the thick, curling eyelashes shading her dark eyes. Brown? Green? Hazel. Then, that absolute mop of pale hair, like an aureole of wavy, disheveled dandelion fluff strewn over the shoulders of her soft pink robe.

He felt he knew her. Certainly he knew every nuance of that delicious voice. What would her reaction be if he told her he'd listened to her every night since Cy had switched on her show?

He must have been staring because the delightful giggle stopped abruptly as she met his gaze. She stared at him wide-eyed for several seconds and then blurted out," Give me ten minutes." With a spin of her wheels, she was gone from view.

In her huge red-and-white bathroom, Jessie washed her flushed face and struggled to bring some order to her recalcitrant mass of hair. She tied it back finally with a pink scarf and traced her lips with matching color. Then she sprayed on an expensive floral cologne her mother kept giving her and gave herself a critical, narrow-eyed once-over. Not great but adequate. She simply wasn't a morning person, and it showed.

"What the hell do you think you're doing, Jessie Smith?" she whispered.

Luke Chadwick was roughly attractive, dark and strong and virile. He was more attractive, perhaps, than anyone she'd met for... Come on, Jess, she chided herself. What's all this fantasy about a guy you don't even like, much less know?

But she was all too aware of the currents of sensuality he aroused in her. He appealed to her, as man appealed to woman.

Hold it, Jess. You know that part of your life is over.

So what was she doing, getting into her clean jeans and a pink-checked shirt and hustling out the door to have lukewarm thermos coffee with a man she had every reason to avoid?

"Here she comes," Denny whispered nervously. "Think we oughta offer to push her?"

Luke got to his feet. "Uh-uh," he cautioned quietly. She'd paused in the kitchen doorway, but now she rolled smoothly down the walk again. She had bright-pink sneakers on her feet, he noticed, and with a queer, aching twist in his chest, he remembered the clean Adidas runners she'd worn in the marathon. What was it like to put shoes on feet that didn't work?

"I didn't remember they made mornings anymore," she commented, rolling up next to them and handing Luke a red-and-white striped mug. She tipped her head back and squinted up at the blue cloudless sky, the sun just clearing the treetops.

Luke took advantage of her moment of distraction to study the delicately carved facial bones, the classic tilt to the nose, the full-lipped, rosy mouth. She was unusually beautiful. Her deceivingly slender frame seemed long limbed, the movements of her head and torso graceful.

"It's very nice," she added in a reflective way, and he silently agreed. "Sort of freshly scrubbed and dressed in new clothes." Denny looked at her as if she might speak in tongues at any moment.

"Guess you usually sleep later than this," Luke remarked, wondering desperately how to get Denny to stop staring at her. He carefully handed her a full cup of his not-so-hot coffee. "Hope you don't mind it black."

She shook her head, and wisps of hair floated loose from the scarf. "I work nights. I'm a radio announcer. We have black coffee in our veins instead of blood." She sipped at the brew and was pleasantly surprised at how good it tasted.

"I know. I've heard your show." Luke caught Denny's astonished glance. Luke hadn't said anything to Denny about what she did.

Jessie shot him a look, eyebrows raised. "Dear old Cy again?" she queried.

Luke nodded a bit sheepishly. "I've enjoyed your program. You're a great host."

Jessie beamed. She knew she was good at her job, but it pleased her to know others thought so. "You listen much to the radio?" she quizzed, her head tipped curiously to one side.

Laconically he nodded and then added, "As long as there's nothing good on TV."

She instantly recognized the quote the ingenuous young caller had made on her show, and Denny looked more puzzled than ever when they laughed together.

"You're really on the radio? What station?" Obviously Denny doubted he'd heard properly.

"CKCQ, a show called 'Night Shift.'"

"I never thought people in—" Luke impaled him with a deadly glare, halting his words, and Denny flushed deeply under his tan, quickly revising what he'd been about to blurt out. "People still listened to the radio," he finished weakly.

Jessie had intercepted Luke's warning glance, and she felt ridiculously touched at his attempt to spare her embarrassment. But what Luke didn't understand was that Denny's reaction was one she'd grown to expect and even welcome. She'd learned that a frank approach was usually the best one when strangers were uneasy on first meeting a person in a wheelchair.

She leaned forward conspiratorially and whispered to Denny, as loud as she could, "Hey, it's okay, I know I'm disabled, they told me about the wheelchair. I don't faint when you mention it."

Both men were shocked for a split second. When she laughed mischievously at their expressions, they grinned sheepishly.

"It's really hard to know whether to talk about it or not," Denny confessed forthrightly. "I've never known anybody in one before, see, and I sure don't want to hurt your feelings. But I honestly never considered what people in one of those chairs did, like where they worked or anything. Then I find out you're a media type. Well, I never met anybody in the media, either. Kinda threw me, there, for a minute."

Luke felt like groaning aloud. Was there one more questionable statement left for Denny to make? Watching Jessie covertly, he tried to gauge whether or not Denny and his freewheeling mouth were making her feel self-conscious.

But she gave them both an engaging grin. "Well, I never knew any Italian-Canadian-Dutch gardeners before, either." She looked at ease, sipping her coffee and tipping her rounded chin up now and then to catch the warming sun's rays on her already golden skin. Luke relaxed and was admiring a dimple beside her mouth when her voice grew a shade steely. Focusing her attention on Luke, she demanded, "Now what, exactly, were you planning on doing here in my backyard, Mr. Chadwick? Without my permission?"

He sank down on the grass, consciously putting himself at her level. "Please, could you call me Luke? I always think people mean my father when they say Mr. Chadwick." She had a determined chin. He'd bet she had a stubborn streak a mile wide. Had to have, to accomplish what she had in spite of... He'd better make this sound good.

"I figure that if you calculate the time, energy and wear and tear on the equipment you must need to go into training for a marathon, there has to be a substantial financial investment involved. So if some bozo comes along and ruins the big day, there's a financial loss."

Jessie was listening with her head tipped a bit to the side, a noncommittal look on her well-modeled features. She had the most engaging eyes, wide and dark and sort of surprised, changing with each new thought and emotion.

His voice deepened. "I feel I owe you, Jessie. And I'm a man who pays his bills. I can't stand being in debt. It keeps me awake at night." If only money were really the reason for his insomnia... How simple that would be.

She gave her head an impatient, negative shake, and he hastily finished what he had to say.

"I want to landscape your back garden. It needs it, and I feel I owe you that much, at least."

He could see the refusal forming on her face.

"Hey, Jessie," Denny interjected just then in a conspiratorial way. "Don't you know nothin' about the male ego? You have to be generous here, see. Luke felt like the village idiot after that race. He's really not too bright anyhow—we sort of protect him inside the family—but we let him out that one day, and you know what happened."

Denny's nonsense brought a twinkling delight to her expression, and she tilted her head teasingly, studying Luke as if pondering this new information.

"So give the guy a chance to make up for it," Denny implored. "Hell, his health is suffering."

Jessie had to laugh at this outrageous claim. Luke radiated good health, from the top of his absurdly appealing dark head right down that muscular frame to the tip of his size—thirteen?—work boots. Once more he was giving her that intent, almost frowning look that she remembered so vividly from their first meeting. Just as it had then, it sent waves of awareness shivering up her arms, across her neck, into her breasts. She didn't want to appear foolishly stubborn, but the last thing she ought to agree to was having a man around for the next few weeks. Especially one who made her feel like this.

Why couldn't her villain have been Denny instead of Luke? She liked Denny, but he sure didn't ignite any sparks.

"What sort of things were you thinking of doing to the yard?" she asked. It wouldn't hurt to hear some suggestions, at least. It was fun sitting here in the early morning with the birds singing and a handsome man crouched at her feet.

Half an hour later, well into a heated discussion over rosebushes, Jessie gave in. It was crazy to refuse such a generous offer, especially when she realized how truly ingenious Luke's ideas were for her yard.

"Okay, if you're so set on doing this, I'll buy the materials, you do the work," she said grudgingly. She had a feeling Luke wouldn't give up until she agreed, anyway. His square jaw had a definite stubborn set to it. He's probably used to having women give in to him, she warned herself.

He beamed at her, and his smile reminded her again why it would be dangerous to have him around. But it was already too late. She'd agreed.

"I'll be over tomorrow morning with a list of materials. There won't be a lot—we'll improvise most of what we need, like I told you. Then I'll come by whenever I've got a few hours, evenings and weekends mostly," Luke added.

Denny heaved an audible sigh of relief. "If you two can get along for a couple minutes without any more arguing, I'm going to get my smokes from the truck."

He hurried off down the path to the fence gate leading to the alley, and as soon as he was out of earshot, Jessie asked the question she'd been too shy to ask in front of Denny. "What about your family? Aren't you stealing time from them if you do this for me?" Jessie told herself hers was a perfectly ordinary question, but she couldn't help tensing for his reply.

"I'm single. My time is my own. And you, Jessie?" He tossed the query back at her, standing up with one easy motion and bending to retrieve his thermos. Cy hadn't said so outright, but he'd given at least the impression that she was unattached. Still, Luke wanted to hear her say so, for some odd reason.

"I'm divorced," she said briefly. "Years ago." She turned away from him then, wheeling recklessly back over the rough earth to the sidewalk, struggling to get the chair up and over the edge of the cement.

Luke was behind her in an instant, effortlessly easing the chair up and over the barrier. Jessie snapped furiously, "I could have done it myself, thanks. I'm not helpless, you know, and I'm sick of you shoving me around when I don't need it."

She hated herself the instant the words were spoken. It had been a long time since she'd felt the futile, angry need to lash out when someone performed a task she knew she could do herself. She's thought herself far too self-confident and poised these days to resort to such insecure responses.

It was Luke. It was something about this man that kept her off balance. But it wasn't his fault, really. It was her own reaction to him that made her feel unsettled.

His face was stern, the blue eyes remote and guarded when she finally dared to look up at him. Remorse swept over her. She hadn't meant to hurt him.

"Luke, I'm sorry. I shouldn't have snapped at you like that." Impulsively she reached over and put a hand on his forearm, just below the careless roll of his shirtsleeve. The contact was both pleasant and disturbing. The hair-roughened skin, several degrees warmer than her fingers were, stretched tautly over sinew and muscle and tendon. She imagined his blood pulsing strongly, sensed the potent life force of the man who was Luke, and she snatched her fingers away.

But he caught her hand before she could settle it safely in her lap, holding it lightly, turning it over and running his rough thumb up and down her palm, stained from the wheels of her chair. He made her ridiculously aware of her callused skin and the tiny nerve endings beneath.

"I seem to make a habit of doing the wrong thing around you, Jessie. I can understand, though, how it must feel having somebody pushing at you all the time, whether you need it or not. People have pushed me at times, and I hated it, too. Be patient with me.''

Jessie felt a combination of surprise and pleasure at his words, but the light touch on her hand was disconcerting. She pulled gently and a little shyly away and smoothly steered for the kitchen door just as Denny appeared around the corner.

"I'm starving," she blurted out, feeling warmly self-conscious in front of Denny. "Do you two want to join me for muffins and cheese?"

The men exchanged a questioning glance, and then Denny said, "We'd like to, but we've got a driveway to finish this morning, eh, Luke?"

Luke nodded with little enthusiasm, and they both said goodbye.

"See you tomorrow morning," Luke promised as he disappeared through the back gate. In another moment she heard their truck roar to life and drive away.

Silence descended. Jessie sat for another minute in the heat of the sun, staring blankly at the weeds and grass and choking moss that composed what passed for her back garden.

"The old order changeth, yielding place to new," she muttered softly. It was one of Cy's haphazard quotes. Then she shrugged and headed for the phone.

Using a special buzzer, she rang upstairs, and when Cy picked up his receiver, she barked, "You get down here, you old schemer. What's this nonsense about your having a bad back, anyhow?"

Jessie grinned wickedly as Cy sputtered explanations, and by the time he came sheepishly downstairs, she had cheese melted over bran muffins and two steaming mugs of fresh coffee waiting on the table.

"There's a whole routine of exercises just for backs," Jessie teased mercilessly. "Why, in just a few hours a day using my weights, we'll have you as good as new, poor dear," she said solicitously, enjoying Cy's alarmed protests. He despised working with weights, as Jessie well knew. He put half a muffin into his mouth, chewed contentedly for a moment and bolted down half a cup of his coffee. Then he sat back and studied Jessie thoughtfully.

"Okay, I lied to Luke," he admitted matter-of-factly. "There's nothing wrong with my back, as you well know, you brat. So stop spoiling a perfectly good meal with threats of torture." He shuddered. "However, I jeopardized my immortal soul for a reason," he went on, buttering one last muffin. "Two reasons, as a matter of fact." He laid the knife down and studied the tabletop, frowning. "As you know, I don't believe anything in life happens accidentally, Jess. I believe in patterns, you might say. Now Luke doesn't have a clue why he grabbed your chair in that infernal race, any more than you have. He's not your ordinary weirdo, by any means. Quite the opposite. I like him—he's what we used to call 'a man's man' before you women decided that was barbaric use of the language." He munched his muffin thoughtfully, washing it down with another cup of coffee. "So perhaps he's appeared in your life for a reason. As a bystander, I'm curious," Cy finished ingenuously, giving her an impenetrable look.

"Yeah," she agreed sarcastically. "Everybody needs a cripple in his life, all right." She could use the despised word to Cy because he understood. Everything.

Except maybe this matter of Luke Chadwick.

"If that's your harebrained first reason, I can hardly wait to hear the second. You said there were two."

"There are. The second is that maybe you need somebody like him."

"Me? What on earth for?"

Cy stowed his cup and knife and plate in the dishwasher and sauntered over to the stairs. He cast a deeply satisfied look over his shoulder at Jessie, who sat glowering at him.

"To use a machete on that jungle out there, for starters. After that, why not just make it up as you go along? You're way too independent for your own good, woman. You need to learn to have fainting spells once in a while, like the belles of the Old South."

He sprinted up the stairs, and Jessie stared after him, exasperated.

"One of these days, my boy, you'll go too far," she muttered. "You think you're far too clever, Mr. Cyrus Grant."

But for the rest of the day and all through the hours she worked that evening, Luke Chadwick was never far from her thoughts.

CHAPTER THREE

AT WORK THAT EVENING Jessie deftly inserted a cassette, monitored the first few bars of a romantic ballad, then removed her headset and punched the button that allowed her to respond to the flashing telephone summons off the air.

In spite of literally having risen with the birds that morning—thanks to her early visitors—she felt wide-awake, keyed up and on top of everything as she steered "Night Shift" competently through the evening hours. Judy, who worked the switchboard during the day, went home at six, and after that the announcer answered the incoming calls.

"'Night Shift,' Jessie here," she murmured into the phone and listened sympathetically as a teenager she'd spoken with several times in the past month begged for advice on yet another crucial problem with her love life. Why the listening audience turned to a radio announcer for the answers to life's problems was a mystery to Jessie, but she seemed to get more calls all the time like this one.

"I've tried everything, and he doesn't even know I'm alive," the adolescent girl wailed. "You figure it would be okay to phone and maybe ask him to a party, but I'd just expire if he turned me down, whatd'ya think, Jessie?"

Jessie thought privately that anyone else in the thick Vancouver telephone directory might be better qualified to advise the girl on matters of the heart. She did her best however.

"If there's nobody else he's seeing regularly, well, it's worth a try. And if he says no, just dust yourself off and go to the party, anyway. Things like that happen to men all the time. It's not the end of the world to get turned down. We gals are just as resilient as they are, don't you think?"

Mollified and hopeful, the girl thanked her and hung up. Jessie checked the cassettes of music and commercials a final time against her setup charts and waved through the glass at Barry Daniels, the news announcer, wandering past her booth with a coffee mug balanced in one hand and a Danish in the other. He stuck his balding head in the control room door and said cheerfully, "Hiya Jess, how's it going? Did you hear about Morgan leaving to do the morning show on LK-FM?"

They chatted for a few moments, and then Barry remarked, "A weird guy wandered in here looking for you last weekend. The late-night newsman saw him in the corridor and called the cops about midnight on Saturday. Apparently he was a fan of 'Night Shift,' and he wanted to give you a poem he'd written—harmless kind of guy. The police suggested we get better locks or some kind of improved security system, though."

Jessie groaned. "Evan's going to go into his lecture about how all these things weren't necessary before I came along, I just know it. Remember how he complained about having to make the washroom larger for my chair? And the ramp into the records library?"

Evan Rathmore was the station manager. He was not, in Jessie's opinion, a likable man or even a fair one. But he was her boss, and this latest incident would add to his petty list of grievances about females in general and disabled ones in particular.

"Ever thought of changing stations, Jess?"

"Haven't we all?" Evan was not a popular man with his employees. "But I love doing 'Night Shift,' and I've built up a listening audience. It takes time to reestablish yourself at another station, unless you're a superstar like Morgan."

Barry wandered back to the newsroom while Jessie read her listeners a news item she'd come across in *Billboard* about a local singer making it big in Japan, gave the station's call sign and her name and then sat quietly through a taped commercial for a car dealer and more music.

The phone was blinking again.

"CKCQ, good evening."

Jessie heard breathing with muffled noise in the background.

"CKCQ, hello?"

There was more breathing and then a whispered sound that might have been her name.

Jessie hesitated and then firmly hung up. Occasionally most announcers attracted a crank caller, and she'd forced herself to view these unfortunate souls as simply a hazard of the job. The last one had been loud and vocal, phoning every day for several weeks to protest a Safeway commercial he insisted was spawned by the devil.

Now it seemed she'd attracted a heavy breather, as well as the guy Barry had told her about. If the crank caller kept it up, she knew she should report him, but she wondered uneasily how much of this sort of thing Evan would tolerate before he decided to replace her. With an able-bodied male, of course. Well, there wasn't time to dwell on it now. With a cheery weather bulletin predicting sunshine and blue skies for several days—"we must be doing something right for a change, Vancouver,"—Jessie played the final medley of tunes before the ten o'clock news.

She was sipping a fresh cup of horrendously strong coffee and monitoring Barry's fast-paced and expert reporting of world chaos and idiosyncrasies when her phone blinked again, insistently.

Jessie let it blink for long moments, smoothly bridging Barry's news reporting with another medley of music. When she couldn't delay any longer, she answered the telephone with a resigned sigh, fully prepared for the breather.

"Hello, Jessie."

The mellow, rumbling voice was instantly recognizable.

"Oh, Luke, I'm so glad—I mean, I thought it was the breather again."

"The breather? What breather?" Understandably, he sounded confused, and his tone sharpened slightly.

Jessie silently cursed her blurted admission and hastily said, "Let's try this whole thing again. Hi, Luke, how are you this evening?"

Now why should her heart be pounding so loudly? Irritated with herself, she strove for the lightest tone she could muster. "You're phoning to say you've come to your senses and decided not to have anything to do with my garden, right?"

There, that was just the right touch of teasing humor. She swallowed the persistent lump in her throat and wondered dazedly where her usual aplomb had gone.

Luke's chuckle was soft and somehow intimate. "No luck there, lady. That garden is the challenge of my career, and I intend to have it fit for coverage by *Better Homes and Gardens* before I'm done."

"Well, all I can say is good luck," she bantered, wondering why exactly he'd phoned, checking the timer to see how many minutes were left her before she was on the air again.

"I got thinking after we talked this morning, and I wondered if you had any objections to hot tubs."

"Hot tubs?" Mystified, she glanced again at the clock. She'd have to go any second now. "No, hot tubs are fine.

I've never actually used one, but I understand they're great. Why?''

''Just wanted your opinion. See you tomorrow, Jess.''

He was gone. She shrugged and shook her head. Now what had all that been about? And why should she feel such glowing pleasure about an ambiguous phone call?

She hurriedly donned her earphones and forced her attention back to her program, wondering if her listeners could hear the difference in her voice when she had a silly smile plastered all over her face, and wondering, too, whether Luke was listening to her and if he could detect it.

You idiot. You're getting childish in your middle years.

She knew that for the rest of the evening there was effervescent sunshine in her voice, and the breather didn't call again.

THERE WAS STILL SUNSHINE, the real article this time, when she wheeled out into her garden the following morning. Luke had said he'd come by about ten-thirty, and for the first time in months, Jessie had set the alarm on her clock radio. Normally, she simply slept until she awakened naturally, but she hadn't taken any chances that morning. She'd wanted to be showered and ready when he arrived, but there was no sign of him yet.

Her hair was still wet from having shampooed it, and she shook it back and rested her head on the back of her chair, letting the deliciously warm sunlight spill over her and seep into her pores.

Luke came in quietly through the alley gate, closing it softly behind him. It was almost hidden amongst overgrown lilac bushes that formed a scented tunnel into the backyard, and he had to crouch and duck his head to avoid the branches.

When he straightened, he caught sight of Jessie.

Her face was upturned to the sun like a delicate spring flower, and she wore a soft blue track suit, its V-shaped neck revealing the long, graceful lines of her neck. He could see the pulse beating softly in her throat. Her lashes swept down across her cheekbones, and there was a contented half smile on her lips. Soft bits of pale, fluffy hair curled around her face, and Luke stood silently on the grass studying the relaxed figure before him, vaguely aware that a knot of tenderness clenched and unclenched inside him.

Something about Jessie, an indefinable feminine something, affected him deeply.

It wasn't pity, either. Belatedly he realized that today he'd been unaware of the wheelchair she sat in until that moment. Just as Cy had predicted, he was beginning to see only the woman, and that woman was poignantly beautiful.

"Morning, Luke." She hadn't moved a muscle, and her eyes were just as firmly closed as before.

"How'd you know it was me?" There was laughter in his voice.

How could she admit that the tiny hairs on her arms stood on end each time she was around him, that the pleasant lemony scent of his after-shave was ingrained on her senses?

"I heard you come in the back gate." Her hazel eyes opened wide, and she smiled mischievously up at him. "I could even hear you thinking about whether you dared wake me up or not. Scared you yesterday morning, huh?"

"Not badly. Actually, I was thinking that you looked like Sleeping Beauty." Now the mischief was all his. "It's been a long time since I read that story, but if I remember correctly, the prince . . ."

Jessie flushed, caught prettily in her own web and suddenly anxious that he might think she was flirting with him.

"Thirty-two is a bit old to be cast as Sleeping Beauty," she objected tartly, squirming stiffly upright in her chair and running her fingers through her nearly dry hair in an effort to tidy the rebellious mass. She succeeded only in setting it even more on end, and it glowed in a curly, attractively messy halo around her face and down her back.

Luke pulled over a white plastic chair and straddled it comfortably, folding his arms along the back and resting his chin on them. A few houses away, a dog yapped incessantly, and children's voices rose and fell in quarrelsome play from another yard. Here in Jessie's garden there were only birds and the hum of bees exploring the dandelions that flourished in the tall grass.

"It's great to have a house and a backyard like this," he remarked.

"Where do you live, Luke?"

"In a bachelor apartment in the West End." For the past few years he'd wanted nothing more. He wondered if it was time to start thinking about buying a house of his own. He could afford it. His severance pay from the RCMP and most of the profit from the business had gone into investment funds simply because he had nothing he cared to spend it on.

"Like some coffee?"

At his enthusiastic nod Jessie disappeared through the clumsy screen door into the kitchen. A wide sliding patio door would make the garden much more accessible for her. Luke gave the nook's glass windows a calculating glance, making mental adjustments to the plans he'd sketched.

She returned quickly with a wicker tray balanced neatly across her legs, steadying it with one hand and guiding the chair with the other. Obviously, she'd carefully prepared it ahead of time. A fat thermal coffee maker, two brown pottery mugs and a plate of huge carrot muffins vied for space with spoons and napkins.

"Bring that small table over here, please, and we'll put this on it," she instructed briskly, and Luke hurried to do her bidding, easily lifting and repositioning the circular lawn table beside them. He was careful to let her arrange the tray by herself, mindful of the dressing-down he'd received the day before for offering help where none was wanted. Jessie was a graceful hostess, pouring rich brown mugfuls of steaming coffee for each of them, handing him a muffin without asking and taking one herself.

"There," she pronounced happily, surveying the arrangement of cups and plates and butter, and she sounded so smugly pleased he couldn't help smiling at her again.

"Are you usually up this early?" He took a bite of his muffin and a gulp of the aromatic coffee. "You work until one, don't you? Then you need time to wind down after your shift, too."

"You sound as if you've worked nights yourself." Jessie liked the easy way he was sprawled in his chair, obviously enjoying everything she served. There was a lazy grace about him, an ease with his body that likely came from being physical, working hard outside. "Lots of times it takes me till three just to relax enough to go to sleep," she confided. "You get yourself all keyed up, and then you can't let go."

He nodded understandingly. "I used to work nights when I was in the RCMP," he commented.

"You were a mounted policeman?"

"Yup. But that was a long time ago." A tiny note of tension radiated from him, and she wondered why. "I quit eight years ago. Denny and I started up the business not long afterward."

"Ever been sorry you left?" Jessie had caught the hesitancy and wondered if perhaps he had regrets.

"Never," he said firmly. "It took me three months to get toughened up to hard physical work, though. You think you're in good shape until you start laying cement bricks and shoveling dirt for hours. I find a certain peace in what

I do now that I never even came close to finding before.''
There was a finality in the statement, and he changed the
subject smoothly, refilling their coffee cups. "How about
you, Jessie? Did you always want to be an announcer? It's
quite a new field for women, isn't it?''

"It is, yes. I was one of the first women in the business
here in Vancouver. The public grew much too accustomed
to hearing only men on the airwaves. But announcing wasn't
my first career, either. I was a dancer, you see. A ballerina
with the Royal Canadian Corps de Ballet until I was twenty-
two. I'd started training when I was four, so I had a lot of
time to hone my skills.''

Too late, Jessie realized the effect this news usually had
on people, and she looked anxiously at Luke. If only he
wouldn't react with the usual horror and embarrassed
clucking she usually encountered when she forgot herself
enough to mention her dancing.

His soft blue eyes held her gaze unflinchingly, and his
expression betrayed nothing except friendly interest.

"Is that when you were injured, Jess? When you were
twenty-two?''

She breathed an invisible but heartfelt sigh of relief. Luke
was different. She should have trusted his reactions—except that she hardly knew him that well yet. But that was
changing rapidly now, due to the openness of his question,
the perhaps stern, but certainly composed, lines of his face.
There was no horror, no pity, there.

Oh, Luke, thanks, Jessie thought gratefully.

"Yeah, ten years ago this June. I was in a car accident a
week after my twenty-second birthday.''

Her matter-of-fact statement didn't stop Luke from adding up in his mind all the things that must have changed for
Jessie after that.

A dancer who'd never dance again. A kid, a beautiful young woman, sentenced to life in that wheelchair. Dreams, aspirations, goals—destroyed all at once.

Wrenching, agonizing recognition and sympathy tore through him, and for a terrible moment he was afraid he wouldn't be able to swallow the bite of muffin he was chewing so nonchalantly or conceal the reaction her words had caused.

Six blind, tumultuous seconds passed as he struggled. But there was value in his years of discipline as a policeman, and he used every atom of that training now to conceal his horror and his shock from Jessie.

He must have succeeded because, after that first guarded, intense, almost frightened glance at him, she seemed to relax, leaning forward casually to butter another muffin and place half of it in front of him before she refilled their mugs once again, chatting to him in a free and easy fashion.

"It's difficult to explain, but you see, broadcasting really is the first livelihood I've actually chosen. At the age of four, when I started to dance, I wasn't what you'd call either mature or career-oriented." Her head tipped to the side, and again that slightly wicked, mischievous smile flashed at him. "So when I had to change direction, I had an awful time deciding what I could do that I wanted to do. I'd had no practice at making career decisions, and of course a lot of jobs weren't possible for me." She glanced at him, anxious suddenly that perhaps he was bored with hearing about her life. But Luke's face, set only moments before in a rather stern cast, was now animated and relaxed. He was obviously interested in what she was saying.

"I always talked a lot, anyway, and one day I was asked if I'd mind being interviewed for a radio show about spinal cord injury. Of course I agreed, and when the show was aired, one of the announcers made the fatal mistake of telling me I had a pleasing voice. At that time women were being actually courted by radio stations—you know, part of the big feminine awareness thing that happened in the seventies. So I headed straight for the Royal City Academy of Broadcasting in New Westminster—it's gone now—and when I graduated, I was hired to read the news and do a few interviews for a small station miles out in the suburbs. Then I tried for and got a job as night deejay at CKCQ, and finally I was offered the job I have now." She slumped back in her chair, and her eyes widened. "There, see what I said about liking to talk? Bet you're sorry you ever asked, huh?"

But he wasn't at all. Luke had an insatiable urge to learn all he could about Jessie, and instead of the urge diminishing the more he was around her, it seemed to grow stronger all the time.

Looking across the table into her lovely and now familiar face, seeing her body gracefully draped in the chair, Jessie seemed vibrant to Luke, sparkling with the pleasure of simply being alive, golden and beautiful in the sunny morning. Her shape was pleasing to him, gently curved and womanly.

Most disconcerting of all, Luke felt an incredible wave of desire for her wash over his body, so powerful it shocked him.

"Well, you two, are there any of those muffins left, or have you eaten them all?"

Cy's hearty greeting startled them both. Jessie turned to him with such a fond and welcoming smile that Luke actually felt a stab of jealousy before he chided himself and stood to shake the hand the older man was proffering.

"Hello there, Luke." Cy didn't seem at all surprised to find him with Jessie this time. "Discussing plans for reclaiming this tropical rain forest, are you? Let me get a mug for some of that coffee and I'll give your ideas the official stamp of approval, whatever they are. Anything has to be an improvement over this." He waved a cheerful hand at the proliferation of ferns, weeds and general chaotic but lavish growth surrounding them. The area where they sat was something of an island, reminding Luke that, so far, he hadn't said one word to Jessie about the plans he'd spent hours working on the previous night—while he listened, of course, to "Night Shift" and her entrancing husky voice.

Luke retrieved his briefcase from where he'd thrust it under his chair, and when Jessie had cleared a space on the table, he spread out several sketches.

Cy carried a chair out from the kitchen to sit on, ignoring Jessie's syrupy, "Cy, dear, do be careful of your back, won't you?" The older man simply shook an admonishing finger at her and, with the familiarity of one very much at home, found a mug for himself, poured coffee and thickly buttered the last muffin.

"Lead on, Macduff," he then ordered Luke dramatically, and Jessie rolled her eyes and pulled a face.

"Honestly, Cy. We've got to enroll you in a course teaching modern aphorisms. You use these expressions, and I pick them up, and soon I catch myself saying something like that over the air. Lead on, Macduff, indeed. Lordy, I could lose my job."

"No appreciation for the classics," Cy muttered around a mouthful of muffin and craned his neck to see what Luke was pointing out.

"I can't figure this out upside down," Jessie complained a moment later. Almost immediately she could have bitten her tongue for saying anything because Luke got up and came to kneel beside her chair as if it were the most natural thing in the world for him to do. He spread the diagram casually across her knees, forcing Cy to take a position on her other side if he wanted to see.

Luke's dark, curly head with its lavish sprinkling of gray was suddenly at Jessie's eye level, and his thickly muscled forearm was resting easily beside hers, touching her now and then as he pointed out this shrub, that plot of grass, this flower bed.

"Now right here I thought we could make a patio from interlocking bricks, forming a small courtyard, and it wouldn't take much to make this bit of the kitchen wall a sliding door, providing access..."

She could smell the cleanly washed fragrance of his hair, the trace of shampoo it exuded, and the scent of a man perspiring lightly in the May sunshine. It was a deliriously wonderful smell, she thought dreamily.

"And right here we could put a raised kitchen garden. You mentioned you'd like to try growing some vegetables, didn't you, Jess?"

She nodded her head and breathed in, taking his essence and making it part of her experience, thinking dazedly that nothing had ever smelled so good to her as Luke did this moment kneeling at her side.

"Then in this section we'll put several stands of bamboo against the cedar fence and an ivy ground cover so there's no maintenance required, and over here..."

She imagined she could feel the vibrations from his huge body, the leashed power he exuded, like an aura surrounding them both in pulsing awareness.

Get hold of yourself, you foolish woman, she urged herself, wishing he'd move away, wishing he'd kneel here at her side forever....

"Hot tub? What do you mean, a hot tub?" She came out of her sensual trance with a jolt, grabbing the edge of the meticulous diagram and paying close attention for a change.

"Right here, in this sheltered area between the largest trees, is an ideal location for a cedar deck and a hot tub.

This area's plenty large enough to accommodate it, and the upkeep on the kind of tub I have in mind is absolutely minimal.''

Jessie was shaking her head, and she interrupted him. "I thought we'd agreed on a very modest amount of work here, Luke. If you're going to get into major changes like a patio and a hot tub, I insist on paying you. Although I'm not sure I even agree with your plan. What you're suggesting will take you all summer to finish.'' She shook her head again, decisively. "For pity's sake, I don't need a hot tub. How would I even get in and out of one? Have you considered that?''

He had, it turned out.

"You get in and out of a swimming pool, don't you?''

Jessie realized right away that she shouldn't even have asked.

He had a friend who just happened to be in the hot tub business and who had suggested modifications and handholds so that she could transfer herself as easily as she would into a bathtub.

And now Cy, traitor that he was becoming, insisted grandly that he would happily pay more rent if it meant having the sybaritic pleasure of such luxury available in his landlady's back garden.

"Cy, you know it's not just the money," Jessie objected, and Luke added his deep rumble to Cy's loud arguments in favor of the tub. The discussion had grown louder and louder, and it took several minutes before any of them became aware of the sound of a female voice just inside the back gate, a pleasing hesitant voice.

"Excuse me." The woman gave the group a tentative smile and picked her way daintily towards them over the rough path.

She looked about fifty, Jessie noted, although it was hard to guess. Her luxurious white hair was smoothly braided into a coronet on top of her regal head, and she gave the impression of meticulous, careful grooming with her dark skirt and impeccable white shirt.

"My name is Amanda Simpson. I've just bought the house next door. I couldn't help but notice gardeners doing pruning here yesterday. My kitchen window overlooks your yard," she explained to Cy. "My trees are desperately in need of care, and I wondered..."

Cy sprang to his feet and with a courtly gesture offered the newcomer his chair. He introduced Luke and identified Jessie as his landlady, then held a hand out in a formal greeting to Amanda.

"Cyrus Grant, delighted to meet you, Amanda," he announced, taking her carefully manicured hand in his own. Jessie was intrigued by the fact that he held it a shade too long before releasing it again.

Amanda sat down, crossing her shapely legs primly at the ankle, politely refusing coffee or muffins. In a business-like manner she arranged with Luke for the care of her yard.

She was an elegant, attractive woman, Jessie thought, listening as Cy cleverly found out that Amanda was alone. Jessie was absolutely fascinated when the woman revealed that she wrote romances for a major publisher and that she'd never owned a house before.

Jessie wanted to ask her more about her writing, but Cy managed to monopolize the conversation. All too soon she rose to leave, and Cy walked with her to the back gate.

Jessie distinctly heard him offering his help with any heavy lifting or house repairs Amanda might need, and Jessie exchanged an amused glance with Luke.

Jessie gave the old reprobate a cynical glare when he sat down again.

"That's a tricky back problem you've got, Cy," she commented, and he gave her an innocent look.

"It comes and goes," he said and immediately started pushing the case for the hot tub once again.

Jessie was weakening. She couldn't help but imagine the absolute pleasure of sinking chin deep in steaming hot water after an exhausting session with her weights or a ten-mile run in her chair, or just on one of those desperately gray, depressing Vancouver rainy days...with a fascinating book and a glass or two of wine....

"You agreed to it when I phoned you last night," Luke stated unfairly, squinting up at her with beetled eyebrows and an injured expression she knew was totally phony but was nonetheless appealing.

"As a former physician, I believe the tub would be therapeutic, Jess. I'll bet we could get it written off as a tax deduction," Cy insisted.

Jessie threw her hands in the air and yelped, "Okay, okay, you've convinced me, I give up, we'll have a hot tub. Now shut up, both of you, before Amanda calls the cops on us for disturbing the peace. She probably thought she was buying a house in a quiet neighborhood."

Before she knew what was happening, Luke put an exuberant arm around her and gave her an impulsive hug.

His cheek grazed the tender softness of her face, and he inhaled the floral perfume he'd come to associate with Jessie.

"Good decision," he said heartily, and then, realizing what he was doing, he flushed a deeper shade of reddish bronze and moved away in what he hoped was a casual fashion.

Cy smacked a huge kiss on her other cheek with absolutely no hesitation, hugging her affectionately as he did so. He left one arm draped over her shoulders.

Once again Luke felt jealousy stab at him. He got to his feet, looked at the watch on his tanned forearm and said, "I'd better get going. Denny's meeting me in the university area in a few minutes." He gathered up his papers and stuffed them in his narrow black briefcase. Catching Jessie's glance, he gave her a jaunty wink.

"See you tomorrow," he promised. With a nod at Cy, he strode to the back gate and ducked under the lilacs. Jessie listened as his truck motor roared and the vehicle pulled away.

Why did it suddenly seem as if the day had grown a shade duller, the sunshine just a little less warm?

LUKE WAS SIMPLY BECOMING her friend, Jessie told herself firmly, hours later. And there was nothing wrong with making friends with him. She had a number of male friends at the station.

What if he was an unreasonably attractive man? She was woman enough to admire him as she would anything of beauty. There was absolutely no valid reason for the confusion of feelings that swept over her every time she went over the hour or so they'd spent together that morning. There was no basis for the involuntary physical responses his nearness caused, either.

Jessie hurried into the gray-carpeted, mirrored room off her kitchen, the room Cy had not so fondly labeled her torture chamber, where mats and weights and complicated electrical equipment lined the walls. Turning on a tape of disco music, she threw herself into her daily workout, pushing each routine just past the point that yesterday she'd considered her limit of endurance.

Working out consistently was ingrained in her from years of ballet, when strenuous classes were a daily routine. The exercises Jessie did now were different but no less demanding. Sweat soon dripped into the blue-striped headband she had pulled on, and her arms screamed for mercy as she bench-pressed, lifted, wrist-curled and crawled rapidly back and forth, pulling her body with her arms.

The whole time her rebellious brain worked just as hard as her muscles, doggedly refusing to shut off as it was supposed to do when the body was being taxed in such a manner.

Loud and clear, she was reminded that certain things were forever lost to her. It was a fact she'd accepted long ago—ten years ago, in fact.

She did repeated sets of pull-downs.

"...eight, nine, ten," she counted.

She was reminded of dancing, for one thing. She'd never dance again, but as the years passed after the accident, Jessie had finally realized one day that she'd already passed the age when a ballerina would ordinarily be forced to quit the stage. The realization had swept away the last regrets about her lost career.

"...six, seven, eight, nine."

Marriage. Even before her accident, she'd been a failure at marriage, so it stood to reason she wouldn't try again after being disabled.

"...seven, eight, nine, teeeeeen." Ouch. That one hurt...like the admission that she would never have children of her own. Her thoughts flew enviously to her friend Kathleen, who was expecting her second baby. Kathleen had a husband, a stable marriage. There wasn't any point in comparing herself to her friend. Their lives had taken very different paths.

Sex. Physical intimacy was something she'd avoided since her divorce. Oh, there'd been plenty of men since her accident with various offers of solace in that department. Disability seemed to attract those who were morbidly curious, or those who wanted a partner totally dependent on them. Or... *Stop it!* she told herself crossly. *You know there were also a minute number of kind, thoroughly nice, presentable sincere men who seemed to want you just for you.*

Jessie's mouth twisted in a wry grin, and she mopped her face with a towel she kept handy.

The trouble was she'd never been able to feel she wanted any of the men she'd met.

Maybe that was a good thing. She was old-fashioned enough to consider sex an outgrowth of love, and love suggested permanency. Which brought the whole thing back to marriage. Disabled women didn't have a great track record in that department, especially if they'd been married before their accident.

Kathleen and her husband, Joe Dodd, were rarities. Their love had sustained them both before and after Kathleen's accident.

But as for herself, who needed a broken heart to drag along as well as useless legs? She'd already had one broken marriage in her life, and one was quite enough, thank you.

Jessie hooked her long legs up to the electrodes and wires that composed a functional electrical stimulation apparatus. This prohibitively expensive bit of paraphernalia had been a gift from her parents—a gift her mother was sorely disappointed with.

Chandra had been certain from the beginning that if Jessie would only try hard enough, she'd be able to walk again and thus dance again. Jessie suspected that her mother still believed vaguely that the partial paralysis of her body was the result of a lack of willpower, although she'd never said that in so many words.

By touching a switch on the portable control panel, Jessie activated impulses that stimulated the muscles in her legs she couldn't otherwise feel or exercise. The machine quite simply helped prevent atrophy, and Jessie viewed it as her most valuable beauty aid. It had been a wonderful gift, even if Chandra had bought it for the wrong reasons.

Thoughts of beauty aids somehow turned Jessie's thoughts to the subject of men. It had been decidedly simple to negate emotional entanglements before. So what was different now? Why was she getting herself in a state over Luke?

Luke.

Luke and the way he made Jessie feel. He was the difference this time.

But Jessie didn't want to feel this way. She didn't want to feel this way at all. She'd never thought it possible for her.

Why couldn't this traitorous warmth, this quickening excitement, which seemed to have lain coyly asleep all these past ten years, simply have atrophied the way her leg muscles would have if she'd ignored them in a similar manner?

Because, she lectured herself brutally, no matter how she felt about him, there was nothing ahead for her but heartbreak if she let herself—she swallowed the word, but it popped right back into her mind—if she let herself love Luke Chadwick.

She must not let herself love him.

Willpower wasn't going to do a darn bit of good in that area, either.

CHAPTER FOUR

"OKAY, YOU GUYS, come and get it," Lorna hollered out the back door. "Denny, make sure your sons wash those hands before they get near the table, too."

Retrieving the football from where it had landed in a flower bed, Luke helped herd his nephews toward the washroom, which was conveniently situated near the back door of Denny and Lorna's comfortable old home.

"One at a time, men." Luke lined up the three sturdy little boys, standing at the end of the wobbly line they formed and putting Rob between himself and the other boys. Nearly four, Rob was the smallest of the rowdy gang and inclined to be trampled easily in the stampede.

Denny supervised the washing process.

"Better shove those sleeves up past your wrists," Denny ordered. "And use some soap there, Dan. Your mother'll know right away if you don't use soap, she can smell it a mile away. Faces, too," he added, receiving a chorus of disgusted groans from his sons.

"Unca Luke, do me," Rob insisted when his turn came, and Luke hoisted the chubby child up under one arm, and with practiced ease, he used his free hand to clumsily swipe a cloth across dirt-smeared cheeks and soap his nephew's tiny, grubby hands.

"I sit by Unca Luke," Dave declared, and there was a minor squabble as Dan and Rob also demanded that honor.

Finally, everyone was seated, a nephew on either side of Luke and Rob in a high chair placed strategically near his father.

Lorna served the food, a hearty meat-and-noodle casserole with some sort of delectable cheese sauce, plenty of green salad and a strudel-topped apple pie for dessert with great heaps of vanilla ice cream accompanying each generous slice.

Sunday dinner with his sister and her family was a long-standing tradition and one Luke thoroughly enjoyed. Tonight, however, his thoughts were often far away as the dinner progressed, and Lorna finally said in exasperation, "For heaven's sake, Luke, are you listening to me or not?"

"Sorry." Luke gave his sister an apologetic smile. "Say again?"

Lorna scowled at him, and Luke gave her his full attention for the first time that day, realizing belatedly that his twin not only sounded exasperated with him but that Lorna had seemed generally out of sorts with her entire family today, and that wasn't like her at all.

Tall and a shade too thin, Lorna had deep auburn hair instead of Luke's dark mop, and to her everlasting chagrin, she was the twin with straight hair while he'd rated curls. But she'd received identically colored eyes, huge and almost unreal in their blueness with long, thick lashes.

Normally she sparkled with energy and good humor, managing her male household with efficient control and unlimited love.

Today, however, there was definitely something wrong, and Luke wondered guiltily why he hadn't noticed earlier. If he could just stop thinking of Jessie for a while...

"Sorry, I wasn't paying attention. What's up, Sis?"

Denny wasn't any help at all. Before Lorna could respond, he jibed, "You haven't been right in the skull all this week, buddy. Every time I talk to you, you're off wool-gathering someplace. Who is she? You can tell us, we're family."

"Fambly," repeated five-year-old Dave, his mouth full of pie. Crumbs flew from his mouth, and his brothers went into fits of giggles.

"That's enough," Lorna warned sharply, and Denny glanced at her and hurriedly said, "That's it, gang, you're all excused. Come along and you can watch TV for an hour till bedtime. And no arguments about what show. I'll pick one for all of you."

Sons in tow, Denny led the way to the basement family room. Luke frowned at his sister. Lorna was studying the bottom of her coffee cup as if it held the secrets of the ages.

"You're awfully short-tempered all of a sudden." Being twins did away with a lot of unnecessary social politeness. Luke and Lorna had always understood each other almost instinctively, and age hadn't dulled the easy way they communicated.

Lorna's eyes narrowed, and she shrugged in a desultory fashion.

"How's the catering going?" Lorna had started a small cottage industry-type business out of her kitchen after Rob was born, preparing her special brand of good, wholesome food for small weddings, bridge luncheons and parties. At first, her customers had all been neighbors and friends from the Richmond suburb where she and Denny lived. The business had increased through word-of-mouth to the point that Lorna now employed an assistant twice weekly, as well as a young man with a small car who made her deliveries.

"Luke," Lorna demanded, a note of sarcastic desperation in her voice, "do you think it's remotely possible that Denny might have ever heard rumors about the women's movement and the need for us to have careers of our own?"

Luke stared at her, surprised at her outburst, doubly surprised at the bitterness in her voice when she mentioned Denny. The Mason's marriage was one of the few Luke had seen that made him believe such a bond could not only work but be full of love into the bargain.

He pointed in the direction of the kitchen. "I thought you considered your catering a career."

"That's exactly the point. It is my career. But just like any other businessperson, I want to expand. You know the new Market that's opening over by the river?"

Luke nodded. The huge colorful Markets, housing numerous businesses in stalls under one large decorative roof, were becoming the hub for shopping in the Lower Mainland.

"I want to rent one of the stalls and open a combination take-out and lunch-counter service called The Soup Kitchen. I'd specialize in soup stocks and good homemade bread. That way I wouldn't have to carry as much stuff as I do now with the catering, because the emphasis would be on lighter meals. And lots of women want good soup stock and don't have time to make it from scratch."

"It sounds like a good idea, Lorna. Innovative, as well. I've never heard of a store selling soup stocks."

Her blue eyes glittered with frustration and anger. "I know it would really be successful, but you know what? Denny won't hear of it. He won't listen. He won't discuss it. He wants me to go right on like I am now, entertaining myself with my little hobby here at home." Lorna's voice was angry and sarcastic. "And maybe—get this—even have another baby in a year or so. I had the boys late enough in life without starting all over again."

Luke felt as if he'd discovered quicksand in a placid meadow. He stood up and started scraping plates and stacking them. "You do grow wonderful babies, Lorna," he teased gently. "Even if you only use one pattern for them all and I never get a niece out of all this, you're still really good at it." His sister finally gave him the barest ghost of a smile.

"I'm thirty-eight, Brother, same number as you. I'm getting a bit long in the tooth for growing babies, even though I adore them. And if it comes to that, what about you? You're aging right along with me. It's past time you returned the favor," she countered. "I wouldn't mind a niece or nephew of my own, you know."

"Want me to try and talk to Denny?"

It was about the last thing Luke felt like doing. He'd never interceded between Denny and Lorna before. He'd never had to, he admitted wryly.

"I'd be grateful if you'd try, Luke." She turned her expressive gaze on him and said earnestly, "I really need to do this, for myself. You know I worked at that deadly dull law office before the kids came because we needed the money. I told Denny after Dan was born and the landscaping business picked up that I never wanted to go out to work again, that all I wanted was to be a wife and mother, so maybe this situation is partly my own fault. Obviously, he believed me. But darn it all, this isn't the same as typing up legal briefs—this is a chance to run my own business. Something of my very own, that I've created. Other than babies, of course. See if he'll talk to you about it, won't you, Luke? He sure won't talk to me, and I end up getting furious with everyone."

"No kidding? Well, you sure hide it well. Nobody would ever notice you were in a temper, Lorna," Luke remarked. The tension eased as she laughed and aimed a friendly punch at his shoulder.

He was saved from further comment because Denny rejoined them, and they all cleared the table together and stacked the dishwasher in the huge remodeled kitchen.

A HAZY GLOW lingered over the city when Luke steered his small, sporty car over the Oak Street Bridge later that evening. The weather had stayed clear, and the unexpected stretch of May sunshine was already sending hordes of people to Vancouver's miles of beaches, resulting in heavier traffic than was usual for a Sunday night.

Lorna had seemed in a better mood after speaking her mind, Luke thought with satisfaction while waiting for a stoplight to change. Recalling their chat, he considered her joking request for a nephew or niece.

As she'd reminded him, he was thirty-eight years old. If he were ever going to have children of his own, he'd better do so in the next couple of years or content himself with simply being a doting bachelor uncle to his nephews.

Here it was again, that nudging suggestion that he should be getting on with life rather than only marking time.

And then, just as they had an awkward habit of doing these days, his thoughts slipped to Jessie, and Luke wondered with a wrenching ache in his gut whether she ever thought longingly of having children.

Could women in wheelchairs have babies of their own? It was a subject he'd never given a moment's thought to before knowing Jessie.

He clicked the car radio on. It was already set to what he thought of as "her" station, but the voice on the air wasn't hers. She must be off on weekends. He glanced at his watch. It was early, only a little after eight.

Without pausing to debate the decision, he swiftly changed lanes and signaled a left turn onto the through street that would lead most quickly to her house.

Jessie had spent Sunday doing housework, laundry and even preparing extra meals to slip in the freezer for days when she was working. She'd stayed frenziedly busy, refusing to admit she was trying not to think about Luke, disgustedly aware that she was thinking of him, anyway, and had been all day.

She'd grown used to having him there in her back garden this week when she awoke, used to sharing a coffee with him in the evening before she left for work. He fitted the job in whenever he could, early mornings or late evenings, and each day they found a new subject to talk over or argue about. When Saturday came and Luke didn't, she'd been ridiculously disappointed and also annoyed with herself for caring.

She was still labeling aluminum freezer plates when the doorbell rang.

Her heart gave a tremendous thump when she opened the door and saw him standing there, and she realized her faded jeans were covered with splotches from the spaghetti sauce she'd made. She was horrified to realize she hadn't brushed her hair or looked at herself in a mirror since the morning.

"Hi, Luke. Come on in. I was just—"

"Hi, Jessie. I was just—"

She looked up at him, towering in the doorway, and she couldn't help smiling. His dark curls were endearingly tousled, and he had a grimy set of small fingerprints on the pale-blue knit shirt he was wearing, just at the neck. Whose child had he been holding? She asked him, gesturing at his shirt, and he tried to squint down at it, giving it a brush with his hand.

"I have three grimy nephews," he explained. "It could be any one of them."

He was smiling, the same wide, glad smile she could feel on her own lips.

"I was going to drive down to Spanish Banks and watch the lights go on in the city, maybe have a coffee. Want to come?"

The invitation was unexpected. It was offered so casually, as if he were asking just any ordinary woman to come for a ride on a warm Sunday evening. It was the kind of everyday, male-female thing that hardly ever happened to her, and she found herself aching to accept, knowing she shouldn't....

"Oh, I . . . Well, I'm in the middle . . . I'm not, I mean I can't . . ." She drew in a deep breath and recklessly did what she wanted so badly to do.

"Can you wait a minute while I brush my hair?"

His smile widened, the blue eyes with their thick lashes twinkled at her, and he bent forward, running a rough finger lightly back and forth over her chin, making her flinch for an instant until he added, "It might be an idea to wipe off all this red stuff on your chin while you're at it. No point in both of us being stained."

"Spaghetti sauce," she breathed ruefully, gesturing at her jeans and what once had been a white T-shirt. "I guess it looks as if I bathed in it. Come in, sit down, and I'll go wash my face."

It took half an hour to peel off her clothes behind the closed bedroom door, scrub herself down in the shower with hands that shook as if she had palsy and pull on white linen slacks and a short-sleeved cotton blouse in a deep chocolate shade that she knew suited her tan and brought out the brown in her eyes.

You're making a mistake, she warned herself grimly, fumbling with the buttons on her blouse.

You're setting yourself up for a fall, she lectured, lips moving silently while she struggled to tame her wildly tangled mane of curls with the hairbrush.

I'm scared, she thought plaintively, tracing her lips with bronze gloss and remembering how his fingers had felt, stroking across her chin. The memory made her shudder.

She wheeled out finally, praying she looked relaxed instead of on the verge of a nervous seizure, and Luke drank in the bronze and cream tones of her skin, the contained wildness of her white-gold hair, the sparkle in her dark eyes.

Her firmly lush breasts were subtly outlined under the brown blouse and on her feet were matching brown sandals. He noticed her toenails were painted a warm coral.

She looked lovely, well-groomed, sexy. Luke suddenly realized he hadn't even given a thought to the wheelchair, or how he'd get her into his car, or where he'd stow the damn thing, or... Misgivings about his impulsive invitation rolled over him.

Trying not to appear at all uncertain, he stood up and said bravely, "Madam, your chariot awaits," and was rewarded by a bubble of delighted laughter.

"You and Cy must have gone to the same school of bad remarks."

He held the door while she rolled out and down the sidewalk, and he opened the door on his red Thunderbird, beginning to worry about what he ought to do next. Before he had time to puzzle over it, she'd set her brake and transferred from the chair smoothly and with a minimum of fuss into the passenger's seat, looking comfortable and quite at home there as she fussed with her seat belt.

"Just shove the chair in the back. It folds up," she said offhandedly, and he did. Then painlessly, easily, he was driving them along the twilit streets toward the ocean.

"It's so lovely in this city when it doesn't rain, isn't it?" she was saying enthusiastically. "Oh, Luke, did you see that garden? It was full of bushes with huge scarlet flowers on them. Can we have some like that in my garden?"

"They're hydrangea. I'll put half a dozen in if you like."

He kept stealing glances at the clear purity of her profile beside him as she chattered on about the progress he was making in her yard, and once, stopped at a light, he caught the young man in the next car also admiring her, an envious, openly lecherous expression on his face.

Luke shot him a cold, narrow-eyed glare, and the car sped away when the light changed.

The incident made Luke realize that he'd never seen Jessie out of her chair before, never watched anyone reacting to her in an ordinary fashion. Riding along beside him like this, no one suspected that she was disabled. They saw only a remarkably beautiful blond woman, expensively and tastefully dressed, laughing and talking with her companion.

A sudden and overwhelming wave of angry resentment shot through Luke as he began to comprehend the subtle difference in attitudes that she must encounter daily. The idea that anyone would think differently of Jessie in or out of her wheelchair appalled him, and yet, ashamed but honest, he knew he, too, had been a victim of doing exactly that before he came to know her.

"Oh, just look at that violet color on the mountains, and the trees against the sky. I'll bet that's what Hawaii looks like at sunset."

He felt ridiculously pleased that she was enjoying herself. The sleek car sped down the long hill leading to the beach, and below them was the protected inlet. Tankers lay peacefully at anchor on the gray-blue depths, and numerous tiny sailboats bobbed here and there like toys. Across the bay, the cities of North and West Vancouver were still softened by a hazy sunset glow, and to the east, downtown Vancouver, with its profile of dramatically tall buildings, lay mirrored in the still depths of the calm water, the dramatic orange and crimson of the sun's dying reflection shining out from thousands of windows, all of them changed miraculously into mirrors by the sunset.

The road followed the line of the shore westward. There were several parking lots along the way, and Luke pulled into one far down the beach and stopped.

"I haven't been down here in ages," Jessie remarked, turning her head eagerly this way and that to see the view.

It was peaceful, the only sounds pleasantly cheerful ones. A group of teenagers threw a Frisbee, a radio played softly from a convertible parked some distance away.

"I come here often in the evening," he admitted, bravely adding, "I usually listen to you doing 'Night Shift' from down here. That voice of yours blends right in with the surroundings, mellow and soul soothing."

She flushed with pleasure and heard herself confiding after a moment, "I've been asked to audition for some commercials next week, and I think I'll give it a try. Most announcers make extra income that way."

Thinking all of a sudden of Lorna, Luke said, "You get a lot of satisfaction from your career, don't you, Jess? Do you ever think about doing anything else, or will you stay in broadcasting?"

"It's been my life for the past eight years," she answered simply. After a moment she added, "there's my parents, of course, and Cy, and a few other friends I see now and then, but my work is really the core of my life. Yes, it means a great deal to me. It's what I plan to spend my life doing. How about you, Luke? Will you stay in the business you're in now, or will you look for another career?"

She'd managed neatly to pinpoint the major uncertainty in his life at the moment.

"I'm not sure," he temporized. "Someone suggested once that I might try doing a type of counseling, but so far I enjoy landscaping." To avoid another question, he asked, "Is there much job security in announcing?"

She shook her head. "Because it's media, it's highly competitive. An announcer, or a station for that matter, is only as good as its last ratings. In a sense, you're always on trial, striving constantly for excellence in your work, which doesn't allow for much goofing off." She gave a half smile and added matter-of-factly, "Plus, disabled people always have to perform any job twice as well as anyone else, so it's a kind of double challenge for me."

A light breeze blew in from the water, and Jessie drew the scent of ocean and seaweed into her nostrils greedily, unaware of how her bland statement had affected Luke.

He knew that what she said was true. Jessie would have to prove herself in any job situation, but the one she'd chosen was doubly difficult. It had overtones of show business. She was on stage all the time, and she had to be exceptionally talented simply to survive in that environment, never mind succeed.

And yet she did so, day after day.

Her simple courage awed him, made him feel humble. He wanted to ask bold questions about her life, discover what it was that had made her this way.

He turned toward her, reaching almost unconsciously for her hand, holding it firmly in his own and ignoring her halfhearted, shy attempt to draw away.

"Jessie," he began, and the sudden tension in his voice as well as a tightened grip on her fingers brought a surprised glance from her. She waited, studying his sober expression.

What he was about to ask was intensely personal, and he realized full well that she had every right to tell him to mind his own business. But he needed to understand everything about her, without knowing quite why he felt that way, and the only way to gain such understanding was to ask, boldly and bluntly.

"Jessie, can you tell me about your accident, explain what it was like for you, before and . . . and after? How did you learn to be so accepting, how can you be so happy all the time? I keep remembering that you were a dancer, that movement was your very life—"

"Well, it's not courage, that's for sure, so don't ever accuse me of being brave, or I'll punch you, hard." Jessie's blunt and spirited reply was definite and automatic, and Luke had to grin in surprise at her feisty warning.

"It makes me shudder when well-meaning people coo, 'Oh, my dear, you're so courageous,'" she went on disparagingly. "Bravery involves the ability to make a choice, and there was no choice involved. It was simply a matter of survival. And of learning how much I could do, instead of concentrating on what I couldn't do."

The late-evening light was waning, and her expression softened. Her dark eyes lost their aggressive gleam, grew pensively huge, dominating the engaging triangle of her face as she met his intensely frowning gaze head-on.

"You know, the only other person I've tried to really explain all this to is Cy," she commented thoughtfully after a long, silent moment. "Most people avoid asking, of course, as if paralysis is some shameful disease I've contracted. But if you want to hear about it, I'll do my best." Her smile flashed and was gone. "Mind you, it's liable to get boring because I've got to go quite a ways back. Sure you want to hear the sordid story of my life?" Her words were light, almost flippant, but her face was vulnerable.

Luke nodded, maintaining his steady hold on the small hand nestled so neatly inside his own.

She was excruciatingly conscious of her hand in his, the safe warmth his huge, rough palm seemed to convey, the awareness of flesh and strength and maleness the link provided. She was adept at controlling her voice, so none of the turmoil inside her was revealed as she spoke, but Luke could feel the betraying hammer of the pulse at her wrist. He looped his fingers around hers in silent reassurance.

Her eyes were deep pools now, staring into his but not really seeing him, looking into the past.

He waited, and his own heart was hammering so hard in his chest he was certain she must hear it.

"I was such a naive, innocent kid," she began. "I'd led a ridiculously protected, disciplined life until just before the accident. I told you I was a dancer, and a dancer's life is anything but glamorous. It's class every day, practice, performing, then back to your room, exhausted more often than not. It was my mother's ambition for me. My dad is a liquor importer, an extremely successful businessman, and money was no problem, so I was sent to the best schools, given the rigorous training a ballerina must have in order to succeed. Life was strictly regulated. We were closely chaperoned all the time I was growing up, and I was kept so busy I never thought to question my life. Besides, I was competitive and, I suppose, talented, as well. By the age of sixteen, I was dancing with one of Canada's leading troupes, and dancing was my entire life. Then, when I was twenty, I met—" Jessie drew in an involuntary gulp of air before she continued, and Luke could feel the increased tension in her hand.

"I met a country-and-western singer, a man named Wayne Palmer, at a party. He was ridiculously good-looking, twenty-four, talented. He'd cut a record and it was doing well, and I was impressed. He was vastly different from anyone else I knew."

She was quiet for a long moment. A couple strolled past, arms around each other's waists. Jessie's gaze followed them thoughtfully as the echo of their conversation and the woman's soft laughter floated into the car.

"I was flattered that a man like Wayne would be attracted to me. I was very shy and much younger than my years, and he seemed very much a man of the world. He was everything I'd never been—rebellious, impulsive, madly young, a touch wicked. No wonder I fell for him. I'd never met anyone even remotely like Wayne before. We were married only a week after we met, on my twenty-first birthday. My parents were horrified, especially my mother." A tiny, sad smile tilted Jessie's mouth as she remembered Chandra's rage, her attempts to have the marriage annulled. "My mother was right to be concerned but for the wrong reasons. She was basking in my dancing success, and she was concerned only that I might damage my career. My dad was more worried about my happiness. He quietly did some checking into Wayne's background and found that he'd been in and out of juvenile court and that he'd had a pretty rough childhood. Dad tried to warn me, but of course I wouldn't listen."

"Were you living here in Vancouver?"

Jessie shook her head. "My troupe was based in Eastern Canada, so we lived in my apartment in Toronto when I wasn't on tour. Wayne liked to party, and there were always a number of his friends hanging around. During the next months I found out he gambled and drank rather a lot, and most of my savings disappeared. He knew I had an income from my grandmother's estate and that I was an only child of wealthy parents. While he was quite willing to live on my money, he resented me for having it. I wasn't much of a fighter in those days, so I spent a great deal of my time in tears."

Jessie's voice was unemotional, stating facts from long ago, remembering other scenes she wasn't about to describe, sordid and humiliating quarrels with Wayne.

"Miss Priss," Wayne had labeled her sarcastically when she refused to party every night with his rowdy friends. "You figure you're too good for us ordinary folks," he'd accuse. "You might have all the right equipment, rich girl, but you sure don't know how to use it," he'd taunt when she rejected his drunken advances. When he was sober, sex had been pleasant enough between them, but certainly not the thunder-and-lightning experience avid reading and romantic ballet had led her to expect. When Wayne was drunk, Jessie wanted no part of his clumsy, selfish advances, and it never failed to infuriate him.

Why should long-ago accusations still have such power to hurt her? She thrust away the memory of those months of marriage, hurrying to the crux of her story.

"We'd been at a party the night of the accident, and he'd been drinking. I asked him to let me drive, but he refused. He misjudged a turn on a narrow road, and the car overturned. He was thrown free, uninjured. I still don't remember the accident. I remember waking up in the hospital. I was in an electric circle bed, and my bottom felt numb, my legs uncomfortable. In a way I was lucky because my spinal cord wasn't severed. It was bruised, and I still have some sensation in my legs, although I've never recovered enough to walk again." She inclined her head thoughtfully to one side and added, "It's the strangest thing, Luke. The doctors and therapists all tell you what's happened to your nerve endings and bodily functions after an accident like mine, but it used to astonish me that nobody ever simply asked how it felt emotionally. Maybe things are better now, but ten years ago nobody offered much psychological help. Isn't that weird, when the adjustments are so great? It's like living two entirely separate lifetimes, before and after, with nobody to talk to about the shift. My parents came out to Toronto, of course, but they weren't any help at all. I think the hardest thing about that time was the loneliness.''

"What about your husband? Didn't he help you?" Luke's voice was husky, and she felt his warm breath on her face.

"He wasn't around much while I was in hospital, and right after I got out, we were divorced.''

Luke kept his features carefully neutral, but the storm of emotions her calm words stirred in him were like a whirlwind rushing through his body.

As if she guessed at the rage he was feeling toward a man he'd never even met, Jessie said quietly, earnestly, "I don't blame Wayne, Luke. It was an accident. I could have chosen not to ride with him. He was charged with impaired driving afterward, although he wasn't convicted, and the publicity damaged his career. Afterward, when I fully understood what had happened to me, the ramifications of it all, I was a different person entirely than the girl he'd married.''

The light was fading quickly now, and the ocean was pewter, streaked here and there with traces of color left by the lingering sunset whose rosy hues still stained the sky to the far west.

"Statistics show that ninety-nine percent of marriages fail when the woman is the injured partner," Jessie added.

"The bastard. The rotten, selfish bastard, dumping you at a time when you must have needed emotional support the most." Luke's words were barely audible, but the intensity of them shocked her, warmed her with the depth of his concern.

"I did need support, but you've got the details wrong, Luke. I was the one who divorced Wayne.''

CHAPTER FIVE

"I CAME HOME from the rehab hospital one weekend and found he'd moved another woman into my apartment. So I got a lawyer and divorced him, and then I moved out here and started over." Jessie's tone was reasonable, her throaty voice even, as if what she was describing to Luke was a commonplace occurrence. Beyond the windshield night was slowly painting the inlet shades of green and gray and pewter. Inside the car the enticing flowery scent of Jessie filled his nostrils even as the full impact of her words caused fruitless anger to surge inside him, rage toward a man he'd never met. Jealousy and a deep need to protect the woman at his side struggled with his efforts at control, and finally Luke swore, his words short and foul and graphic.

"My attitude exactly," Jessie agreed calmly. "Actually, though, once the shock wore off, I realized Wayne had done me a favor. That was an important turning point in my rehab program because, from then on, I was furiously determined to be fully self-supporting and independent. For the most part, I have been, too." She sounded proud of herself.

"And..." Luke couldn't bring himself to use the man's name. "What became of him?" He realized he was hoping for news of painful death.

"Wayne? I never saw him again after the divorce became final. I knew he remarried somewhere in the States, and that it didn't last. He had a couple of good years as far as his singing went, made several recordings. There's still a single of his played now and then. We've got it down at the station, but he never made it really big the way he'd hoped to. He used to come to Vancouver once in a while for a gig in some pub and I'd see his name listed.''

Her voice was entirely free of malice, and he frowned into the darkness. ''Don't you hate him, Jessie?''

''I thought I did at first, for a couple of years,'' she admitted. Then, very thoughtfully, she added, ''But I don't think so anymore. My life is full now, and I'm happy. It takes too much good useful energy to go on hating somebody year after year.''

''So you don't love him, either?'' Luke understood emotional complications too well to think it wasn't possible.

She shook her head vehemently, and the rising moon made silver rivers of the hair on her shoulders. Her denial was quick and honest, and a tense knot in Luke's stomach relaxed.

''Good grief, no,'' she declared. ''I think of him occasionally, the way you do about things in the past. Everyone makes mistakes, and I guess marrying Wayne was my big one, but you learn from them.''

Night had deepened even as they talked. The inside of the car was full of shadows, and Jessie hardly knew Luke had moved until she suddenly found herself encompassed by his arms.

''Luke, I...'' she started to protest, but he slid her gently, firmly, across the seat into his embrace, and bending his head swiftly down to hers, he kissed her lightly. There was hardly more than a flicker of his firm lips across the softness of her own before he drew back.

''You're a lovely woman, Jess. I need to hold you, kiss you.''

Surprise held her frozen at first, and then a piercing sweetness engulfed her as his lips claimed hers a second time, more confidently now.

Again she resisted a little, frightened by the confused welter of sensation pouring through her but totally unable to make her resistance more than a token murmur.

He gave her time to get used to him, kissing her softly, gently. She needed time. There was the strangeness of being held so intimately, his body warm and hard and alive, touching hers, the slight and pleasant tickle of his mustache against her skin, the heady man smell he exuded.

He was patient, gentling her, cradling her, silently questioning instead of demanding, and when she relaxed slightly in his embrace, he again narrowed the distance between her lips and his own until they met a third time, this time with all the pent-up longing and the male passion Luke had struggled to conceal till now.

At that blazing instant, for Jessie, there was the disconcerting knowledge that Luke was very, very good at kissing. His firm lips knew just how to caress and tease and question, his tongue drawing circles of sweetness on the sensitive rim of her shy lips until she opened for him, not conscious of deciding to do so, only needing to feel the sensuous headiness of his tongue exploring the interior of her mouth. The world narrowed and blurred, and she was astonished and thrilled by the burning urgency he stirred in her breasts. Now she no longer had the slightest desire to stop.

Her hands had come to rest on his broad chest with some confused idea of pushing him away, but as their kiss deepened, she spread her palms, feeling the mighty surging of his heart like an echo to the pounding of her own.

She couldn't seem to resist touching him, her hands greedily stroking their way up to his shoulders where the bunched muscles tensed beneath her fingers, further up around his strong neck to the softness of the wildly curling hair.

His large, warm hand was stroking her rib cage lightly through her thin blouse, moving upward towards her breasts. Jessie, lost in a dream of delight, longed for that hand to reach its goal, ached for his touch on her suddenly sensitive flesh.

Luke's heart was hammering, and his breath came in short gasps, matching the raggedness of her own breathing... and then, headlights and young voices calling ribald comments through the open windows as a car full of teenagers drove slowly through the parking lot.

Jessie pulled back, her eyes wide and frightened at the interruption. Luke held her firmly, protectively close to his chest, shielding her with his body until the other car accelerated past them with a scream of tires and honking horn before it finally sped off down the highway.

"Easy, love..." Luke stroked a hand over the silken softness of her hair, trying to calm the panic he sensed in her, silently cursing the other car and its youthful occupants.

But the spell was broken. Jessie drew back jerkily, using the armrest to draw herself over to the passenger's side of the car, lifting her legs with both hands and swinging them back to safer territory.

Then she sat quite still, staring blindly out into the darkness and wondering dazedly what had happened to her brain, kissing Luke like that. She knew she was trembling more from the aftereffects of his embrace than from the intrusion of the other car. Passion, a word she'd always considered hugely overrated, was suddenly a force to be reckoned with, and she felt off-balance.

Worst of all, she didn't have the vaguest idea what to say next, how to treat a situation of this sort. She was thirty-two years old, and any one of the fifteen-year-olds who phoned her regularly for advice could probably have given her some right then.

There was an endless moment of strained silence between them, and then he said gruffly, "I've wanted to do that for a while now, Jessie, so there's not much point in apologizing."

She felt a painful constriction in her throat at his words, a dreadful gnawing ache of desperate, futile longing for the normal life long since lost to her and a burgeoning anger at his choice of words.

"I don't expect an apology, Luke." Her voice was harsh and more than a shade bitter. Would he even think of apologizing for a kiss if she were able-bodied?

Of course not. He'd probably be speeding right now for his apartment, or hers, to fulfill the cravings their embrace had created, a perfectly healthy, normal male anticipating nothing more than a delightful affair with a normal female.

Pain knotted her soul, and Jessie knew why she'd always avoided scenes like these. The potential for mistakes was simply too great.

After her divorce she'd been emotionally numb, loathe to explore what had to be severe limitations in her body's ability to respond to a man. Up till now she'd never been tempted to experiment.

Until tonight. Why tonight? The answer, of course, was Luke. There was a sort of inexplicable energy between them she'd never experienced before.

She'd wanted his kisses, and that wanting had outweighed years of determined—and sensible—avoidance.

This single episode had to be the end of any physical relationship, however. Jessie couldn't, wouldn't, carry it further.

How could she stand it if she disappointed him? What if he were repelled by her clumsy attempts at loving? She'd never been very assertive sexually, even after months of marriage, and Wayne had been quick to mock her shyness.

It was far too late to try again. The time had passed for her to learn about physical loving. Suddenly she wanted only to retreat to safety, to a place where she'd feel secure.

"I want to go home, Luke."

To her dismay, he didn't start the car immediately. Instead, he reached across and insisted on taking her tightly balled up hands in one of his. She resisted, but he was far stronger than she.

"Jess, we're not kids, we should try to talk about this." His voice was rougher than he'd intended because Luke felt completely off balance at the moment. "What is it you're so afraid of?"

Kissing Jessie had been impulsive, an affectionate response to her candid conversation. *How wrong can a guy get?* he wondered.

It had been like innocently lighting a tiny match that suddenly ignited a full-scale forest fire. Physical desire for her raged inside of him even now with a shocking intensity. He wanted to taste her, explore the contours of that slender body, learn every nuance of touch that gave her pleasure.

And he knew she'd felt the same way only moments before. He'd felt it in her body, in the wild response of her kiss . . . yet now she was snatching her hands away and huddling against the door with her face turned from him.

Hell, he was good and scared of feeling this way about her, too. What did he know about her limitations, about what was even possible when a woman was disabled? But he'd learn, he wanted so much to learn.

He glanced over at her, and his heart contracted. She looked so small and vulnerable, crouched down miserably in the corner. She was undoubtedly even more scared than he was. Luke tried again, coaxing her gently.

"Jess? Talk to me. Don't just clam up and shut me out this way. If there's anything I did that hurt you, if I was rough—"

"No, it's not that at all. It's not physical. For God's sake, do you go around treating other women as if they'll break or something if you kiss them?" she asked furiously. For a moment the anger flared higher than the fear inside her. But defeat quickly took its place, along with disgust for her quick temper when she saw the withdrawal, the hurt, on his face.

"Please, please, Luke, just take me home."

He turned the key, and the motor roared abruptly to life. He backed up and swung the car around, and his face was set in hard, cold lines as he accelerated down the highway.

With every long, silent moment she felt increasingly ashamed of the way she was acting. She owed him an explanation of some sort. After all, she'd responded to his kisses in a way she'd never responded before in her life. Taking a deep, cleansing breath and planning her words carefully, she attempted to explain at least some of what she was feeling.

"Luke, I'm sorry. It was unfair of me to snarl at you like that. It's just that, since my accident, I've never dated, or—" she gulped and forced herself to finish "—or had an affair with anyone. Even before the accident, there was . . . was only . . ." Her breath ran out, and she gulped a bit before she was able to add, "only . . . Wayne. And I wasn't very good at . . . I think I was terribly bad at . . . so if I'm acting silly over what must be very ordinary and casual to you, it's because . . ."

She couldn't go on. It was horrible to sound so gauche, to make so much out of what had only been a kiss, after all.

He must think her a complete idiot by now, and rather than make it even worse, she gave up, her cheeks burning with shame.

Luke didn't answer immediately. She'd made him furious, going on about other women when all he was trying to do was find out what the hell was wrong with her.

Although her admission brought a deepening of the growing tenderness he felt for the woman at his side, it also provoked grave self-doubt. What right did he have to come along and cause ripples in a life Jessie confidently described as "full and happy?" He, of all people, understood the need for isolation of the spirit, for caution when it came to emotional entanglements.

The best thing to do was back off, or the growing friendship between them would disintegrate. And he valued her friendship too much to jeopardize it, didn't he?

Or was this only friendship? He suddenly didn't really want to examine his feelings for Jessie too closely.

So he forced a light and playful note into his voice and said, "Tell you what, Jess, let's blame what happened back there on the full moon. Moons like that can make people crazy. When I was in the RCMP, we always had more problems when the moon was full than at any other time of the month. I remember once..." Luke launched into a complex and funny story, and though Jessie wasn't fooled by his tactics, she was charmed and comforted.

For the rest of the drive, Luke continued to relate curious tales out of his past. Jessie relaxed, and she was even laughing when he pulled to a stop in front of her house, which made it easy for him to rescue her chair for her from the trunk, stand prudently back and let her transfer there on her own, then walk beside her to the front door. When she paused awkwardly, half in and half out, unsure of how to leave him, he rubbed his knuckles lightly down her cheek and said casually, ''Night, Jess. See you sometime this week.''

She watched him stride back to his car, heard the powerful, smooth motor purr into life and saw the vehicle glide down the quiet street. Her fingers touched her face where he had touched her.

An awful sense of failure and loss overwhelmed her as she rolled into her house and slammed the door unnecessarily hard behind her.

Then she stared around at the comfortable, familiar, empty rooms, and she burst into tears. It had been so ironically easy during all these years to turn her back on romance, to sensibly decide it could have no part in her life. And it had been simple before she'd had a concept of what it was she'd relinquished.

Tonight with Luke she'd skimmed the surface of what might have been. What would have been ... if.

In an agony of longing, Jessie pummeled her useless legs with her fists and sobbed like a child for what she'd accepted years before was lost to her forever. Hadn't she even been relieved at times that sex and its complications were no longer a part of her life? What a fool she'd been, what an empty, stupid fool.

For the first time in many years, she despaired again, the way she had after the accident. It didn't last.

The years of acquiring self-esteem, of exploring potential and developing respect for herself and her abilities imposed their own presence. Like specters, they came now to stand invisibly on either side of her chair, old friends, reassuring, comforting, familiar.

You're strong, Jessie, they said.

There are many more things you can do than things you can't, they reminded.

No one has it all, they whispered.

She sobbed one last time, found a towel and mopped her eyes, gulped a glass of water and finally went to bed.

IT RAINED MONDAY and Tuesday, a gray and chilling Vancouver downpour that seemed to go on and on. There was no way anyone could work outside, and of course Luke didn't appear. Jessie was both profoundly relieved and childishly disappointed.

She used every ounce of professionalism she possessed in order to inject the necessary carefree, full-of-zest "sunshine" into her voice while doing "Night Shift," and it was a mark of her competence and ability as an announcer that she succeeded. All the same, she was limply grateful when the taping for commercials was delayed for another week.

Wednesday was the day Jessie always shared an early dinner with Cy. It was her turn to cook this week, and although she didn't feel like it, she prepared a hamburger-and-noodle casserole and grated carrots for a salad while she watched the rain dribble down the windows in her eating alcove. She tuned the radio to a bouncy rock station in an attempt to lighten the black mood that still plagued her.

As usual Cy arrived from his last class at about three, and he brought a large pitcher of his latest batch of beer down for Jessie to sample.

"It's great, Cy. It's a lot darker than your last batch, and there's more malt in this, isn't there?" Jessie did her level best to sound enthusiastic, sipping at the mug Cy had filled to the brim and rolling back and forth as she made the last-minute preparations for their meal.

Cy was staring out at the muddy mess the excavated backyard had become in the rain, and she missed the puzzled glance he shot her way when he caught the note of desperate cheeriness in her voice.

"How's the hot tub coming?" he demanded. "Damn rain, without it Luke could have made real progress back here this week. How you two getting along, Jessie? Still arguing over everything?"

Jessie rescued the casserole from the oven, resting it on a heatproof board across her knees and then plopping it down on the table.

"I haven't seen Luke this week," she said stiffly. She was serving the casserole, and as she spoke, she slopped a spoonful onto the woven yellow place mat. "If you want to know about the hot tub, why not ask him yourself?" She scraped too hard, and the sticky mess fell to the floor. Jessie muffled a curse and said petulantly, "What makes you think I see him any more than you do?"

Cy shrugged and took his usual place at the table. "Just figured you might know," he said innocently. "I thought I saw you climbing into his car Sunday night," he added, shaking out drops of Worcestershire sauce onto his plate. "I was glad to see that, Jess. It's about time you started getting out, and Luke's a real nice guy, even though I didn't think so in the beginning."

Jessie reached across and stilled the hand still shaking the sauce bottle. Cy raised his eyebrows at her in surprise, and she met his eyes with a level glare.

"If you're having any delusions about matchmaking, Cyrus Grant, you can forget them right now. Maybe you haven't paid too much attention here, but Luke is a nice, normal guy. An 'AB,' Cy. Able-bodied. Which, in case you haven't noticed, I'm not."

She was far angrier with Cy than she had any right to be. Anger had been building inside her since Luke's kiss, she now realized. And Cy was unwittingly providing the outlet for her frustration.

She brought her trembling hands down from the table and curled them into a tight ball on her lap, struggling to regain her composure. Her face felt hot and flushed, and Cy was still staring across at her, a frown making his thick eyebrows meet over his kind blue eyes.

"No, he's not physically disabled, but then I never thought you'd hold that against anybody, Jess. It's not Luke's fault he's able-bodied. Hell, after the years he spent in the RCMP doing what he did, you'd have to say he gave every type of disability a fair chance of happening to him, now, wouldn't you?" He calmly forked a mouthful of noodles and meat into his mouth and chewed appreciatively. "This is really great. How come the same darned recipe never tastes this way when I make it?"

She opened her mouth and snapped it shut again. She absolutely wouldn't give this infuriating man satisfaction by picking up on his bait about Luke.

They ate in silence for a few long moments, and then Jessie put down her fork with a clang and said grumpily, "Okay, you rotten old man, spill it. You win. What exactly did Luke do in the RCMP that was so dangerous, anyhow?"

Cy sipped his beer maddeningly slowly before he answered. "I've got a nephew in the force, think I mentioned him to you a coupla times. Well, first time I met Luke, after the marathon, that is, he told me he knew the sergeant up where Kenny's stationed in Yellowknife. I write to the kid all the time, so I just happened to mention meeting Luke."

Jessie shot her crafty friend a look that said she perfectly understood just how accidental that mention of Luke must have been. Cy ignored it, munching his way through another gigantic mouthful before he continued.

"Well, only this week, back comes a long letter. Seems Luke Chadwick's kind of a well-known name in police circles, even though he's been out of the force maybe seven years by now. He was what they call a high-power hostage negotiator, apparently the best in the business. One of those guys they send in when the prime minister gets kidnapped, or some nut holds a whole planeful of people for ransom, you know? Luke was so good at it they used to loan him out to other governments at times. Most of his jobs were damn dangerous.''

Jessie had given up all pretense of eating. She was gaping openmouthed, astonished at what Cy was saying, incapable for the moment of linking the Luke she knew with the person her friend was describing.

Cy helped himself to another generous amount of food, liberally sprinkled on the sauce again and attacked the casserole hungrily. He chewed quietly for while and then continued. ''Nobody seems to know why he quit. Kenny says the sarge up there told him Luke walked into the OC's office one day and handed in his resignation, right at the peak of his career. Threw the whole works of them for a loop, guess they had big plans for him.'' Cy inclined his head and asked curiously, ''He ever mention any of this to you, Jess?''

She shook her head, feeling dazed with the new picture Cy had presented.

''Well, you can bet he had good reasons to keep quiet, whatever they were. You can bet, too, it wasn't easy for him making the decision to leave his career. I remember all too clearly how I agonized over retiring from medicine. Nearly worked myself into cardiac problems—the very illness I was leaving in order to avoid. Luke's lots younger than I was, though.'' Cy buttered a thick chunk of bread and munched on it. ''Well,'' he added, ''it's interesting but none of my business, really. Wouldn't want him to think I was prying into his life. I'd never have repeated any of this, even to you,

Jess, if you hadn't been on this 'poor me' kick of yours, either. You know, girl, life socks it to all of us, one way or another, inside or out. Maybe you're lucky yours is so obvious. You ask me, the hidden kind can be every bit as bad.''

Cy drank his beer down in one long draught and added sternly, "I'm warning you, though. The last thing I'll stand by and watch you do is get on your high horse and turn your stubborn back on someone that could make you really happy. Luke has feelings for you, Jess, and don't go shaking your head at me that way, either." He shook a remonstrative finger at her. "I'm a man, and old or not, I've not forgotten the way a man looks at a woman he desires. Yes, Jessie, desires. Don't shy away from a good English word. Sparks fly every time you two are together. And you're no end of a fool if you let a goldarned wheelchair stop you from taking him up on whatever he proposes."

This kind of brutally honest conversation was one of the reasons she loved Cy as much as she did, but it didn't stop the tears from burning behind her eyes or making her voice thick when she answered him.

"What you're talking about should be the coming together of two whole people, not a crawling of one incomplete person toward the other, Cy."

Exasperation made him sputter and thump his fist down with a crash on the table, causing both Jessie and the cutlery to jump.

"Hogwash. What've I just been saying? There's not a one of us on this earth hasn't got problems of one sort or the other. Not one single whole soul around, if you ask me. So don't go setting yourself up as unique because you're not. And don't be too proud to accept whatever gifts life sends you." He poured another mugful of beer and took a long, appreciative swallow, giving Jessie a meaningful look as he did so.

Tension ebbed and flowed between them until at last Cy inquired hopefully, "Any dessert around?"

Just as he'd planned, the inane request shattered the strained atmosphere. Jessie served the apple crisp she'd made and nearly forgotten about, and Cy spooned it up with greedy enjoyment.

"Could I just have one more small bowl of this, Jessie, me love, before I have to start cleaning up this horrendous mess you've made of the kitchen?"

That evening at work Jessie kept thinking of Luke, of how he hid his complexity behind a simple gardener's facade. She couldn't keep his image or Cy's lecture from popping into her mind at the most inconvenient times.

The phone lines were unusually busy, probably, she surmised, because of the wet weather. When the blinking lights demanded her attention for perhaps the twentieth time in her second hour of work, she remembered Luke's tales of full moons and madness, and her smile was reflected in her voice when she took the call.

"'Night Shift,' good evening."

Silence. Breathing. *Another call from the nut case.*

Then, just as she was about to disconnect, an eerily familiar male voice purred, "Hello, Jessie. Long time no talk."

The raspy tones were muffled and indistinct, and disbelief kept Jessie speechless. It simply couldn't be. Was it possible to conjure someone up just by talking about him? An icy wave of shock made her shiver, and it was long seconds before she could bring herself to answer.

"Hello, Wayne. Why are you calling me?"

"Hey, c'mon, is that any way to talk to a guy you once lived with? I'm in town, I decided to give you a call."

Why make contact after all these years of silence? Jessie realized she was holding her breath and consciously exhaled as he mumbled, "Pretty fancy job you got there, darlin'. I been listening to you for a couple weeks now, ever since I came back. How come you never play any of my songs, Jess?" Petulance crept into the slurred tones, and then he gave a nasty little laugh. "Little old Jessie, on the radio. Y'know, you don't even sound crippled, y'know that, Jessie?"

He was drunk. The realization came simultaneously with the knowledge that Wayne Palmer had lost the ability to hurt her with his words. Years had healed the wounds he'd created long ago, and the scar tissue was thick and impermeable.

"And you don't sound sober, you know that, Wayne?" Even minor sarcasm took more energy than she cared to waste on him. Wearily she added, "Look, what happened years ago between us is ancient history now, and I don't care to resurrect it. Don't call me again. We have absolutely nothing to say to each other."

Yet for all her coolness on the phone, her hand was shaking violently when she adjusted the headset to go back on the air. Her lead-in to the next medley seemed rich in irony.

"It's late evening here on 'Night Shift,' a perfect time for romance. Here's a song guaranteed to put every one of us in the mood for love on such a wet Vancouver night." The song traveled smoothly over the airwaves, and Jessie stared at the insistently blinking light on her telephone line, counting the number of times it flashed angrily.

Twenty-two, twenty-three, twenty-four—she exhaled softly and forced herself to relax when at last it stopped.

Barry knocked on the glass just then and mimed a swallow from a coffee cup, and she nodded eagerly. A few minutes later he arrived in her cubicle carefully balancing two brimming cups.

"Given any thought to running away with me?" He gave her his professional leer, and she felt ridiculously safe and comforted at having him nearby.

"Darn, I can't tonight, Barry. I'd have to leave a note for my milkman, and I didn't bring the right makeup with me."

"Offer's open anytime," he teased expansively, and when the phone blinked again, she pretended to fuss with papers and said offhandedly, "Get that for me, Barry?"

It was only the young woman who worked nights at the convenience store down the street asking Jessie to play her favorite ballad.

"You get a lot of phone calls in response to this show, Jess. You must be doing something right." Barry was munching on a candy bar. "Have you talked to Evan this week?"

Jessie grimaced and nodded. She'd spent an unpleasant half hour with the station manager Monday afternoon, and he'd gone on at great length about the cost of the new locks he'd had to install and the general problems women announcers caused. "He's on the rampage because we slipped a couple of notches in the last ratings. Think heads are going to roll?" Her flippancy covered the tiny pang of anxiety about her job that had niggled ever since Monday's conversation.

Barry shrugged and swallowed the last of his chocolate.

"I doubt it. Evan always blows hot and cold." He picked up his coffee cup and started out. "There's not much I can do with the news and weather to help the ratings, anyhow. Unless I fictionalize them both."

For the rest of her shift, the phones were relatively quiet, and Jessie found her thoughts divided equally between Luke and where their relationship was going, and the problem of ratings. She forcibly kept herself from wasting one single thought on Wayne Palmer and his bizarre reappearance in her life. But strength of will didn't stop her from feeling anxious every time the phone rang.

There was little she could do about her feelings for Luke, she finally concluded. But perhaps there was something she could try to help the station.

She sounded her idea out on Barry at the end of their shift when the night announcers had taken over.

Barry mulled over what Jessie had told him. "You're talking about a sort of advice to the lovelorn segment so people can write in with a problem and get it answered on the air?"

"Something like that. I'd have to think the details through, but I seem to get so many calls like that I just figured it might be a good idea to emphasize it."

Barry nodded thoughtfully. "What would you call it?"

Jessie shook her head. She hadn't gotten that far yet. "I don't know. 'Love Line,' maybe?"

He groaned. "Have a heart, Jess."

"That's brilliant, Barry. That's what I'll name it. 'Heart Line.'"

He rolled his eyes and demanded skeptically, "You going to be the guru who answers all the questions?"

"Nope. I'll have the listening audience phone in suggestions for each problem. Listener involvement, Barry."

Cy had been giving out advice for years, and there had to be a lot more people out there like him, with answers to everything. Every different listener must have an answer for at least one problem, she figured. And if Cy were any example, the opportunity for handing out advice should be tremendously enjoyable to everyone.

Jessie felt exhilarated as she drove home, thinking through the details for the addition to her show. She pulled up in front of her darkened house, and a stab of longing swept through her. It would be wonderful to have someone at home to share a late-night glass of milk with and talk to about her idea.

And not just any someone.

Jessie was honest enough to admit she wanted Luke.

THE WEATHER CLEARED during the night. Early Thursday morning Luke hefted another wheelbarrow full of damp soil and pushed it to the area where he and Denny were preparing to lay an instant lawn.

"Why did this dude decide he wanted a full acre of grass to cut, d'you suppose?" Luke asked as he dumped the load, following Denny's bare perspiring back as they returned to the dirt pile.

"I figured he'd go for that minimal care sketch I showed him. It would sure have a lot more visual appeal than lawn," Denny agreed, swiping a filthy hand across his forehead. "His wife loved the idea, wanted a little fountain, but he insisted on grass."

"Well, when you've got this guy's money, you can have a lawn for a month and then tear the thing out if your wife doesn't like it," Luke commented, heaving the barrow so that the dirt spilled out in an even black stream.

"Speaking of wives, I guess you noticed that mine is on the warpath," Denny said morosely, patting his jean pocket in an absentminded search for his cigarettes. His usual cheerful expression was gone. He looked out of sorts and worried as he pulled a cigarette out of a crumpled package and lit it impatiently.

"She's still on that damn fool idea about the soup place. Jeez, to begin with, the rate of bankruptcy in a business like that is nearly ninety percent. I told her, but she won't listen to reason." He tossed his cigarette to the ground and ground it out viciously with his boot. "C'mon, I got some lemonade in the thermos today. That sister of yours is one stubborn broad when she gets her mind set on something, y'know?''

Luke was about to ask lightly why Lorna was only his sister when she was being a "stubborn broad," but one glance at Denny as they found a spot in the shade to share the icy drink changed his mind. Denny was obviously in no mood for smart remarks.

"Lorna mentioned it. She sounded as if she really wanted to try her idea out, Denny. I know what you're saying about the poor outlook for business starts right now, but she's done pretty well with her catering, hasn't she? Maybe you ought to let her go ahead and try. If it's a case of start-up money, I can always—''

"God Almighty, it's not just the money." Denny scowled. "You know this business is doing great—that's the point. There's no need for her to work like she did before the kids came. Why can't she just relax, join a bridge club or something, take up tennis? I don't want one of these career households like you see on TV, everything rush, rush, whose turn to make the goddamn dinner. I just want a good old-fashioned marriage here, Luke, y'know what I mean?''

He raised his thermos cup to his lips and drank steadily. "You take somebody like this Jessie friend of yours, now. In her case, I figure it's essential for her to be ambitious, get ahead. She's never gonna get married, have a family, she needs a career like she's got. But Lorna, with the kids and me, the house, the nice little catering stuff on the side, what's she need with ten million more problems?''

Luke's anger didn't start slowly. It filled him like too much air forced into a balloon, and he exploded.

"You chauvinistic, condescending ass." Blood pounded in his temples, and he didn't even notice the astounded surprise on his brother-in-law's homely face. "Don't you ever let me hear you making assumptions like that again about

Jessie, you hear me? What the hell do you know about her life or the choices she's made? You talk as if being married is some bloody great favor a man does for a woman. Let me tell you, the guy lucky enough to have Jessie . . ." Luke suddenly heard his voice, raised in anger against Denny. What was he saying? Denny was his friend, his partner, to say nothing of being his brother-in-law. The tirade finished as rapidly as it had started.

"Sorry," he mumbled.

Denny sat and watched him for a while, staring unblinkingly while Luke felt his skin growing warm with embarrassment.

Finally, Denny let out a long, low whistle. "That's what's been bugging you, isn't it? And I've been too dumb to see what's right under my nose." His brown gaze bored like an auger into Luke's frowning face. Denny's expression was a mixture of self-satisfied comprehension and affectionate concern.

"You're in love with her, isn't that it? You've fallen ass over teakettle in love with that woman, haven't you, Luke? Man, this is serious. This is heavy stuff, falling in love with a woman in a wheelchair. So what the hell do you intend to do about it?"

CHAPTER SIX

DENNY'S QUESTION HAMMERED into Luke's brain, and he wanted to snarl out a denial, or laugh easily and negate his emotions, or lash out with his fists and punch someone.

It was the unexpected violence of his response that made him face the truth for the first time. And that truth was— Luke felt the blood pound into his temples—that truth was yes, he did love Jessie. The mental image of her, which was never far from his inner imaginings, flashed through his mind, and his gut wrenched painfully.

He didn't want to be, and yet he was in love with Jessie. The realization terrified him, in a way that irrational maniacs with machine guns and planeloads of hostages never had.

Denny and Luke were staunch friends, and they stayed friends because they never lied to each other. When he'd retired from the RCMP, Denny had been the only person Luke had finally found himself able to confide in other than Graham Marshall, the psychologist from the Justice Institute.

Luke didn't lie to Denny now, either.

He cleared his throat hard. "Yeah," he finally said in a gruff voice he hardly recognized. "Yeah, you're right. I didn't know myself until just now."

Denny's voice was hushed and deadly serious. 'Whatcha gonna do about it?'' he asked again.

Luke expelled a long, hopeless sigh. "Y'know, Den, till now I've never put a whole lot of myself into a relationship with a woman. Before I left the force, I was too, well, I guess arrogant is the word."

Denny gave him a skeptical look. "Lucky is the way I remember. Steady stream of bimbos, I never could get their names straight. I was too busy ogling the landscape, Lorna used to say. Then there was that one you lived with for a while, Carol, now she was different. She was a bright lady as well as beautiful."

Denny was right on both counts, Luke mused. Carol had been smart, beautiful, ambitious. And Luke had come close to destroying her and himself before she finally—wisely—walked out on him.

"Ever hear from her, Luke?"

"She's a pediatrician now down in San Diego, married with two kids of her own. We exchange Christmas cards."

"Seems to me she was the last one you ever brought to dinner."

Again Denny was right. The kind of temporary companions Luke had chosen over the past few years weren't the kind you took home to meet your family.

"So what d'you figure on doing about, uh—" it seemed as if Denny were hesitant about even naming her "—about . . . Jessie?"

Even without remembering Carol, Luke knew what had to be done. He'd probably known last Sunday when Jessie had said proudly, "My life is full now, and I'm happy."

"The only thing I can do. I'm going to finish the landscaping and then get the hell out of her life. The last thing Jessie needs is me around, messing up her head."

Denny considered this and then said hesitantly, "Don't get me wrong, Luke, I don't see it quite that way, but what I do see is that . . . Oh, hell, making a life together is tough under any circumstances. But with one of you... Well, all I'm saying is whatever you do, give it lots of thought, don't jump into anything,'' he concluded uneasily. "Look at me, with a perfectly normal wife, and all we do is fight lately.''

Black despair settled over Luke like a shroud. He grasped the handles of the wheelbarrow and growled, ''Let's get back to work.''

Plagued by separate demons, the two of them labored like men possessed for the rest of the day, and they scrupulously avoided saying anything else to one another that even bordered on the personal. By the end of the afternoon, the lawn, which should have taken them at least another six hours of hard work to complete, lay like a variegated patchwork of green, complete. Within two weeks the long, narrow strips of instant lawn the men had carefully unrolled and arranged would root and spread, making it impossible to tell where the divisions had been, smoothly covering the telltale seams of today's raw earth.

Too bad, Luke mused bitterly, that life didn't have the same capacity to knit the human soul together without scarring.

DURING THE BUSY DAYS that followed that conversation with Denny, Luke used every spare moment to implement his plans for Jessie's garden. He was determined to do just what he'd told Denny he would do—finish her yard, then get out of her life.

Keeping that in mind, he did his best to avoid her as much as possible for the first few days, doing most of the yard preparation after she'd gone to work in the early evening or arriving shortly after dawn and working as quietly as he could before she awakened.

It wasn't easy being this close to her and trying to maintain distance. Inevitably they met, and he couldn't ignore the tumultuous reaction just the sight of her stirred in him.

She didn't really do anything more than smile at him, or incline her head a certain way, or give him a look from under her long eyelashes. But for Luke, just being around Jessie was enough to awaken all the feelings he tried so hard to deny.

He attacked her garden as if by doing so he could subdue his emotions. He brought in a backhoe one evening while she was at work and excavated a sizable hole for the hot tub. Next he decided he might as well level most of the existing undergrowth while he had the machine. A stray rosebush he hadn't realized Jessie prized fell victim to his orgy of upheaval.

He was there the following morning when she stared at the carnage of her yard, and he had to admit it was probably difficult to envision what it would eventually look like. Just now it looked awful, rawly gouged and full of roots.

Still, he thought irritably, Jessie was overreacting.

"You've wrecked it. This is the worst mess I've ever seen," Jessie shouted, exploding with rage. "I knew letting you start this was a mistake, I knew that damn hot tub was a bad idea. I should never have let you and Cy railroad me into this. I liked it fine the way it was. And you've mowed right over the rosebush I loved," she wailed.

Furiously she rolled ahead of Luke over the chewed-up earth to see what was left of the bush, carelessly ignoring the raw, rutted ground. Giving a furious heave when her wheels stuck, she overturned and tumbled ignominiously into the moist dirt.

"Jessie!"

Luke was aghast. He leaped to her rescue. Righting her chair with one hand, he bent over to scoop her up and received a solid thump in the chest from her balled-up fist for his trouble.

"You just leave me alone, Luke Chadwick. I can at least try to get myself up. I'm not an idiot invalid made of porcelain that you have to move around."

It was partly the thought of being in his arms again that bothered her, as well as the confusion she felt about the way he'd been acting all week. Jessie used all the uncertainty that had built in her since last Sunday night to fuel her rage now. He'd been remote and cool to her ever since, and now he'd gone berserk in her yard with some machine, and when she'd objected, he'd scowled at her.

She simply didn't understand men.

She heaved herself up with her arms and somehow, using absolute force of will, dragged her body into her chair, punctuating the procedure with grunts of effort and angry exclamations.

"I'm a...totally healthy...perfectly normal...woman...who simply happens...to be...in a wheelchair."

Jessie glared at him, shoving her tumbled hair back with an angry hand, and he looked as if he wanted to shake her. They were both breathing hard.

Then amusement slowly began replacing the anger in his eyes. His lips began to twitch, and he reached a cautious finger down to touch her cheek. "You're the grubbiest normal woman I've ever seen," he said. "Your forehead is filthy, and there's dirt all over your nose. And that tracksuit..."

She gave him a haughty glare and tried to roll in the direction of the house, only to find her wheels were well and truly stuck. He let her struggle for long, maddening moments, and then he said quietly, "Need some help, Ms Smith?"

She hesitated, hating to admit defeat. Finally, she had to nod silently. But even she thought the ridiculous situation was funny, and by the time they reached flatter ground, she was stifling giggles. They caught one another's eye, and the laughter exploded. The tension that had hung like a cloud for a week was suddenly gone.

"Why have you been so...different with me lately, Luke?" Jessie blurted out the question before she lost her nerve and he'd had enough time to retreat into his guise of polite stranger.

He was sitting in a plastic chair drinking the iced tea she'd brought out after her necessary shower.

Luke studied her, his eyes going slowly over her scrubbed face. Then he leaned over smoothly and cupped her wet head in his hands, claiming her lips in a burning kiss that sent tremors into her fingertips. It was an insistent, hungry caress, and it left them both shaken. He drew away finally, still devouring her face with his gaze.

"I've been trying to stop myself from doing things like that," he said quietly. "But I don't think I'll bother anymore."

While Luke worked just outside that afternoon, Jessie automatically did household chores indoors and tried to calmly and dispassionately evaluate what was happening in her life.

Both calm and dispassion were entirely lost after the first five minutes of thought. The arrival of Luke Chadwick in her carefully ordered life had caused an upheaval tantamount to an earthquake, forcing her to consider issues she'd avoided for years.

Issues like love. Issues like sex. Jessie whispered the words to herself. The fiery stirring she experienced in Luke's arms disturbed and excited her, made her aware of how minuscule her knowledge was about the physical responses of her body, what her limitations were. What was even possible for her, sexually?

Folding the bundle of clothes she'd just rescued from the dryer, her hands stilled, and she swallowed hard. How silly to be thirty-two years old and not to know more. But ten years ago there hadn't been the counseling services for the disabled that she understood were now available. Even if they had existed, certainly Jessie hadn't had the courage back then to do much asking. Not after the things Wayne had said.

Kathleen had asked, though.

A wry grin came and went as she remembered the rehab hospital in Toronto, and her first meeting with the woman who'd become as close to her as a sister during the traumatic months just after her injury.

Jessie had been transferred one morning by ambulance to the rehabilitation center, and she was propped in a heavy, antiquated hospital wheelchair in the double room that would be her home for the next few months. For the first time she'd allowed herself to fully comprehend the fact that she was about to learn how *not* to walk again, that the purpose of being here was all negative—to teach her how to live without dancing, how to get through the murky years ahead without the use of her legs. It was a trauma too deep even for tears, and she sat staring stupidly into the brilliance of a June afternoon wishing desperately that she had died in the accident.

The door to the room crashed open, and Jessie jumped, struggling clumsily to turn her heavy chair toward the door. A pixie of a girl with a flaming mass of carrot-red curls and thousands of freckles scattered across her piquant face exploded into the room, freewheeling a chair identical to Jessie's as if it weighed nothing, pulling to a flourishing stop scant inches away.

She was crimson with rage, and she started talking just as
if she and Jessie had been in the middle of a conversation.

"Can you believe this? The nerve of that woman. I was
kissing Joe goodbye in that little room off the corridor. It's
the only lousy place in here with one single iota of privacy,
and along comes that skinny nurse who looks like a rabbit,
and without even knocking, she barges right in and says,
just as if we're both twelve years old, 'We can't have you
hiding in corners like this, Kathleen, it's a poor example for
the others. You know we have physio in ten minutes.' You'd
think we'd all been neutered, for cripes' sake, or should be,
to listen to her." An Anglo-Saxon expletive completed the
recital, and the outraged expression on the triangular face
quickly changed into the widest, friendliest smile Jessie had
ever seen.

"Sorry about that. Welcome to purgatory. I'm Kathleen
Dodd, and I peeled everything I could about you out of the
aide this morning, seeing that we're going to be roommates
while we're incarcerated in this joint. Listen to this. Your
name is Jessie Palmer, and you're female. Do you believe it?
That's the full extent of what they'd tell me. I mean you
could have been ninety-three and senile instead of disgustingly gorgeous and...how old are you, anyhow, Jessie?"

The utter hopelessness Jessie had felt a moment before
began to recede. No one could possibly stay despondent
long around Kathleen, and within half an hour they were
fast friends.

Both women were almost the same age, they had com-
parable injuries, both had been married less than a year—
there had been many similarities between herself and Kathleen, Jessie remembered now. There were also differences.
Jessie grimaced, remembering the most painful difference.

Kathleen's boyish husband, Joe Dodd, was a garage me-
chanic, and his openly expressed love and support for

Kathleen shone on his angular face whenever he was around her.

Jessie had drawn unwilling comparisons between Joe, who was with Kathleen every chance he had, learning right along with her how to cope, and her own husband, Wayne, who was conspicuous by his absence.

Kathleen was the only real friend Jessie had. The dancers from her troupe had visited often at first, less as the horrifying extent of her injury became apparent and finally, not at all, but her friendship with Kathleen flourished.

After Jessie left the center and moved west, she missed Kathleen badly, but as years passed, their letters and calls had dwindled, discouraged by distance. There'd been a jubilant birth announcement when the Dodds' daughter, Chrissie, had been born. Then last Christmas a card and a note had arrived from Kathleen with the news that she and Joe and Chrissie were moving to the Lower Mainland to a small farm they'd bought in Langley. *Guess what?* Kathleen had added gleefully at the end of the letter. *I'm once again with child, as that proper English nurse we had would say. Jess, I'm so happy.*

After the move Jessie had driven out twice to visit, and it was as if the years since she'd last seen Kathleen had disappeared. The core of their friendship was as strong as ever, even though their lives were now vastly different.

She hadn't talked to Kathleen since the night of the marathon. Impulsively Jessie wheeled over to the telephone and dialed her friend's number.

"Hello?"

The buoyant voice always brought a smile to Jessie's face. A long, delightful conversation later, she'd accepted an invitation to drive out to Kathleen's home for lunch the following day.

The forty-minute drive out to Langley the next morning took Jessie from the heart of the bustling Vancouver metropolis into the green serenity of deep countryside. She crossed the Petulla Bridge, a graceful arch over the mighty Fraser River, and within a few more miles houses on either side of the busy freeway suddenly acquired breathing space, with fields and woods and horses and sheep around them.

Winding along quiet country roads, Jessie located the Dodds' low cedar cottage with its tidy outbuildings, set on a small wooded acreage.

Jessie's arrival was a confusion of delighted greetings from Kathleen, who was gloriously, hugely pregnant, and from a cocker spaniel so friendly he nearly wagged himself in half. Her arrival also elicited the frightened wails of Chrissie, age two and shy, a tiny girl with Kathleen's flaming curls and Joe's quiet eyes.

"It's absolutely great to see you, Jess. You look lovelier all the time, and I look like a watermelon. Is there no justice? I listen to your program whenever I can, and I brag to my friends about my show-biz friend."

Kathleen smoothly made order out of chaos, shooing the dog outside, scooping her little daughter onto the scant inches that remained of her lap. Jessie offered Chrissie the bright puzzle toy she'd brought for her, and the tiny girl became brave enough to toddle over and accept it, giving Jessie a watery smile and trotting off to play.

Kathleen poured them each a steaming cup of peppermint tea in the cozy kitchen.

"I can't stand the smell of coffee now, hope you don't mind, Jess."

"Not at all, I love this."

Radiant and effervescent as ever, Kathleen giggled as she intercepted Jessie's involuntary glance at her swollen stomach.

"More of me than you expected, huh? I'm bigger with this one than I was with Chrissie. I'm not due for another six weeks, so don't panic, Jess. I promise I won't go into labor over lunch."

Kathleen was exactly the same outspoken, lovably audacious person she'd always been. Jessie teased, "It's not labor that worries me, it's the fact that if you lean forward, I swear you'll overbalance and fall out of your chair."

"Joe keeps threatening to tie me in if I get much bigger. Now enough about me. Tell me about your exciting career, your risqué life as a swinging single, all the famous people you meet. C'mon, Jess, liven up a dull housewife's day."

For a full hour they caught up on each other's lives. Kathleen fed Chrissie, and the child grew comfortable enough to crawl into Jessie's arms and fall asleep. Kathleen tenderly took the warm bundle and rolled off to put her down for her nap, and Jessie absorbed the peace and the aura of calm happiness the little house and its occupants seemed to exude.

The windows that gave a view of the back of the property revealed a well-tended vegetable garden. Honeysuckle vines with their crimson-and-white shooting-star blossoms trailed up a trellis on the back porch, and their enchantingly sweet perfume floated in through the open kitchen window.

I should ask Luke if he thinks honeysuckle would be nice against that back fence....

Luke. He was always there, in one way or another, just beneath the surface of her mind.

Kathleen rolled briskly into the room again, slipping a seafood quiche into the oven, putting the finishing touches on a butter lettuce salad.

"I grew the ingredients for this with my own two hands, right out there in that kitchen garden. Joe made me raised beds, and I just pull on a pair of huge plastic coveralls, slip out of my chair and grub around to my heart's content."

"A . . . a friend is remodeling my backyard, and he's making me a small garden plot." To her chagrin, Jessie felt her face flush revealingly at the mention of Luke, and Kathleen was quick to notice.

"This the man in your life, Jess?"

It was the perfect opening, and Jessie gathered her courage.

"Remember I told you about the man who grabbed my chair in the marathon? That was Luke. I've gotten to know him. He's renovating my backyard, and, Kath, this is going to sound incredible to you, but . . . I need advice."

Timidly Jessie talked about the years since her divorce and how she'd avoided sexual encounters.

"Then Luke came along, and everything's changing. It's scary for me. I, well, I want our relationship to have a chance, to be as normal as possible, but I don't know how to go about it. I don't doubt my capacity to . . . to love him. It's the physical part of that love that I'm scared about, Kath. I just don't know how to get over the awkwardness, I suppose. And I've never wanted to before."

Kathleen had set out their lunch, and now she served Jessie generous portions of the delicious food.

With a wry grin wrinkling her freckled nose, she remarked, "This reminds me of when I was in the rehab center. That's exactly how I felt with Joe, and nobody would give me any straight answers. I guess because nobody really knew back then. If we tried to fool around a little and find out for ourselves, there was absolutely no privacy, and we'd get into trouble. Remember the time I stole the keys to the lab and Joe and I locked ourselves in?"

Jessie had to laugh at the remembered fiasco. "The charge nurse called the locksmith and then accused you both of being 'morbidly oversexed.' I think that's how she phrased it? Oh, Kath, I used to envy you like mad.''

Kathleen reached across and squeezed Jessie's hand in a loving gesture.

''I used to be so scared for you. You never talked about Wayne or how things were between you. I despised that guy the one time I met him. I was so relieved when I heard you were divorced.''

Unbidden came a recollection of the recent shock of Wayne's whiskey-hoarse voice on the telephone, her ex-husband's unexpected and unwelcome reappearance in her life. Jessie suppressed a tiny frisson of fear. Surely he wouldn't call again. She forced the thought out of her mind, concentrating instead on all the things she needed to know.

There was so much to ask Kathleen, so much to learn from her. And the only way to go about learning was to be absolutely honest with her friend.

''Kath, since my injury I've never had sex with anyone. It was all right with Wayne during my marriage, but afterward, I never had the courage to try again.'' She nibbled at the mixed salad, aware that Kathleen was waiting for her to continue.

''Maybe I'm just not a passionate woman. I know Wayne was often impatient with me, complaining that I wasn't responsive enough. I was such a romantic in those days—you know, all the ballets, like *Sleeping Beauty* and *Romeo and Juliet*. Well, it was hard to make the adjustment from romance to real life when I was newly married. Wayne was the first man I'd been with. I was pretty innocent, and he, well, I've thought since that maybe he just didn't always take enough time. Sometimes I felt as though I didn't exist as a person, as if my body belonged to him. Other times it was fine, but it wasn't an experience I felt confident about. After the accident I never had the courage to try again.''

The words were difficult, but a feeling of relief came with confession. "If it wasn't any big deal before I was injured, I could imagine how it would be for me afterward, without even normal sensation. I grieved over it sometimes, but I never met anyone I trusted or loved enough to want to try again."

Until now.

Kathleen's first reaction was to call Wayne several favorite pithy words. "You just got a bad start, that's all. Lovemaking isn't like that with a thoughtful partner. It's terrible to turn away from relationships because of one bad experience, Jess."

Jessie toyed with her fork, then said, "Don't you see, Kathleen? I don't have the vaguest idea what's even possible for me. All the movies, the books, the articles about sex are for normal women. What about us?"

Kathleen patted her bulging midriff and said dryly, "Obviously there's hope. As far as the physical side of lovemaking is concerned, stop worrying. Our lovers have to take charge a little more, but modern research has proven that sexual response and orgasm are just as possible for us as for anyone. Ninety-five percent of what we think we 'feel' is actually happening in between our ears, anyway, disabled or not." She smiled across at Jessie, dimples flashing. "I could have told them that a long time ago, the part about women on wheels being sexy. Anyway, now they pompously announce that the brain contains what they've labeled 'pleasure centers' and that we're capable of transferring the sensation we feel in one area to make it seem as if we're feeling it in another. Erogenous zones above the level of our injury take over for those below, and bingo."

Jessie choked on a mouthful of food at the word, and for the next hour she listened intently and asked everything she needed to know about all aspects of lovemaking.

Kathleen was marvelously open and willing to share her experiences, detailing for Jessie the special times of pregnancy and delivery, the joys of being a mother and a wife, but especially emphasizing the wonder of lovemaking with a beloved partner.

"You better go see your doctor, though, unless you really want to end up like this." Kathleen patted her hard, round tummy lovingly. Her face softened, and joy shone from her eyes. "I can't wait to see this little guy. Having babies for me is a real miracle, just like the love Joe and I share. That's a miracle, too."

Jessie didn't doubt it for a moment, and a sense of longing filled her. To love and be loved, to carry a child conceived in passion and in joy—Luke's child. The future had suddenly become a promise instead of a threat, thanks to Kathleen.

Before it was time to leave, they took a tour of the small, well-ordered farm. Kathleen insisted that Jessie take cuttings from the fragrant honeysuckle vines for her own back garden.

As Jessie drove back through heavy afternoon traffic, the perfume of the carefully wrapped plant on the seat beside her hung heavy in the air, full of portent. The plant was like Kathleen, rich and ripe, a beautiful symbol of all that was sweetly possible with care and tending and, most of all, with love.

There was a cheery note on the door when she arrived home, and she was pleased to see that a great deal of work had been completed in the backyard. The pink lock-stone deck now stretched in a smooth apron from her back door, an irregular shape that would probably branch into crooked paths when it was finished, invitingly wide to accommodate her chair. Every area of the garden would be accessi-

ble for her, due to Luke's clever planning. The ugliness of
yesterday's upheaval was disappearing already.

There was still a deep, gaping hole under the cedar tree
where the hot tub would be placed. An electrician would
install the wiring for the pump and heater.

She unpinned the paper and smoothed it out on her lap.

Hi, Jess. Missed you. All preparation now complete for
installing hot tub on Saturday. Think the weatherman
could manage some sunshine? See you then.

                                        Luke

She studied his handwriting, the decisive downward
slashes, the confident loops and uncluttered letters. Feeling
silly but responding to a need she couldn't explain, she
folded the scribbled note and tucked it carefully into her top
dresser drawer.

SHE AWOKE SATURDAY morning to a cacophony of men's
voices and the sound of trucks coming and going in the alley. Scooting to the window, Jessie peeked out. Luke was
standing with his back to her, his T-shirt stretched tight
across his shoulders, his narrow hips encased in faded, cut-
off jeans. He was talking to a deliveryman, and a huge
boxed shape, which had to be the hot tub, sat squarely on
her deck.

By the time Jessie had showered and dressed, the yard had
become a mad scramble of people and activity, including
Cy, a teenage boy Luke had hired for the morning, the delivery driver, Luke and an electrician. With a great clicking
of high heels and a jangle of bracelets, Amanda Simpson
arrived from next door, a cloud of her musky perfume
wafting from her each time she took a step forward.

"Despite the noise and the interruption to my work, all this activity is stimulating," she said by way of greeting to Jessie, the writer's deep voice purring the words in the sensual manner she employed for even the most casual statement. This morning Amanda was wearing a one-piece jumpsuit of soft blue velour. As always, her makeup and dramatic jewelry were securely in place, her smooth white hair drawn up into a coronet of braids. Jessie noted that Cy seemed to materialize beside them as soon as Amanda appeared, but then Luke strolled over to talk to her, and Jessie soon forgot to notice anyone else.

She felt her cheeks flush as she met his forthright gaze. All she could think about was how his kisses had burned, how his embrace had locked her against his hard, lean body. How stupidly prim she'd acted with him. Would there be another chance?

"Well, Jess, by tonight we'll have your tub in operation, if I can get this crew organized at all," he said easily.

He'd stopped fighting his feelings for her. They remained, no matter how he tried to deny them, so he'd decided he might as well extract every ounce of enjoyment out of his hours with her. Seeing her now, her crisp white shirt against her deep tan, the soft cotton outlining the gentle roundness of her breasts, the single thick braid on her neck throwing her clearly sculpted features into relief, he felt a clutching warmth in his body, an invisible bond that seemed to draw him to her.

Lord, she was beautiful. She always had that freshly scrubbed, appealing innocence about her.

How he wanted her.

"Okay, crew, let's get to work," he suggested roughly.

Amanda seemed in no hurry to leave, and she retreated with Jessie to the kitchen as the men maneuvered the huge tub into place.

"Join me for breakfast?" Jessie suggested impetuously, and the older woman hesitated, then accepted with her crooked, enigmatic smile.

They sat in the sunny alcove over toast and poached eggs, getting to know each other, chatting about Amanda's writing and their mutual love for classical music. Amanda was extremely interested in Jessie's job, and after a few minutes Jessie found herself describing her idea for the "Heart Line" show.

"I've suggested it to the station manager, and I think he might go for it."

Amanda considered the idea thoughtfully.

"It would certainly interest me, but then we writers are insatiably curious about other people's lives and problems. Especially," she added a trifle pensively, "if our own lives have been rather dull."

The windows afforded a front-row-center view of the activity outside.

"Luke has an exceptional imagination," Amanda commented thoughtfully, looking outside and then peppering her eggs until they were almost black. "I may just use this fairy-tale garden he's making you in one of my books. Where on earth did you meet him?"

Jessie laughed and related the tale of the marathon. Strange how long ago it seemed, yet it had been barely a month since that May morning.

"And Cyrus? How long have you known him?" Amanda asked as she casually smeared strawberry jam on a slice of toast. Jessie, smiling to herself, agreeably filled Amanda in on large portions of Cy's habits, interests, personality and pet peeves, skillfully ignoring the existence of his string of lovelorn women admirers. There was no point discouraging Amanda's interest at this stage.

After the sneaky matchmaking Cy had done on behalf of her and Luke, Jessie felt not one smidgen of guilt about giving Amanda inside information. It served Cy right to have Jessie doing some scheming on his behalf for a change, and Amanda was totally unlike the usual scatterbrains who phoned him.

Amanda was a lady, from the tip of her aristocratic nose to the toes of her elegant shoes. She was about as different from freewheeling Cyrus Grant as anyone could be, Jessie decided, and that made things much more interesting.

"I must go home and try to work my way through the vagaries of chapter eight. Thank you, my dear. I have a feeling you and I are going to be great friends." Jessie found herself hoping Amanda was right. She found the writer both intelligent and stimulating.

Jessie tidied her kitchen and started a pot of vegetable soup for the men's lunch, but the sounds of activity in the garden drew her constantly to the window.

As the sun rose higher, the mid-June day grew blazingly hot. Luke stripped his shirt off, and healthy sweat made his tanned nut-brown skin glow like polished leather. Jessie's gaze lingered on his tall, virile form as he lifted, shoveled and used brute strength to shift the heavy tub into its resting place.

The dark mat of hair stretching in a V across his broad chest narrowed and disappeared intriguingly into the low-slung waistband. His torso was free of even an ounce of extra flesh. His legs were long, well shaped and extremely strong below the ragged bottom of his makeshift cutoffs. He grinned suddenly at something Cy said, and Jessie caught her breath at the hard male beauty of him, the sense of dark power in the muscular frame mixed with the faint trace of vulnerability in his smile.

By late afternoon the tub was in place, and Jessie went outside just as Luke finished planting clumps of woolly thyme around its cedar apron. The purply-blue flowers and soft gray leaves were a visual feast against a larger terraced area that boasted golden-headed lilies, branching spikes of delphinium and blue and gold irises. Clever arrangement of the tall perennials, interspersed with emerald ferns, would make the tub intimately private, nestled as it was beneath the overhanging branches of the tall cedar tree.

"It's like a little pool in some forest glade," Jessie said, her voice full of awe. "I keep expecting a beautiful wood nymph to appear and do a shampoo commercial."

She and Luke and Cy were admiring the scene and sipping the chilled wine Jessie had thoughtfully stuck in the fridge that afternoon. The men were sweaty and dirt stained. There was a new camaraderie between them, the result of a day's grueling shared physical labour.

The tub was filling slowly with water.

"It'll take several hours before that heats up enough to be comfortable," Luke remarked. "I'd like to keep an eye on it, just to make sure the heater's working properly." There had initially been a faulty connection, and Luke and the electrician had replaced several wires.

"I'll barbecue steaks and make a salad for dinner if you two want to be the first to try it out later," Jessie announced, and she felt her pulse accelerate when Luke accepted her invitation and Cy shook his head regretfully.

"I've got a date," he announced a trifle smugly. "Amanda has invited me to dinner and an art exhibit at Brackendale this evening."

"Brackendale? Isn't that way up Howe Sound on the Squamish Highway?" Jessie was both intrigued by Cy's date and a tiny bit relieved that she and Luke would be alone.

"Yes, ma'am. A good hour and a half's drive each way. We may just have to stay over at some romantic little inn," he concluded, smiling. Glancing at his watch, he swallowed the final drop of wine in his glass and reluctantly got to his feet. "I'd better go and iron myself a shirt." He sighed. "I have a definite hunch this occasion calls for more than the usual clean T-shirt and blue jeans."

"Knowing Amanda, I'd say you're dead on," Jessie agreed. "I'd shave, too, if I were you."

Cy gave her a scandalized look and rubbed his chin. "Twice in the same week? Don't get fanatical about this, Jess. It's only a date, after all, not a proposal of marriage."

"Heavens no," Jessie agreed gravely. "It's much too soon for that. Wait for the second date, at least."

Cy went off amidst friendly laughter, and the heavy stillness of a hot afternoon filled the shady glen. Luke and Jessie shared the silence companionably, as well as the remaining wine, but with each passing moment an awareness grew between them, unspoken but potent. They were alone, and although neither had deliberately planned it that way, an entire summer evening stretched ahead to be spent with each other. Eager anticipation arose, unspoken but recognized.

"I'll go home and clean up," Luke said huskily, "and I'll be back within an hour to light the barbecue and help grill the steaks."

As soon as he left, Jessie headed purposefully into her bedroom, showered quickly, sprayed herself liberally with the light floral scent she'd grown so fond of and pulled on lacy bikinis. Then she tugged a hanger from her closet and wriggled into the thin cotton length of a jumpsuit she'd seen in a boutique window and purchased impulsively the week before.

The garment was vertically striped in wide lemon and white bands, with a zipper closure up the front and elastic around the waist. The top was a backless halter, with a charming shirt collar and two bands of fabric cleverly covering her in front, leaving her toffee-tanned arms, shoulders and back totally bare to the waist.

Jessie caught her hair up on her head in a high chignon of loose curls, with frothy, soft ringlets escaping in wisps over her ears and her nape.

She added touches of golden eye shadow, brown mascara and light coppery lipstick. Then Jessie rolled the legs of the suit to her calves in casual, stylish flair and polished her toenails bronze. The barest of bright-yellow sandals, bought to match the jumpsuit, and a huge sun-yellow bangle on her arm completed the outfit.

Studying herself critically in the full-length mirror, Jessie was thankful for the tedious hours she spent each week in her "torture chamber." Her body reflected the hard work in long slender lines of arm and shoulder, a minute waistline and firm breasts that required no bra beneath the silky fine weave of the cotton. However, she knew the sparkle in her eyes had more to do with Luke than with exercise.

"That's it. You'll have to do, lady," she whispered. She arranged her legs and feet in demure lines and hurried to answer the doorbell, heart pounding in anticipation.

Luke was back. The evening was beginning. She rolled across the room and flung the door wide.

CHAPTER SEVEN

ON THE WAY OVER Luke had stopped impulsively and bought more wine. The liquor store was beside an ice-cream store, and he bought a pint of pecan double nut. Then he noticed a little Chinese grocery with buckets of fresh flowers outside, and three bunches of colorful strawflowers joined his loot.

Awkwardly balancing all the packages, he knocked at Jessie's door with the flowers dripping wetly down his pale-blue cotton pants.

The door swung wide, and he gazed at her. The white-and-gold sun-bronzed beauty gazing up at him stormed the defenses he'd carefully erected during the drive.

Keep it cool, Luke, he'd advised himself. *It's only a matter of days now till the job is finished. Don't make leaving her any harder than it is already.*

"Hello, beautiful," he said softly, and it was fortunate his arms were full because if they hadn't been, he would have kissed her. The shy, excited eagerness in her dark eyes, the soft high color beneath the golden, glowing skin, made him foolishly happy as he deposited all his bundles on the table.

Her outfit was both sassy and sexy. She had absolutely beautiful skin. Was all of Jessie as soft and smooth as the generous portions that were displayed in that crazy striped overall? He forced his attention away from the firm, high, tilted breasts, the graceful long arms and vulnerable throat bared by the upswept hairdo.

Fortunately, the first awkward moments were neatly smoothed by searching for a vase for the flowers, stowing the ice cream in the freezer and putting the wine in the fridge door to chill.

"The briquettes for the barbecue are under the utility sink in the laundry room. I put the potatoes on to bake a while ago because I figured after all that hard work today, you'd be starving. Are you?"

The scent that was Jessie, a whiff of flowers and spice and a more intimate perfume that was hers alone, wafted over him as he passed close to her, and he was suddenly ravenous—but not for food.

He hurried outside and lit the barbecue, singeing his finger and quietly cursing because he couldn't keep from sneaking glances at her as she moved smoothly in and out, setting the small round table in the garden for their supper, humming absently along with the soft ballads she'd put on the stereo.

Dusk was falling by the time they ate. The air was drowsy and full of the thick warmth left by the sun, and birds called sleepily from the trees around them. Cars passed the house, children were called home by their mothers, teenagers played rock music across the street, but all the sounds were muffled and distant in the tranquility and privacy of Jessie's garden.

"Thank you for this." Jessie raised her stemmed glass in a salute, indicating the hot tub and the surroundings Luke was creating for her. They'd laughed and teased and argued heatedly over the cooking of the steaks. They'd eaten the delicious food in greedy camaraderie and sipped the wine, each conscious of the other but relaxed and easy in their awareness.

"You're making something beautiful and lasting out of a wild mess of underbrush," she commented. "In spite of me," she added with a rueful grin.

Luke glanced around, for the first time really seeing the difference he'd made in the yard instead of only gauging what needed to be done next.

"That's the great part of this job, Jess. There's a positive result to it every time. Guaranteed success, as long as nothing gets root weevil. It's a great confidence builder, gardening. Lots of mess but no stress." There was a faint trace of irony in his tone that prompted her impulsive question.

"Is this what you want to go on doing with your life, Luke, or do you ever think of returning to police work? You were a hostage negotiator, weren't you? It must have been challenging, rewarding—do you ever miss it?" She saw the sudden curious sharpening in his blue gaze, and haltingly she explained about Cy's nephew and the sergeant who'd known Luke, adding quickly, "Skip the question. I just realized it makes me sound like an old gossip. I didn't mean it that way, though." She felt embarrassed and concerned lest he think she was prying.

"There's no escaping your past," Luke said with a crooked, rueful smile. "But as far as going back to it is concerned, the answer's a definite no." He felt the faint but familiar anxiety that memories of that time always stirred in him. Yet with Jessie his usual reluctance to discuss what had happened was missing. He wanted her to know, he realized wonderingly. He needed to tell her how it had been, spell it out to her so that she would understand.

"Jess, remember telling me that your life was divided into two parts, the time before your accident and the years since?" Luke was sitting upright in the lounge chair, his legs no longer stretched out indolently. There was a subtle new tenseness about him, and Jessie felt suddenly apprehensive about what he might say.

"My life is like that, too, Jess. Before and after."

"What was before like, for you?" Her query was soft, but as Jessie watched, pain flickered swiftly across his face at her question. She knew this discussion was hard for him.

"I joined the force young, and I loved the excitement, the charisma of it all. I had a knack for staying cool in an emergency, thinking on my feet, making quick decisions that usually worked out, and I had several promotions, heady stuff for a young guy. Then they trained me as a negotiator. Back then, hostage taking was a relatively new thing, so there weren't a lot of people in the field. Well, soon after they trained me, there were a whole rash of hostage incidents. It seemed to become the 'in' crime of the era. I was successful on one highly publicized case, an international diplomat held at gunpoint by members of a radical group, and there was a mass of publicity. Suddenly it seemed I was in demand all over the place, loaned out to other law enforcement agencies all over the world, given the red-carpet treatment with hotels and expense accounts. It was a huge ego trip for me."

Jessie nodded understandingly. "Like being unknown, and all at once chosen by the National Ballet to dance the lead in *Swan Lake*," she commented. Her words had the desired effect on him because he gave a lopsided grin, and his tone was a shade less terse.

"That's about it, although I'd never have made it in a leotard. But yeah, same scenario. A star is born, and it's not long before his hat doesn't fit anymore because of his swollen head. I was flying high for several years. It was party time.

"There was even a woman I fell in love with, a medical student named Carol Hudson. I felt as if I had the world by the tail. I was the fair-haired wonder child of my detachment, and slowly the cases I dealt with, the tension of the situations, began to be less important to me than the game I was playing of being a hero. The victims, the hostages I was fighting to free, were becoming more like chess pawns to me instead of real people. Yes, it was all a game. Fortunately, it was still a game I usually won.''

The bitter self-condemnation in his voice surprised Jessie.

''Luke, you're being too hard on yourself,'' she protested. ''I'm certain...''

''I'm just being honest, Jessie. I want to be totally honest with you, so shut that lovely mouth and listen.'' The gentle rebuke was accompanied by a tight-lipped smile, but it soon faded, and he averted his eyes as he went on, staring unseeingly out across the garden toward the blank wall of Amanda's house.

''There was an armed bank robbery late one afternoon, not a big hoist, just a branch bank. The guys who did it weren't professionals, they were small-time grease balls who'd been in and out of minor scrapes for years. They were spotted and chased to the waterfront area where they abandoned their car and commandeered a boat from the marina as a last-ditch effort to escape the hordes of policemen on their tail. Trouble was they picked a boat with a father and his fourteen-year-old daughter on board, getting set to go out for a day's fishing.''

Luke's smooth, deep voice was choppy all at once, his delivery flat and rapid. Instinctively, hardly realizing she was doing it, Jessie reached across the small distance separating their chairs and gripped his hand in both of hers, sensing that what was to come was tremendously difficult for him to talk about.

"That's when I was called in. They rushed me down to the police boat. We gave chase. They had a head start, so they were already in U.S. waters when we caught up with them, and it was getting darker by the minute. A fog bank was rolling in."

His clear blue eyes were clouded with painful memories.

"Luke, you don't have to tell me this," Jessie said softly, but he shook his head impatiently and continued.

"With an electric megaphone I contacted the men on board. I honestly was arrogant enough to feel that I'd been called out on a minor matter not worthy of my talents." He gave a mirthless laugh, and silence stretched between them for endless seconds. Jessie felt his hand involuntarily tighten in her grasp.

"Negotiation is always a matter of buying time, you see, of prolonging contact, hoping that the criminals get tired, have second thoughts about what they're doing. In this case, I knew if they sailed off in the fog, we'd certainly lose them. And I was heavily into winning. I was Superman and James Bond, all rolled into one."

Luke had moments when he craved a cigarette more than any other single thing in the world, and this was one of those times. He reached for the wine bottle instead and poured Jessie and himself another glass. The bottle was empty when he set it down.

"They were scared, I could tell by their voices. It gave me an edge, a sense of superiority, and of course I'd underestimated them all along. I was used to dealing with professional criminals, and surprisingly, a pro is predictable to a degree. These bastards weren't, and that's where I made my mistake."

His voice was flat and hard and ruthless, the lines in his face deeply etched. He looked dangerous this way, older and tougher and hard edged.

This was a different Luke than the man Jessie knew. This was the man he'd been, she realized, in the time he called before. It was like looking at old photos of herself in her parents' family album and realizing that the smiling girl standing straight and tall and wearing a ballerina costume was actually her. She'd been that tall, she'd held her body that way, in the graceful stance of a dancer. She'd never even thought about the functioning of her spinal cord then.

Before, and inevitably, after.

Luke was abruptly talking again.

"They kept yelling, 'Back off, you've got ten minutes to back off,' and I procrastinated, telling them we needed more time because they were in U.S. waters, we had to talk with the U.S. Coast Guard. I offhandedly assured the guys with me that these men wouldn't shoot the hostages. They were just punks. I should have offered them a running start, but I was cocky. I held a hard line, and then they shot the girl."

Jessie felt an icy shudder run over her at the quiet statement.

"In disbelief I heard the gun go off, heard them throw her overboard. Then they ran for it, and we hooked the body and I dragged her in." A long, hopeless sigh accompanied his words. It was a scenario he was fated to relive time after time, through a million nightmares, a million waking regrets. His voice was tired when he continued. "I looked at that lovely dead young face, Jess, and knew that if it hadn't been for my arrogance, she might have lived. The criminals got scared and dumped the father overboard, but we picked him up alive. They were caught and sent to prison, but for me, nothing seemed to register after I pulled that girl from the water."

Jessie was silent. Too often people had mouthed platitudes when she told them about her disability, minimizing it not to comfort her—it was, after all, hers alone to deal with—but making it more bearable for their own tender sensibilities to accept.

She'd never do that to Luke. She loved him too well to minimize his handicap. What had happened in that boat was his to live with as best he could, just as her confinement to her chair was hers. Nothing she could say would minimize that fact, and she didn't even try.

"What happened next wasn't a sudden thing," he added evenly. "It crept up on me over the next months, a blackness of the spirit I couldn't shake off, no matter what I did." There was a mirthless humor in his tone. "Believe me, Jess, I tried everything. Liquor, parties, women, even though I was living with Carol. Brawls, more liquor. It soon became obvious to my commanding officer that I wasn't fit to negotiate anything, and he ordered me to take an extended leave of absence. At least work had given me some reason for getting up and gluing myself together each morning, but now there wasn't even that. I was foul-tempered and impossibly unreasonable, and finally, Carol left me. We'd been living together for nine months, and how she ever stood those last few, I don't know. Losing her shocked me into finally getting professional help. The man I saw became a good friend. His name is Graham Marshall. It helped a bit to find out that what had happened to me wasn't unusual at all. They even have a fancy name for it now—Post-Traumatic Syndrome. With Graham's help I was able to take a good long look at myself and come to terms with what had happened."

"Is that when you quit the RCMP?" Jessie's question ironically pinpointed the part of Luke left unhealed. He'd told her this much. He might as well tell her the rest. He nodded in answer to her question.

"I couldn't do the job I'd been trained for any longer. The one thing you have to have in negotiation is confidence, Jess. I never got mine back enough to want to try again. Rather than go back and start all over in some other field, I decided to get into a line of work totally unrelated to law enforcement.''

The weariness in his voice tore at her soul. She wanted desperately to comfort him, to tell him it didn't matter. But she knew it did, and again there were no words to say.

Instead, she did what she would never have dared to do even an hour before. She leaned out and wordlessly took his shoulders in her hands and drew him steadily toward her, impelled by the need to give solace.

Surprise flashed across his face, and then it was Jessie's turn to be surprised, for he took charge, smoothly lifting her out of her chair as if she were featherlight, settling her on his knee as easily as if he did so every evening at dusk.

''Jessie.'' His rough whisper was a rumble under her ear. ''God, sweetheart, it feels so good just to hold you.''

Jessie felt the thundering of his heart beneath her palm, the warm hardness of his hands on her bare back. She tilted her chin up recklessly, and his kiss was deep and sure of welcome.

Her skin was teased by the bristles of his mustache as he explored the soft recesses of her mouth, his warm lips firm and coaxing as she held back at first, uncertain and still a trifle shy.

His hands continued their restless course up and down the sensitive skin on her back, and a shudder went over her. Every nerve ending in her upper body was alive, clamoring for still another caress from his seeking hands, still deeper kisses from his lips. Like the trail of a comet, his lips found a path from her mouth down the line of her throat, and automatically Jessie tipped her head back to give him access, hoping desperately he'd find the sensitive spot under her ear…there, yes, and the tip of her earlobe…his teeth nipped gently and followed a lazy line to the base of her throat as the quivering he caused inside her grew and spread alarmingly.

"You're so soft, you smell so good." A small fraction of Luke's brain still warned him against what he was doing, but the intoxicating delight of having Jessie in his arms, on his lap, outweighed the caution.

Just another few moments and he'd stop, he told that voice. But her skin was like the flower of an African violet, downy and tender and wonderfully delicate, and he ran his fingers lightly up her bare sides, feeling her breath catch and hold as his hands neared the dangerously tempting area where the yellow cotton barely concealed her breasts.

The warmth and slight weight of her on his knees was accelerating his desire, each shifting motion driving him nearer a time when his burgeoning flesh would demand fulfillment.

Another few moments, and another... He stroked a hand over her hair, finding it strangely warm and alive, as if it, like her skin, had somehow captured the sun. It was a mass of fluff as dainty and thick as dandelion spores. A few pins came loose, and more of her curls escaped enticingly to frame her face.

Careful, Luke. You ought to go.

But the inner warning went unheeded because he felt her trembling, saw the languorous hot passion urgently pulsing in his own body reflected in her half-closed eyes, her flushed and rosy skin, her swollen mouth even now shyly seeking his for one more kiss, one more, again, as her impossibly long lashes drifted down lazily.

His lips closed over hers for a long, urgent time.

Jessie had never before experienced the drugging ecstasy now growing inside her. Sensation had never been as acute, as demanding, as that which poured over and through every cell in pulsing waves. She couldn't guess where it was drawing her or how rapidly. She knew only that there was a place she wanted Luke to take her, a place she'd never been before, and she pressed herself tightly against him.

It was his need for her that drew him on, long past the point when he should have stopped, could have stopped. And then Jessie did something that made stopping impossible.

She reached her hand up to the neckline of her yellow jumpsuit and deliberately, seductively, drew the front zipper down until her uptilted breasts, full and firm, sprang free of the fabric and swelled until they filled his large, hot palms.

She was golden and glowing in the twilight, the paler petal softness of her wonderful breasts lighter than the skin the sun had bronzed.

He could feel their nipples, like seedpods about to burst, thrusting into his hand with a wordless and uncontrollable message of desire, and he felt his own tumescence throb dangerously against her curved bottom.

His lips found her nipples. Jessie felt a stab of wonder that any sensation could be so intense, could afford her such rapture as his knowing mouth afforded.

"Luke?" Her voice was rich with passion, and he released her breast with exquisite slowness, nipping gently with his teeth, soothing again with his tongue, knowing she was about to retreat from him, knowing it would be the hardest request he'd ever fulfilled.

"Luke, could you take us into the house now?" Her whispered request was uneven and shy.

Cradled in his arms, Jessie felt him get to his feet in one smooth motion. The moon was just rising, and its gigantic roundness floated overhead for the moments it took him to slip through the door into the still darker kitchen, then pause uncertainly until she told him again what she wanted.

"My bedroom, please." Jessie hardly recognized her own voice. In a few strides Luke found the doorway. The illumination from her clock radio dimly lit the spacious room.

Her water bed moved sluggishly beneath them as he laid her on the goose-down duvet, stretching himself close beside her, smoothly taking up the rhythm of their interrupted kisses until he felt the slight tension in her disappear once more.

Luke had taken and given pleasure countless times with numerous women over the years. He was an ingenious lover, with all the many techniques a worldly man learns to master, unusually adept at the control so essential to pleasing a female—perhaps because he was always slightly removed from his partner.

Tonight there was no thought of technique, however. His feelings for Jessie seemed to obliterate any measure of distance or control, any attempt at self-discipline. Tonight there was only a raging, primitive urge to make the breathtakingly lovely woman in his arms a part of him, to blend with her in the ancient dance of love. He wanted to give her pleasure, and he struggled with his impatience, willing himself to go slowly, to give her time to adjust to him.

"Jessie, darling, beautiful Jessie . . ."

His words sang to her as he carefully slid the jumpsuit collar over her head, unzipped the front still farther down over her abdomen until her body was bare to his hungry eyes and lips and hands, his kisses, his caresses. He murmured soft and lovely words, tasting every inch of skin greedily as he uncovered it.

Fumbling, he unfastened the ridiculously tiny buckles on her sandals and tossed them and her garment to the floor. The bed swayed softly, and he absorbed into his very pores this new Jessie, feminine and delicate in lacy panties, floating on her watery bed like a mermaid beneath his restless seeking hands.

She writhed beneath his caresses, coaxing him to the areas rendered hypersensitive by his touch, stroking timidly at first down his body until she encountered the glorious proof of his desire for her straining against his clothing.

"Jessie," he groaned in delicious agony as her hands found his manhood and jerked away. He took her hand gently in his and replaced it, shuddering, sending echoes of his delight through her. He moved away, and when he returned two heartbeats later, he was bare beside her, his heated naked skin burning against her own with the same fire threatening to consume them both, but his body was bold and hair roughened, strong as steel, where hers was smoothly satin.

Now her hands were braver, and she gasped at the heat and power he exuded. Timidly she ran her lips in a line down his throat, down until his flat male nipple grew pebble hard between her lips and his desire for her vibrated through him.

He slipped the tiny silk panties down and off her long legs, marveling at the lovely elongated lines of her body even as his desire pulsed nearly out of control.

Naked, it was obvious that Jessie had been a dancer. Where there had been rock-hard muscles in her legs, however, there was now only a shapely fragility, inspiring an overwhelming wave of tenderness in Luke.

He wanted to protect and cherish her forever.

He wanted to keep her from ever being hurt again.

Most of all, he wanted to possess her. Quickly.

"Luke, come closer to me, please come closer."

Yet when he gently arranged her legs and answered her plea, there was a moment of disappointment for her. She knew with her intellect where sensation ended. It was unreasonable of her heart to expect more.

Below the level of injury, Jessie was aware only of movement and pressure. Her brain understood that Luke caressed all of her, but it was only her upper body that responded with liquid lightning, with feverish urgency. Still, she longed for him to become a part of her this way, for his hair-roughened length to encompass her fully, and when the moment came and he gently parted her thighs and entered her, it was her brain that signaled they were joined, but it was her heart that exulted in that joining.

He was poised above her, every tendon of his beautiful physique outlined beneath the dark skin as he hovered, and with terrible need stroked, then paused, waiting, endlessly, it seemed to Jessie, for her to follow.

And she couldn't. The beguiling sensations he created grew intense but faded, as if she'd lost her place in an engaging story and had trouble finding it again.

"Jess?"

The blueness of his eyes was molten fire, burning down into her, and his choked, whispered query was followed by lavish praise of her beauty. It was balm to her parched soul.

But the physical delights that she longed for didn't quite happen. The intense love she felt for the man devouring her with his eyes, his body, his words, was still too new and strange for Jessie to totally relax the inhibitions of the past long years.

Wordlessly she shook her head, her eyes so huge they seemed to Luke to overpower her face. And with a desperate moan he knew he could wait no longer. Too soon, too soon...

She felt his muscles tense and ripple, his body convulse. She watched as unbelievable rapture suffused his face, and then his wild cry was smothered against her shoulder.

Being the source of Luke's obvious joy and gratification gave her intense emotional pleasure, and she was overwhelmed with a sense of peace and satisfaction.

Luke, however, was instantly remorseful.

"Darn it, Jess, I'm sorry. I wanted it to be good for you, and then I couldn't wait." There was astonishment as well as chagrin in his tone. Absolute abandonment wasn't a problem Luke had often experienced before, and it had taken him entirely by surprise.

He embraced her, winding his spent form around her like a teasing octopus, and whispered contritely, "It'll be better after I have a chance to practice more, I promise."

His lighthearted teasing wasn't enough to reassure Jessie. Was it really possible that their loving had been as good for him as it seemed to have been, or was he simply letting her down easily? Doubts and painful insecurities bobbed to the surface of her mind.

"Luke," she blurted out hesitantly, "Was it, um, was I...for you, I mean. I know I'm not very good at this." Her statement was matter-of-fact and apologetic, as if it was a thing she knew to be true but which she regretted.

Murderous rage for the man who must have sowed the beginnings of such doubt in this lovely creature surged through Luke like a storm.

He propped himself up on an elbow and reached across her slender body to flick on the bedside light. He wanted her to see him when he answered, watch the truth in his eyes, read the love for her that must show on his face, still nakedly marked with spent passion.

This was one injured part of Jessie that Luke felt confident he could heal forever, if he only had enough time with her. This uncertainty had been the reason for her withdrawal that other night, and he felt a stab of panic at the thought that she might even now retreat from him again.

Already he needed her far too much to dream of letting her go.

"I know this wasn't perfect for you, and that was entirely my fault," he murmured softly, earnestly, loving the way her color mounted and her lashes fell to shyly conceal the traces of unfulfilled desire still lingering there. "I can't describe what it was like for me. You drew me onward with such intensity I couldn't even wait for you, but you must see that you gave me rapture, Jess. You're a wildly passionate woman, an absolutely ravishing, sensuous woman, a beautiful woman. You're all a man could ever want as his partner in loving. Do you think I could have pretended what happened just now?"

She shook her head, uncertain at first, then with more confidence. No actor in the world could have pretended his cataclysmic response. Jessie sighed deeply, as if she'd taken his message in like nourishment. After a moment's thought she gazed up at him candidly.

"Thanks, Luke. It's just that I really don't know much about this, you know," she said ingenuously, her dark eyes wide and guileless. When he had to grin at her candor, she surprised him by adding, "But I asked my friend Kathleen, and she gave me a lot of pointers."

Luke's amused grin faded into a frown, and he folded his arms behind his head thoughtfully, sinking into the pillow behind him.

"You're full of surprises. Who's this Kathleen?"

He was disconcerted, a bit uncertain how he felt about being part of what sounded suspiciously like a carefully planned campaign. He paid attention as Jessie described her colorful friend.

"What sort of things did you ask?" His voice was deliberately neutral.

She told him, outlining every doubt she'd harbored, every mistaken concept about her own potential as a partner for him. She did it with the wonderful honesty he was beginning to take for granted in Jessie. She went into some detail on several technical facets of human sexual response in relation to disabled women, and he paid close attention, starting to understand why she would have felt the need for counseling.

He could be no less than totally honest with her in turn.

"Jessie, this must sound incredibly naive of me, but I never had any of those particular fears, and I certainly don't now. Remember the other day when you tumbled out of your chair in the garden, and in the process of telling me off for treating you—I think your term was 'like an idiot invalid made of porcelain'—you gave me a lecture on the fact that you were an absolutely totally healthy, normal woman who simply happened to be in a goddamn wheelchair? Well, I laughed because those things are perfectly obvious to anyone who knows you. After I met you, Jess, I didn't consciously try to forget about the chair. It just happened somewhere along the line. So why should lovemaking be any different for you than for any other woman?"

Tears slid silently down her cheeks, and she was certain that if she hadn't loved Luke before, she would have adored him after that prosaic little speech.

He heard her sniffle and turned, surprised, to comfort her.

It was only then that he fully realized how frightened she must have been, how difficult it must have been for her to ask anyone for advice about matters so personal and what that asking said about her feelings for him.

She had guts, this lady.

Not for the first time, he pondered her spirit. What made Jessie emotionally courageous while he was just the opposite? He'd take on a cell full of drunken wrestlers single-handed before he'd do what Jessie had done, baring her insecurities and fears, asking for help with them. He'd almost destroyed himself before he'd finally found the courage to do that.

This time his kiss was gentle, a tribute for one wounded warrior to another.

They were drifting and dreaming and idly chatting when the phone shrilled. Jessie groaned.

"Who can that be this late?" But when she glanced at the clock, she was astonished to find it wasn't yet ten. She could have sworn an entire night had passed.

Reluctantly she lifted the receiver.

"Jessica?"

It was Chandra. Jessie greeted her and then hurriedly moved away from Luke as if her mother could see their embrace. Chandra sounded annoyed.

"Jessica, your father had to go down to the warehouse unexpectedly—some nonsense about security—and we were planning on seeing that French movie on Tenth Avenue that everyone's talking about. I really hate to go alone, dear. I thought you could come with me. I'll pick you up in half an—"

"Sorry, Mother," Jessie interrupted smoothly. "It's not convenient tonight." The words flowed effortlessly from her mouth, words she'd seldom used with her mother, no matter how thoughtless Chandra's last-minute invitations had been.

Stunned silence greeted her announcement. Then Chandra demanded, "And why is that?" Her tone insinuated that nothing could or should take precedence over such a royal dictum, and Jessie felt a rebellious flash of satisfaction when she said quietly, "Because I have a date tonight, Mother. Luke is here with me."

Feeling Luke's hand reach over languidly and caress her shoulder gave Jessie reassurance and comfort as Chandra digested the information and came to her own conclusions.

Trust Chandra to have the last word, and make it succinct.

"I only hope you know what you're doing, Jessie. From your description, he's an attractive man, and women in your situation are particularly vulnerable. I wouldn't want you to get hurt, dear."

Jessie hung up slowly. Her mother's final comment reverberated in her head.

"Your mother?" Luke had met the lady one day when he was working in the yard. She was the type of person Denny usually labeled a "barracuda," and Luke considered the label fitting in this instance.

Jessie nodded wordlessly, squirming herself over until she was touching him again. She didn't repeat what Chandra had said. Instead, she asked with a trace of wistfulness, "What's your mother like, Luke?"

She could almost feel him smile fondly. "Mum? She's a real estate agent in Calgary. I grew up on a large ranch in the Alberta foothills, and Dad decided a few years ago to sell out and move to the city for a rest." Jessie felt the bed tremble with Luke's chuckle. "Some rest that was. Within six months he'd bought a business, a hardware store, and Mum was taking a real estate course. They're working harder than they ever did and loving every minute of it. Lorna and I were really lucky, getting parents like those two."

"You're lucky to have a sister, too. Being an only child is difficult." Being Chandra's only child had been much worse than difficult, Jessie mused. "It's so strange, lying here like this with you and talking about our parents, Luke."

He flopped from his side onto his back, liking the gentle undulations of the water beneath him, and he drew Jessie into the curve of his arm. "This is the best time for talking. No inhibitions."

Jessie felt her face flood with embarrassed warmth, remembering suddenly just how lacking in inhibitions she'd been a short time before.

The bedside light threw shadows into the corners of the room. Luke had been staring up at the ceiling without really looking at it. Now he gradually became aware of the mural covering the whole expanse above his head, a strange and lonely vista of a pockmarked, gray and rocky surface in the foreground, with a backdrop of distant space, planets and strange stars that seemed to stretch into infinity. It seemed an unusual and rather eerie scene for a room as otherwise feminine as Jessie's.

"That's the surface of the moon?" He pointed upward, and Jessie nodded, her hair pleasantly tickling his shoulder.

"Yes, I had a picture that was taken during a moon landing blown up and made into a mural, then pasted onto my ceiling."

Puzzled, he frowned up at the lonely scene.

"Why not a picture of the earth taken from up there, if you're absolutely set on outer space? Why the moon?"

Jessie laughed a bit self-consciously. "It's a dumb fantasy, but it got me through the worst times after my accident. All I could think about then were all the things I'd never be able to do again. There was so much to relearn, so much to relinquish. I was at the lowest point in my entire life because I felt I couldn't do anything, be anything, ever again." She paused, lost for an instant in bittersweet memories.

Luke felt his own insides wrench in understanding and empathy. And love.

"I was feeling pretty sorry for myself, and finally I reached a point when I didn't want to go on living. The doctors agreed I'd never walk again, and I was a dancer. Dancing had been my life for as long as I could remember. Nights were the worst. Ironically, every single night I dreamed I was dancing, and every morning I woke up to legs that didn't even move. It got so I didn't want to go to sleep at night because that first moment of waking was so awful. I started watching television later and later every night, fighting off sleeping and thinking. Television's great for that." She turned her head to grin wryly at Luke, and it was all he could do to nod in response.

Jessie, involved in her story, continued, "Then one night there was a long program on space exploration. They showed satellites and planets, and finally they reran the first footage of the original moon landing. I didn't pay much attention at first. Then I saw these astronauts bouncing around, taking ten-foot jumps without any effort. Hardly any gravity up there, see? If you could manage to stand up down here, well, heck, it was a cinch you could dance on the moon." She reached out a hand and stroked it across his chest reflectively.

"There was still a place in the universe where I could dance, and if dancing wasn't absolutely impossible for me, then nothing was, and I could learn to live with myself." Jessie chuckled, more than a little embarrassed at her revelation. "It was straight off-the-wall, I know, but it gave me strength, that nutty idea. I used to put myself to sleep, moon dancing."

Luke didn't laugh with her. Her words tore at his emotions, touched his heart and his soul, and he enfolded her so hard in his arms he startled her with his ferocity.

He hadn't meant to take the route he had tonight, this blissful, blinding journey into passion, but he knew now it was the right path, the inevitable direction for them.

Right now, with the summer moon streaming through the gently billowing curtains, dimming the faint light in the room, he needed to tell her what was in his heart.

"Jessie," he said, and his tone was rich with certainty as he nuzzled his lips into the living perfume of her hair, "Jessie, I love you. You know," he mused thoughtfully, "I think I've loved you ever since I saw you on that hill in the marathon. And if I could, I'd draw down the moon and dance with you in my arms, tonight."

Her heart seemed to stop and then race with panic and elation, terrible fear and utter bliss, at his quiet declaration.

Luke was in love with her... as she was with him. It was so much more than Jessie had ever felt life had in store for her, the love of this gentle, thoughtful man.

"And I love you," she admitted. It felt wonderful to finally say the words out loud. "I love you, Luke." They seemed to gain in strength and power each time she repeated them, and her tremulous voice grew stronger with each repetition.

"I...love...you," she repeated wonderingly.

She gazed up at the silent and peaceful vista on her ceiling and thought of her mother's cutting remark. The world was still out there, and they'd have to contend with it somehow. Jessie knew from experience it wasn't always generous or kind, or even fair. Would love be enough to sustain them?

"I only wish we were up there instead of here," she said wistfully, jabbing a finger at the moonscape.

"Not me, Jess." His deep voice rang with quiet certitude. "Everything I ever wanted is right here on earth, right here in this room."

He gathered her close and gently kissed her, and in moments she was asleep.

Luke lay awake a long time, cradling her, staring up at the ceiling.

CHAPTER EIGHT

IT WAS LATE Sunday morning when they awakened, each moving up from the depths of sleep, conscious that their immediate world had altered overnight.

For Luke, waking was always instantaneous. Full awareness arrived the instant he opened his eyes, and the warm softness of Jessie's drowsy form evoked erotic images of the previous night. He turned to rekindle the delight of having her in his embrace.

For Jessie, having Luke's hard male body intimately near her own while she slept provided a deep and wondrous peace, a new sense of being cherished and protected, and as always, waking was reluctant and gradual.

"Morning, sleepyhead." He kissed her, nibbling, friendly kisses that traveled from her swollen lips to her cheeks, from the tip of her nose to a tender bite on the chin, and she gradually managed to open her eyes. Barely.

She squinted sleepily up at him through the curls that always seemed to be over her eyes in the mornings.

"What time is it?" Her voice was sleep numbed and slurred.

"Nearly ten." Luke squinted at the clock and resumed his tantalizing journey down her throat, putting his tongue on the slow, even pulse at the base and matching the deep heart sounds with pulsing gentle jabs that caused languorous response to stir in her.

She wrapped her arms around him, loathe to reach the surface of the delicious dreams still half capturing her, sleepily aware of his caresses.

"What day is it?" A puzzled frown wrinkled the smooth skin of her forehead. Her eyes were tightly closed again.

Luke laughed, loving her morning stupor and the vulnerability it gave her. She was usually so alert and independent, so much in control that it made him feel ridiculously pleased to have her like this—warm, sleepy, confused. There was intense pleasure in this intimate new contact with Jessie.

"Let's see, now. Yesterday was Saturday all day, so today must be—don't hint now, I'll get it—why, I do believe it's Sunday," he announced triumphantly, running his hands down the incredible silkiness of her shoulders and then cradling her breasts, his thumbs lightly flicking the nipples into pulsing life.

Her eyes were still closed when he rolled her over on top of him, limp and warm and unresisting, floating just below the surface of sleep.

Her legs obligingly slid apart on either side of his body, and she wriggled her torso languorously until it rested comfortably on his broad chest.

Jessie felt movement, glorious pressure, and thought of her every nerve ending touching and being touched by the man she loved. She reached a barely awake hand down and felt the power of his hot, wet, stroking maleness seeking, finding, entering and leaving and entering again, slow and purposeful.

"That's nice, Luke," she murmured dreamily, and he propped the pillows behind himself so that her breasts were accessible to his seeking lips.

Half awake, half asleep, Jessie allowed sensation to pour over her as his mouth tugged and sensitized, his hands stroked lightly, provocatively, along her neck, down her shoulders, around her torso, teasing, lingering, learning by her quickened breathing and slight gasps just where to hover, where to tantalize.

Incredibly, between one drugged, lingering kiss and the next, it seemed to Jessie that there was nothing she couldn't feel, no sensation of fullness or heat or motion absent in the spiral of intensity unexpectedly gripping her.

With gasping, sobbing breaths she tried to tell Luke of the miracle happening to her, the unbearable tension growing and increasing, coaxing her higher and still higher, until the apex of loving gripped her, forcing her into an arch of straining bliss, her arms and torso locked to his body in unbelieving joy.

"Luke, Luke..."

Jessie uttered a wailing cry of release and relief. Gratitude more profound than she'd ever known came welling from her throat unconsciously, and Luke felt all that he was and all he ever would be spill like a thundering promise up into the woman he loved. The rightness of their union overwhelmed him.

When at last she could speak again, it was to say shakily, "I should phone Kathleen and tell her the good news." But the seemingly flippant comment was accompanied by a rain of tears spilling down Jessie's cheeks and over Luke's chest. It was a long time before the sobs she couldn't control finally eased.

"I didn't know it was like that. How could I know it was like that?" she said, gasping at last. The depth of her responsiveness both thrilled Luke and awed him with its force. Never had he felt as totally united with another human being or felt so responsible for someone's happiness.

A niggling unease intruded, and he pushed it away. Once before a woman had loved and trusted him. He'd failed that trust and nearly destroyed the woman who gave it.

He mustn't fail Jessie.

MUCH LATER they breakfasted with Cy on the brick patio, and Jessie felt a trace of shyness. It was quite obvious that Luke had spent the night with her.

But if Cy was surprised to find Luke with her, it wasn't evident in his offhand, friendly greeting, and within a short time he invited Amanda over to join them.

The older woman arrived, smartly casual in expensive spotless white sharkskin pants and an up-to-the-minute safari shirt, bearing fresh, hot cheese bagels she'd driven down to the Bagel Factory to buy.

As Amanda walked toward them, Jessie figured Cy wouldn't have noticed if a whole battalion of men had suddenly exited naked from her bedroom. It was fascinating to see the usually self-possessed, opinionated Cy flustered and obviously smitten with Amanda. Their evening must have been a landmark occasion for them, as well, Jessie thought smugly.

The day promised to be gloriously sunny and hot, and Luke suggested that the four of them go for a long walk on the shore and then out to dinner.

"Let's drive to Ambleside in West Van," Cy suggested. "I'll give you a guided tour. West Van was my hometown."

Jessie drove, and Luke admired the aggressively competent way she managed the heavy Sunday traffic. The hand controls on her van looked easy to manage, but he suspected Jessie's proficiency with them was deceptive.

The trip took them through the heart of the city and its concrete towers, then over the rainbow arch of the Lion's

Gate Bridge, which channeled them into the municipality of West Vancouver, and finally down to the oceanfront.

The bridge overlooked Stanley Park and the Seawall. The marathon had included two circuits of the six-mile concrete walkway around the periphery of the park, and Luke stared down at it, thinking of the day they'd met.

"Think you'll ever try another marathon, Jess?"

Glancing down at the park as she drove, her thoughts had also been on the fateful day. It all seemed to have happened so long ago, those rigors of training and the tension of that morning, then the calamitous meeting with Luke.

"Only if you wait for me on that final hill," she said softly. Her words eased the last of the guilt Luke felt. The marathon ceased to be an awkward memory and became instead a memorable one.

Both couples seemed lost in thought as they parked and began their walk along the well-maintained beach pathways of Ambleside Park.

"I grew up just up the hill there," Cy announced, "in the part of town called Dunderave. My father was a family physician in the old tradition, and we had a huge English-style mansion with his offices on the main floor. The whole place used to be derisively called Tiddley Cove then because of the strong British influence. Fish and chips in newspaper, crumpets and tea, ladies strolling along here with hats and gloves on, church members over for Sunday dinner and hymn singing." Cy painted a vivid picture for them of an affluent and, Jessie mused, a curiously staid childhood. Such stuffiness seemed to have produced the Bohemian character Cy had worked so hard at becoming.

"It's great to hear stories about olden times, isn't it, Luke?" Jessie said wickedly. "When was all this, Cy, around the turn of the century?"

Cy grabbed Jessie's chair and threatened to roll her straight off the cement path and into the ocean, to the shocked disapproval of two plump ladies in hats strolling behind them.

"When I first moved to this city," Amanda remarked, "I didn't think anybody was actually a native of Vancouver. Everyone always seemed to be from somewhere else."

"Where are you from, Amanda?" Jessie asked curiously, envisioning Toronto or New York, or maybe even Europe. There was a big-city patina to Amanda that suggested sophistication and, possibly, wealth.

"A little village in eastern B.C. called Fernie." Amanda shook her head ruefully. "My father was an underground coal miner in the mines that tunnel through the mountains in that area." She glanced at Cy walking beside her and grimaced. "I had seven brothers and three sisters, and we were desperately poor. My parents seemed to be fighting constantly over money. I left home at fifteen, determined not to have a life like my mother's. There were no crumpets and tea or ladies in hats in my childhood, believe me."

Jessie was flabbergasted by the honest disclosure. When she thought about it, however, her childhood revealed a great deal about Amanda's choice to live a single life, her attention to grooming, her obvious love for fine clothing. What remarkably diverse backgrounds the four of them had, Jessie marveled.

Cy and Amanda headed for a concession selling coffee, and Luke and Jessie continued along the pathway. Luke rested a warm hand on Jessie's shoulder, now and then stroking a finger beneath her heavy braid to touch her neck. It was a disturbingly familiar and yet strange sensation. Occasionally he rubbed the back of his fingers down her cheek in a wordless caress.

With each absentminded gesture of affection, Luke wove the bright ribbon of Jessie's love for him more firmly around her heart. It gave her such pleasure to be touched in this way, to have Luke demonstrative and open about his feelings.

"This is the first time we've been together for a whole day away from the house and garden," he remarked once, and she nodded thoughtfully, thinking of all the wonderful firsts still to come in their relationship and then, with an anxious pang of warning, of all the not so wonderful ones.

There would be his family and Jessie's parents to confront somewhere along the way, and Jessie knew those meetings might prove difficult. Would prove difficult, she corrected, with Chandra a part of them.

There was also the unwelcome reappearance of Wayne in her own life. The thought of her former husband cast a shadow over the brightness of the day, and Jessie shuddered. He'd called twice more in the past week. She'd hung up immediately, but now she was constantly tense every time the phone rang.

A rush of anger and an accompanying feeling of helplessness washed over her. Wayne both frightened and repelled her. She should report the calls to Evan, but she hated the idea of explaining who Wayne was, dreaded the thought of yet another lecture about the inconvenience of women announcers.

"Hey—" Luke planted a quick kiss on her cheek "—can't you see the signs? No daydreaming allowed. These are respectable beaches."

Jessie gave him a smile, loving the way he matched his stride to the pace of her chair as he walked along.

She was sorely tempted to spill out the whole problem of Wayne to Luke, but she hesitated. She had to be careful, she reminded herself, not to begin relying on Luke to solve her problems for her. It would be far too easy to lean heavily on his strength—and soon he'd begin to resent her dependence.

"Race you to the pier," she challenged and was yards ahead of him in seconds.

The rest of the afternoon was full of laughter and conversation, and Jessie pushed all her concerns to the back corner of her mind to deal with another time.

This was today, and today was wondrous.

Across the gentle waves of the inlet, Vancouver lay like a sparkling city of promise, its downtown towers gleaming in the late-afternoon sunshine, the grayness of the concrete jungle balanced as if on a measured scale by the thousand-acre tropically lush Stanley Park on the left and the equally verdant thousand acres of the University of British Columbia campus on the far right.

Over it all hung a sky as deeply and richly blue as . . . Jessie's eyes flew to Luke's face. As blue as his eyes, she decided, returning the private smile he gave her, admiring him as if he were a stranger she'd never seen before.

He'd had her stop for several moments near his apartment building in the West End when they were passing, and he'd changed the rather bedraggled-looking blue trousers and shirt for a pair of navy shorts and a casual T-shirt. Its tight bands emphasized the obvious muscles in his arms and shoulders. Luke's robust body was lean and fit from landscaping. His crisply curling black hair with its smattering of gray and the generous mustache contributed to an air of macho handsomeness, rugged and unstudied.

She remembered the words he'd used to reassure her the night before, and she now applied them to him in her mind.

Luke was all any woman could ever want as a man, a lover, a friend. The depth of her love for him awed Jessie, mixing with an unreasoning fear for all the unknowns that must be met and countered if they were to succeed in their relationship.

It wasn't going to be easy.

DURING THE NEXT WEEK it seemed as if they didn't see one another enough to have a relationship at all. Their work schedules were impossible.

Luke started work at dawn, and the job he and Denny were currently doing was miles out of the city. He arrived home past four, showered and drove to Jessie's. They ate dinner together, but then there was barely an hour to share before Jessie had to leave for work. After two nights of picking her up at midnight and making passionate love until dawn, Luke reluctantly admitted to Jessie on the third night that he was falling sound asleep in people's gardens during coffee breaks.

It was already two-thirty in the morning, and Luke was delaying the inevitable moment when he'd have to go home.

He wanted nothing more than to stay, but common sense told him it just wasn't practical to fall asleep now and have to fumble out of bed at 4:00 a.m. just to drive down to his apartment to shower and shave for work.

Jessie made leaving even harder by snuggling closer to him, her cheek resting on his shoulder.

"Next week's my birthday," she announced, stifling a yawn.

"The twenty-third, isn't it?" he surprised her by asking.

"How'd you know? You're right, too. The point is, I always schedule a week of holidays around my birthday."

He gave her a smacking kiss on the lips and climbed out of bed, tugging his pants on.

"Luke? Why are you leaving in such a hurry?" She squinted sleepily up at him.

"I'm going home to get rested up so Denny gets two good days' work out of me before I tell him I'm taking an entire week off."

Jessie giggled up at him, delighted. "You are? You will? That's absolutely fantastic."

He had to laugh at her enthusiasm, but there was no trace of laughter when he propped one knee on the bed and took her in his arms.

"Jessie, I hope you know how much I love you. I want to be with you every spare minute of every day." His deep voice was charged with the power of his emotion, and it touched her to the core.

Her eyes filled with tears, and she could only nod in response. Life had taken a turn toward perfection, as long as she forced her mind away from thoughts of Wayne.

The remainder of the week inched past, and finally the weekend came. Again there were uninterrupted hours to spend together.

"It's crazy to drive back and forth to your apartment all the time," she reasoned on Saturday afternoon when Luke mentioned having to drive down and get the suit he needed to take her out to dinner. "Why don't you bring some of your things over here for the week?"

"If that's a lewd invitation, lady, I accept."

They raided his apartment together, stuffing random belongings in paper bags and cleaning out his fridge. That night Jessie felt a satisfied permanence in having his underwear sharing a drawer with hers, his shoes aligned neatly beside hers in the closet. It was temporary, of course, she reminded herself, but all the same it was delightful.

"How many pairs of shoes do you own?" he asked in amazement when she showed him where to stow the several pairs he'd brought with him. There were shoe racks in the bottom of her closet that held pair after pair of neatly aligned footwear.

He'd noticed with tender amusement how she matched a pair to every outfit she wore.

"I adore shoes, I always have," Jessie said by way of explanation. "And they're a great investment, too, because they never wear out on me." Her roguish grin flashed, and he shook his head at her.

"Jessie," he declared, "you're one crazy lady, you know that?" And beautiful. So beautiful inside and out that she took his breath away. There was enchantment in her arms, and he sensed that he'd unlocked a deep untapped well of passion in Jessie.

With love and honest openness they explored together the myriad ways their bodies could bring them joy that week.

They laughed and loved and talked and argued their way through the precious hours of freedom.

They wandered the beaches and went to a movie they both wanted to see, then argued forcefully over it afterward.

They complemented each other intellectually. Luke was interested in politics and foreign affairs, Jessie was fascinated by people and their crazy foibles.

On the morning of her birthday, Luke woke her early, tickling her nose with a pink rosebud he'd picked from the garden.

"Wake up, sleepyhead."

Her arms slipped around his neck, her eyes still firmly shut. She'd learned quickly how to lure him back into bed in the mornings, but today he resisted, giving her one greedy kiss and throwing off the covers and hauling her unceremoniously out of bed. He plopped her naked and objecting into her chair and earned himself a scowl that gave way to a sleepy smile when he kissed her again. She was rosy and tempting, and he steeled himself against the need to sweep her back into his arms, back into the tumbled bed.

"To the showers, birthday lady. We've got a full day ahead of us, no time to lose."

Baffled but excited, as well—her birthday was usually spent the same way every year, quietly, with a sizable check from her father and a new dress from Chandra, then a pizza dinner shared with Cy—Jessie put on a brightly printed wrap skirt and a cotton T-top that left her shoulders and arms bare.

He drove to Robson Street in the very heart of the city, parked and whisked her to an outdoor table at one of the hotel restaurants, delighting the waiter by ordering a bottle of expensive champagne and two of the most lavish breakfasts the chef could concoct plus a pot of coffee.

"A celebration, sir?" the young man asked with a smile as he poured the sparkling wine into long-stemmed glasses, and Luke nodded. "My lady's birthday today," he announced, loud enough for the large group of German tourists at the next table to hear.

The next thing Jessie knew, total strangers were smiling and tipping their coffee cups at her in a toast, and when the waiter brought a bud vase with a pink carnation and set it by her plate, their boisterous neighbors broke into a noisy chorus of "Happy Birthday."

Luke's eyes shone with amusement and pleasure as she blushed and smiled at her well-wishers.

"That was fantastic, Luke, but I can't eat another bite," she moaned forty minutes later, and Luke nodded in satisfaction.

"Good. You're going to need your strength—we've got a busy day ahead." He tipped the last of the champagne into her glass, and the well-wishers clapped and cheered as he whisked her away.

The stores were opening, dozens of colorful and unusual boutiques, jewelry stores, delicatessens, groceries and ethnic restaurants that made up what locals and visitors fondly called Robsonstrasse because of its resemblance to the quaint and beautiful shopping areas of Europe.

"I decided to bring you along to pick out your own birthday gifts so I don't get the sizes wrong," Luke told her. He proceeded to buy her everything she was rash enough to admire or he thought she might like.

He bought her a pewter pendant styled by a native Indian artist in the form of a sun god. "To wear on rainy days."

From an Indonesian boutique he bought her an outrageous straw hat with daisies on the brim—to wear on sunny days.

He bought her four plastic bangles from a street vendor in different ice-cream colors to match the four pairs of plastic gumdrop slippers she'd idly admired, and instantly acquired, from a shoe store.

"Enough, you madman," she protested, weak from laughing. But he ignored her and ducked into a lingerie shop, coming out with a dazed, trapped expression, slightly less aplomb and a huge bag stuffed with wisps of scanty satin and lace.

Her next gifts included a bouquet of violets tied with a red satin ribbon, a huge bag of fat, ripe Okanagan cherries, an assortment of wickedly scented oils from a store called the Loveshop, which Jessie refused to enter, and tiny gold earrings shaped like starfish. Finally, Jessie became truly concerned.

"Luke, that's enough, this is crazy, I don't need all this stuff. I won't have you spending all your money on me."

"But I need to buy it for you," he claimed airily, whisking her into a doorway and kissing her by a bank machine.

"Besides, didn't I tell you I'm filthy rich?" He considered that for a moment and amended, "Well, maybe not quite, but Denny and I did collect on a big job."

When at last they stopped long enough to sip cool drinks in a tea shop, Jessie's chair was festooned with bags and packages and flowers.

"This is the best birthday I've ever had in my life," she said with a sigh. "When I was little, my birthday parties were stiff little catered affairs that Mother organized and invited her friend's kids to. I hardly knew them because I spent so much time dancing. What I really always wanted was a noisy party like the kids have nowadays at Mc-Donald's," she confided.

While she was in the rest room, Luke made several phone calls.

That evening, in the party room of a restaurant sporting golden arches, the staff prepared the cake and gathered to sing "Happy Birthday."

"How old is the birthday kid?" asked the boy with the candles.

"Thirty-three," Luke said with a perfectly straight face.

Amidst dozens of balloons, scaled-down furniture and rather puzzled patrons, Luke and Cy and Amanda ate hamburgers and toasted Jessie with Coke.

So MUCH JOY in the space of five short days. Jessie basked in the pleasure of loving and being loved, and not one incident spoiled her happiness. She put her trepidation about Wayne into a box in her mind and sealed the lid. When Luke was with her, it seemed absurd to be disturbed over a silly matter like a few phone calls, anyway.

In the same manner she tried to guard against thoughts that crept into her mind now and then concerning the future of herself and Luke, living, instead, in blissful suspension of reality for those five whole days.

Nothing so perfect could possibly last much longer, Jessie assured herself apprehensively on Friday, and, of course, it didn't.

Chandra phoned that afternoon and demanded Jessie come to dinner on Saturday, with this "Luke person" she was seeing.

Not an hour later Denny arrived with shrubbery Luke had ordered for Amanda's garden and the message that Lorna expected them both for dinner on Sunday, no excuses accepted.

"I'll go if you will," Luke groaned when he and Jessie compared royal commands that evening. He thought up wickedly outrageous remarks for them each to make, sensing Jessie's nervousness and trying to put her at ease. He described his nephews in humorous detail, trying at the same time to give Jessie some insight into his sister.

Luke seemed totally relaxed about the invitations, although he remarked wistfully that he would much rather spend the weekend alone with Jessie.

She tried to adopt his carefree attitude, but when Saturday came, she grew more nervous with each hour that passed.

Her parents lived on West Marine Drive, the area of the city where the taxes for the vast properties cost more per year than what most people paid for their houses.

They were in Luke's car, and when Jessie directed him past the open wrought-iron gates to the wooded, winding driveway, he let out a long, low whistle of appreciation.

"Mother calls this her 'cabin in the woods,'" Jessie said, her voice tinged with irony. The low, rambling house was West Coast cedar and ringed with wide cedar decks. A tennis court lay on the western extremity, and the property was large enough to allow total privacy. Evergreens snuggled around the house, and the wide back lawns with their careful Japanese-style arrangements of tidy flowers swept grandly down to a ravine and a breathtaking view of the Fraser River and the flat delta lands of Richmond.

"Does it have indoor plumbing?" Luke pulled to a stop in the circular driveway and hopped out to rescue Jessie's chair from the trunk, aware from the manicured surroundings exactly why Jessie had been so insistent on a "wild" garden for her own yard.

Arthur greeted them warmly at the door, firmly shaking Luke's hand and bending down to give his daughter a hug and a loving kiss.

"Your mother will be down in a minute. Her tennis game ran late. Let's get a drink and admire the sunset from the back deck. Luke, what can I get for you?"

"Luke likes beer, Dad. Got some cold, or did you forget to stick it in the fridge?"

Luke noted the warmth and closeness obvious between Jessie and her tall, silver-haired father as they bantered back and forth, sharing the task of pouring drinks at the antique sideboard that served as a bar in the spacious, open-beamed living room.

Luke glanced around the room. Tumble rock climbed to the ceiling along a fireplace wall. Windows took up most of the other wall space to the left, framing the magnificent view.

Then Luke's attention was arrested by a portrait hanging alone on a soft almond-colored space between two windows. It was a full-length study, simply framed, of a delicately slender young girl in a knee-length, ethereally wispy ballet costume, her hand resting on the back of a chair as she paused between postures, her serious, dreamy gaze fixed on something unseen.

Jessie.

Before.

Luke's heart twisted into a peculiar aching knot, and he
took an involuntary step toward the painting before he realized Chandra had appeared at his side.

"She was quite lovely, wasn't she? Jessica was seventeen
in that portrait." The cultured voice held the barest tinge of
bitterness, regret and . . . martyrdom?

"Jessie *is* very lovely." Luke looked straight into Chandra's face as he made the correction, and her eyes narrowed
slightly as she returned his challenging stare.

Lorna had once wickedly described for Luke her inter-
pretation of the Perfect West Coast Woman, and Luke remembered the definition as he studied Jessie's mother.

"Lifted, tinted, pummeled and tanned, worth five
hundred bucks for every ounce of lean flesh," Lorna had
declared with acerbity.

Chandra's short hair was casually, carefully styled, an
expensive and subtle mix of different shades of blond. She
was tanned just enough to suggest leisure, and her teeth, her
fingernails, her skin and her slender body were all professionally, meticulously perfect, showcased by understated
and exact makeup. She wore elegant cream slacks and a
matching silk shirt with dramatic touches of heavy, ornate
gold jewelry at her earlobes and wrist. Her age, which had
to be somewhere in the fifties, was indeterminate from her
appearance and, Luke deduced, would remain that way as
long as Chandra's iron will—and a great deal of money—
could preserve the merchandise.

There was nothing easy, nothing unstudied, about her,
and Luke felt instantly on guard. From the corner of his eye,
he could see Jessie, relaxed and laughing a moment earlier
at something her father had said, become suddenly sober

and obviously tense as she glanced over and noted Chandra's arrival.

"Hi, Mother. How was your game?"

"Hello, dear. My serve was off, God knows why, just when there's a tournament on at the club, wouldn't you know." Chandra, Luke noted, made no move toward her daughter.

"Here's your wine spritzer, love." Arthur handed his wife an oversize wine goblet, and Jessie gave Luke a frosted beer mug, then led the way out the sliding glass doors to the wide wraparound deck.

The conversation was easy and casual. It was obvious Chandra and Arthur were adept at entertaining. It was also obvious, at least to Luke, that Arthur Langstrom-Smith deeply loved both his wife and his daughter and tried his level best to form a bridge between them. Without success, Luke surmised, because although mother and daughter were scrupulously polite to each other, there was none of the real warmth Luke was so accustomed to seeing between his own roly-poly little mother and Lorna when they were together.

THE MOON WAS UP, a gigantic orb hanging over the city, when Luke drove home. Jessie was slumped in the seat, and every now and then she heaved a huge, unconscious sigh.

Luke reached across and drew her close to his side, tucking her protectively under his arm as he drove along the quiet streets.

"That wasn't so bad, Jess," he soothed. It hadn't been so good, either, yet there wasn't anything specific he would pinpoint to explain why.

After her first unguarded remark about Jessie's portrait, Chandra had been cautious.

"Your dad's an interesting man." Arthur had given Luke a fascinating capsule account of the rum-running that had

been part of Vancouver's more colorful history in the past
century, drawing verbal portraits of several characters with
almost professional skill. "I see where you inherited your
ability to captivate an audience with your voice."

"Dad's okay. He's just never gotten over the idea I need
somebody to take care of me. Did you notice how interested he was when you told him you'd been in the RCMP?
I could just see him heaving a sigh of relief that finally, at
last, his little Jessie has her very own trained bodyguard
around. God. And he always takes me aside and asks if I
need money."

Luke laughed, stopping for a light at Broadway. "So
what? He's your father. I'd imagine all fathers feel some-
what that way about their only daughters."

"I'm not looking for protection," she snapped vehemently. "I'm perfectly capable of taking care of myself and
supporting myself. It annoys me Dad can't understand
that."

Luke was silent, surprised at her bad temper. Then she
added in a still harsh tone, "I should be grateful that at least
Dad accepts me as I am." Luke perceived the hurt under the
anger.

"Your mother doesn't?" He didn't need to ask. It was
obvious that Chandra had never adjusted to Jessie's injury.

Jessie snorted inelegantly. "She has an overwhelming
need to excel at everything she does. You saw all those tennis trophies. Life's a competition to Chandra, the person
who ends up with the most trophies wins the game. Because of me she lost out on the perfect daughter award."

Realizing how bitter she sounded, Jessie attempted a
laugh, but it came out strained. "It's silly to still be affected at my age by what my mother thinks. You'd think a
person would outgrow the need to please a mother. She's
never going to change, never going to see me as anything

except a failure in her overall game plan. Most of the time I don't let it bother me. I just don't go home any oftener than I can help.''

''Maybe it'll be easier for us to go over together. Your father and I get along fine, and it obviously pleases him to have you there.''

Luke's casual, unconscious reference to a long-term relationship made Jessie catch her breath. They hadn't talked yet about the future or what it held for the two of them. Jessie had determined not to think about it, to simply delight in each day they spent with one another. They needed time together before they thought of commitment, she told herself.

And there was still the hurdle of meeting his sister the next day. What would Lorna's reaction be to Luke's falling in love with a woman who happened to be in a wheelchair?

Jessie turned her head upward and pressed a kiss under Luke's chin. He swiftly caught her lips with his own and then reluctantly drew away in order to pay attention to the road ahead.

''Wait till I get you home, you tease,'' he growled. His hand reached around her shoulder and provocatively stroked her breast, sending shards of hot desire splintering through her.

''Hurry,'' she whispered, wishing the night could last forever with the two of them alone in the moonlight.

CHAPTER NINE

IF JESSIE HAD BEEN anxious the night before about her family, it was Luke's turn to be on edge the following afternoon.

The first problem was the flight of cement steps leading into the Masons' house. Jessie took one look at them and groaned.

"Either we eat out here in the rain, or you and Denny will have to haul me bodily into the house."

It really wasn't difficult for Luke and Denny to lift Jessie and her chair neatly up those steps. Luke knew it was far harder for Jessie to be lifted, though. It bothered her, the way any lack of independence always did. And there was an audience—Luke's nephews watched the whole procedure closely.

Denny muttered something about locating Lorna and headed for the back deck where the barbecue was sending whiffs of charcoal through the open door.

The boys, who'd been hurriedly introduced to Jessie outside, stared openly at her for two full minutes, taking in every detail of her and her wheelchair.

"Why you can't walk up the stairs?" Robbie was the spokesman, but Luke could see the older two waiting avidly for Jessie's answer.

"Because my legs don't work," Jessie explained forthrightly. "The bones in my back were hurt long ago. It's like a telephone when the lines are down—the messages my brain sends to my legs just don't get through."

Luke felt a rush of pride at her simple explanations, and he wondered curiously what the next question would be.

"How come the doctor don't fix—" Robbie couldn't finish his next question because a flustered Lorna hurried into the room, a tin of barbecue starter in her hand.

"Boys, that's enough. What did I tell you?" Her outraged tone bridged no argument. "Downstairs, all of you, *now*."

Robbie started to wail, and Jessie objected, "It's fine, really, I don't mind at all being asked...."

"I've told them not to be rude. I'm awfully sorry."

Luke, with a sinking feeling in his stomach, could see that Lorna was wound tight as a steel spring. Her tall, thin form vibrated with tension and uneasiness.

Where was the easygoing sister he thought he knew?

Denny did his genial host routine, mixing drinks all round and reciting anecdotes from the job he and Luke were doing, but underneath the surface he, too, seemed subdued and a trifle anxious.

Luke was frankly puzzled. Was it meeting Jessie that was causing the strain, or were the Masons still quarreling over Lorna's business? Luke began to wish heartily he'd never agreed to this dinner.

Jessie's valiant efforts to draw Lorna into conversation about popular music and even clothing styles failed. Lorna bobbed up and down, hurrying distractedly to and from the kitchen, even though Luke knew she could—and often did—feed twenty people with relaxed, offhanded ease.

"I'll get the boys washed up for dinner," he offered a bit later, hoping the boisterous trio would liven up the strained atmosphere a little.

"No need. I fed the boys earlier, and they're going to a Disney movie with a neighbor," Lorna explained. "She'll be here to pick them up any minute now."

Luke felt a frustrated, growing anger with his sister. He'd wanted Jessie to get to know his nephews, and now it seemed Lorna had deliberately excluded them from the gathering.

He found himself wanting a cigarette. Why didn't it stop raining so that they could escape the taut atmosphere in the small living room?

Dinner itself was superb, however—barbecued steak with an interesting assortment of marinated vegetable dishes, hot homemade buns, avocados stuffed with shrimp.

"You're a marvelous cook," Jessie complimented Lorna sincerely. "Would you mind giving me the recipe for this mushroom dish? I've never had anything like it."

For about the first time all afternoon Lorna relaxed a trace and produced a semblance of her usual easy grin. "Growing up on a ranch in southern Alberta, I started learning to cook almost before I was out of diapers. Nothing fancy, just lots of good plain food."

"Luke told me about your catering business. Have you ever thought of expanding?"

Luke felt himself tense at Jessie's innocent question. He hadn't mentioned the soup kitchen idea to Jessie, and he and Denny had mutually avoided private discussions lately.

Lorna glanced defiantly over at her silent husband. "Actually, I've rented space in the new Market that's opening the middle of August."

Luke saw Denny's eyes meet Lorna's in a contest of wills and then fall away. His face was grim.

"Sounds like a great idea," Jessie said enthusiastically, wondering what she could possibly have said to increase the already palpable tension in the room. "You know," she went on brightly, talking to fill the silence just the way she was trained to do at work, "radio stations do on-the-spot shows to help promote local businesses. Why not invite the crew from CKXM, your Richmond station, for a taste of your wares the day you open? Announcers love to eat, and they'd give you excellent publicity."

Lorna became animated for a few minutes, asking Jessie all sorts of questions about advertising, and Denny, who hardly ever had more than a couple of beers, began methodically getting drunk, succeeding so well that by the time Luke suggested he and Jessie leave, Denny was snoring in a corner of the couch and Lorna had retreated into her nervous hostess routine.

They were back in the city before either of them spoke. Then Jessie said thoughtfully, "You know, I do believe your sister thinks wheelchairs are a communicable disease."

Luke couldn't answer her because the comment exactly described the way Lorna had acted.

INSTEAD OF FORMING a barrier between them, the difficult weekend only served to draw them closer together that night.

Using the hot tub each evening had become a delightful habit. Sometimes Cy and Amanda would join them, but tonight both the upstairs suite and the house next door were in darkness. Jessie was relieved. Tonight she needed to be alone with Luke.

The dark garden lay hidden in the fine misty rain, with billows of steam rising in white clouds from the heated water in the cedar enclosure. Jessie felt the tenseness of the past two days begin to slip away as she slid from the deck down into the water, with Luke close behind her.

"I knew this would be fun in the rain." She sighed blissfully, loving the contrast of cold air on her shoulders and bubbling heated water below. "I hope it snows next winter.

I can't wait to try it in the snow. I'll buy a red toque to wear on my head so I don't freeze.''

His arms gathered her intimately close to him, propping her back comfortably against his chest, arranging her so that her body was immersed up to her neck in warmth, his long legs stretched out on either side.

"Better buy two red toques, Jess. I'll need one, too.''

There it was again, his expectation of a future for them. Jessie became very still, aware of his heart thumping steadily against her back, his forearms crossed in a loving knot just below her breasts. His words brought to the surface the depression the weekend had created, the deep-seated fears she harbored about the two of them.

"Luke,'' she began hesitantly, knowing it would have to be talked about sooner or later, "don't feel you have to promise me any tomorrow. What we have together right now is more than I ever dreamed of having, but so many things can go wrong for us. When we're alone together, everything's perfect, but you saw that both my mother and your sister didn't approve of our relationship.''

She tipped her head back so that it rested just below his chin and tried to keep the sadness out of her voice, tried to make what she knew to be true into a simple statement of fact. "Their reaction is going to be pretty typical of what most people will feel about us, and sooner or later it's bound to affect how we feel about one another.''

"Does it bother you, Jess, what other people might think? I can't believe a woman as confident and strong as you are would even consider other's opinions a problem. Because what people think means less than nothing to me.'' He made a derisive noise in his throat. "I learned the hard way that people only see what they want in others. In the RCMP I was a hero, and then overnight I was a drunken failure. Word got around I was seeing a shrink, so I became a nut case into the bargain. Then when I left the force, they labeled me a quitter. It took a while to figure out exactly what I really was.'' She felt his lips touching the tip of her ear, and he paused thoughtfully for an instant. ''I wasn't any of those things. I was just a man, Jess, learning some tough lessons along the way.'' He rubbed his chin on the softness of her hair, loving the wet floral scent of it in the rain.

''Now, though, I'm a guy hopelessly in love with a beautiful woman who seems to be doing her best to get rid of me.''

She made a small sound of protest.

''C'mon, Jess,'' he chided gently, ''does it matter to either of us what your mother or my sister or Joe Blow down the street thinks? The important thing is what we think, what we feel. And what I feel—'' his voice lowered to a husky urgency that sent wild shivers coursing through her ''—is this sexy, nearly naked woman wriggling around on susceptible parts of my anatomy.''

There were no words to express the love she felt for him at that moment, so with clever stroking hands and lips that had learned amazingly well what gave him pleasure, she did her best to show him.

How easy loving was, once she learned to allow the music of it to carry her freely. It was not unlike dance, and now at last she fully appreciated the nuances of ballet, remembering how her instructor had once berated the students, telling them the music had to become part of their souls, the movements secondary to the emotion within, the passion of the music pouring outward and then becoming dance.

So it was with love. The music began in her heart and became the loveliest of dances, movements secondary to the feelings that inspired them. Even the rewards were similar, for just as ballet had given Jessie satisfaction and joy in twofold measure for whatever she invested, the outpouring of her love for Luke was returned to her with ecstasy as interest, and she told him so.

"It's because you give me so much of yourself, Jess," he said wonderingly. "You make me want to give you the world in return. I've never felt this closeness before with another human being."

He'd planned to go back to his lonely apartment that night, but, of course, he didn't.

In the morning he made coffee for his thermos and crept as silently as possible off to work. Jessie slept decadently late. The wonderful week of holiday was over, and she'd be doing "Night Shift" that evening.

When she woke, it was to the delicious odor of the freesia blossoms Luke had picked at dawn and strewn across the pillow beside her.

The station phoned that afternoon with the message that she was to call Evan Rathmore. She dialed his number with trepidation, wondering nervously what her boss had to say to her. After his first few sentences she began to smile and couldn't seem to stop.

Evan and the program director had decided that her idea for "Heart Line" was worth a try. She could do an intro that night and start the segment the next day. Evan had monitored "Night Shift" while she was away, and it seemed—harrumph—that Jessie was popular.

Grudging or not, it was the first vote of confidence the gruff manager had ever given her, and she felt ridiculously happy about it for the rest of the afternoon.

It was good to be back at work again. Jessie settled into the rhythm of her show eagerly for the first hour, and then the phone rang.

"You been avoiding me, Jessie?" The familiar, whiskey-rough voice grated over the wires, and she felt her stomach drop.

"What do you want from me, Wayne?" The question was almost shrill, and she waited tensely for his answer. What could he hope to gain by these senseless, aggravating calls, besides making her nervous and on edge? She'd been so certain that after a week away he'd have given up.

His answer surprised her. "How 'bout meeting me for lunch tomorrow, Jessie, so we can have a real talk, eh? Got a business proposition to discuss with you."

Her automatic first reaction was to say no and hang up, but she hesitated. Perhaps if she met him in broad daylight in a public restaurant and told him firmly, absolutely, to leave her alone, he'd stop making these nuisance calls. Maybe if she confronted him face-to-face and warned him that if he persisted, she would seek legal help or notify the police...

"All right, tomorrow at twelve-thirty at—" Jessie thought of all the restaurants she'd been to and named the one she knew for certain would be safely crowded at lunchtime. "—at Nibbles, on Broadway." She gave him the address and hung up feeling a mixture of dread and relief that the situation with Wayne might come to a head and be resolved.

SHE DELIBERATELY ARRIVED at the restaurant half an hour early the next day and chose a central table, wondering for the hundredth time that morning why she felt so frightened by the idea of meeting Wayne.

What was he, after all, except an ordinary man, a meaningless shadow out of her past? It was those ridiculous phone calls that had created the apprehension. She kept an eye on the door, wondering if she'd even recognize him.

She did, of course. He sauntered in, and for an instant Jessie felt sick and frozen, staring at this man who'd shattered her dreams, her illusions, her youth. She'd wanted so much from him but had received so little.

She watched him, and with incredible relief Jessie recognized that she was seeing a stranger. Any power he might have had over her in the past, the anguish she'd once endured because of him, the lingering doubts he'd sown in her about herself as a woman, even the unreasoning fear he'd stirred in her lately with his phone calls, disappeared with his appearance.

He was—Jessie quickly calculated—only thirty-six, yet Wayne had a vaguely dissipated look about him, even at a distance. It was shocking to find that he was shorter, slighter, less good-looking than she remembered.

He spoke to the waitress, and Jessie watched him flash the extravagant grin that had once captivated her. Now the expression looked contrived. The woman motioned to the table where Jessie waited.

"Hey, Jess, how's it going?" His teeth were yellow.

Even the voice, once mellow and pleasing, was now harsh, as if he'd smoked too many cigarettes, drunk too much whiskey. His blond hair was lank, beginning to thin at the temples, and his clothing, flashy from a distance, looked cheap and not quite clean from across the table.

The cockiness was still there in the way he tipped the chair back and measured her boldly with his dark gaze, but his hand was not quite steady on the drink he ordered and downed thirstily. He snapped his fingers rudely at the waitress for another.

"You're lookin' great, Jess."

Wayne wasn't even looking at her. His eyes were flicking around at the tables nearby.

Jessie's lips pulled down into a cynical smile as she realized he was already worrying about what people would think about him, with her in a wheelchair. Why, his macho image might suffer.

It had been a huge mistake to come here, and she wouldn't stay.

The waitress brought his drink, and Jessie shook her head at the woman's question about ordering.

"I've changed my mind about lunch," she said evenly. "I'll just finish this ginger ale, and I'll be going."

Wayne's attitude suddenly became vaguely aggressive, reminding Jessie of his lightning swift changes of mood and her reasons for choosing this particular meeting place. A twinge of anxiety was replaced with anger when he narrowed his eyes at her and growled, "Where the hell you going in such a hurry? We haven't even had a chance to talk. Sit still. Bring the lady a drink, a gin or something, and bring me another, a double," he ordered the now confused young woman standing patiently beside the table.

Jessie quelled her urge to simply leave. The whole purpose of this meeting was to put a stop to the calls. The best way of doing so was to find out why he was making them, she reminded herself. And with the amount of liquor he was consuming, she'd better make a stab at it quickly because before long he'd be incoherent.

He was tapping his nicotine-stained fingers on the table in a petulant, impatient rhythm, and Jessie asked casually, "Where are you working, Wayne? You in town doing a gig, or publicity, or what?"

The innocent question seemed to fuel his anger, and again she felt a stab of apprehension. There was a banked rage behind his eyes when he sneered, "Don't give me that innocent act, you know goddamn well I'm not working, and you know why, too."

She didn't, but certainly alcoholism and success in the music trade didn't exactly mix. Jessie prudently didn't say so. Wayne leaned across the table belligerently, nearly spilling the full glass now in front of him.

"You and those other bastards at the stations, you're the ones who make or break guys like me," he snarled viciously. "How the hell can we make any money if you don't play our records? I've listened every goddamn night, and I've never heard you play any of my records even once. You could promote me, Jessie, what the hell would it hurt? No skin off your ass, pardon the expression." He smirked. "I stuck by you when you needed it, remember?"

Jessie could only gape at him. What held her speechless was the fact that in Wayne's besotted brain he actually believed the things he was saying. The aggrieved monologue went on.

"It wasn't me who wanted the divorce, y'know. We coulda had an arrangement that suited us both, lived comfortable, money no object."

Her money, she thought wryly. His comfort.

"You needed me. I'd have been a success, the music scene here on the Coast was just starting to open up, but you wrecked it for me. You had to go crying to Daddy about me, and he made certain I couldn't get a gig around her to save my soul."

Jessie had confided in Arthur when she returned to the Coast. She'd needed legal help, but more than that, she'd needed understanding. Her father had given her support, both financial and emotional. His love had helped her through the tough months after the accident and during the divorce.

Fleetingly Jessie wondered if Arthur had indeed done his influential best to blacklist Wayne locally all those long years ago. It seemed unlikely, but if he had, it would most probably have been at Chandra's urging, and strangely, Jessie felt almost tender toward her mother at the thought.

Chandra might be the least understanding of parents, but she was loyal to a fault, and anyone she felt guilty of wronging her daughter had better look out. Chandra hated Wayne Palmer with a passion.

"Is that what you want, Wayne? You want me to play your records, promote you on my show?" Jessie kept her tone rational and even, tried to keep her feeling of incredulity at his arrogance from showing.

"Like I said, what difference would it make to you? After all, we were married once."

Long ago. Another lifetime. He was contemptible.

A sly expression came over his face, and he actually suggested, "Y'know, you must need an escort to some of these media things going on. It would probably do a lot for your image to have me tag along, Jess. An announcer and an entertainer."

How magnanimous of him. He'd even risk being seen publicly with her if it would further what was obviously a delusion in his confused brain—the idea that he still had a career in the music industry.

It was the final straw. Things she wished she'd said years ago bubbled to the surface and spilled over.

"How dare you? How dare you assume that I'd ever want anything more to do with you, Wayne? You despicable creep. I was just a kid years ago, and I believed so much of what you laid on me. Don't misunderstand, either. I don't blame you for the accident, Wayne. An accident is exactly what the word implies. But for what you did to me afterward—for that, I can't forgive you." Her breath was coming in deep sobs, and she was too wound up to notice the venomous look growing on his face, in his red-rimmed eyes.

"You may have conveniently forgotten the details of our divorce, but I haven't." She was shaking with outrage, and her voice was rising. She could see other patrons staring openly, and the waitress was eyeing their table nervously, but the feelings so long dormant erupted and she couldn't seem to stop.

"How dare you blame anyone but yourself because of what you've become? You weak, self-centered drunk. Don't you ever contact me again, do you hear me? I'll have the law on you."

He half rose from his chair and leaned across the table, spitting the words at her. "Bitch. Rotten rich bitch. I nearly went to jail once already because of you. The cops, huh? You'll never get the chance because I'll get you, you hear? You can't talk to me like that." He looked as if he were about to have a seizure.

No, Jessie thought with stark and vivid fear. He looked as if he were capable of murder. What an absolute fool she'd been to go there alone.

His mouth was twisted into a narrow, ugly slash across his face. His eyes were burning into her, and panic welled in her throat.

He looked demented, his eyes red and full of hate, his fists doubled, and Jessie finally understood that he wasn't entirely sane. She tried to stay in control as his hand closed around the half-full glass of liquor in front of him, but Jessie believed for an instant that he was going to throw it at her...or worse.

Two large waiters materialized, one on either side of Wayne. "You having some trouble here, lady?"

She nodded jerkily, her eyes held by Wayne's like those of a bird hypnotized by a snake. A cold and evil grin appeared on his face as he shook their hands off and got unsteadily to his feet.

"I'll get you, I promise," Wayne repeated, his tone soft and ugly.

The men beside him hovered, their muscles tense, not touching him but ready. Wayne glared at her for another endless moment, and then he turned.

But the larger of the two waiters said quietly and firmly, "You better pay your tab, buddy," and waited implacably while Wayne pulled several crumpled, dirty bills from his pocket and threw them viciously behind them. They landed on his chair, and the waiter coolly checked them against the bill the nervous waitress produced.

Without another word Wayne made his unsteady way out the door, still followed closely by his escorts, and slowly the buzz of conversation, which had faded into fascinated silence during the scene, once again began to fill the restaurant.

It took effort for Jessie to calm herself down. The waiters kindly suggested that she call the police, and Jessie considered and then rejected the idea. What could she really charge Wayne with? Being a public nuisance, annoying her at work? She'd met him voluntarily today. The best thing to do, she decided, was forget the whole thing. And if the calls at the station continued, she'd simply hang up and report them to Evan as she should have done in the beginning.

Shaking, she drove slowly home, feeling exhausted and drained from the encounter.

LUKE WAS ALSO FEELING the aftermath of an encounter that day, but black rage was more predominant than exhaustion. He felt ready to throttle his own sister with his bare hands. In fact, he would have enjoyed it.

Because the job he and Denny were doing was far out in Richmond, Luke drove to the Mason's in the morning, parked his car in their driveway and then he and Denny rode out in the company truck to the site.

Monday Denny hurried out of the house immediately, but Tuesday morning Lorna waved Luke in for a coffee as soon as he climbed out of his car.

"Denny's late," she announced. "He's just in the shower now."

"Morning, guys," Luke greeted his delighted nephews, each eating a bowl of his favorite cereal.

Luke stretched his legs out comfortably under his sister's kitchen table and scooped a pajama-clad Robbie up on his lap. The little boy smelled deliciously of soap and sleep, and Luke loved the feel of his sturdy body wriggling into a comfortable position against his chest.

"Did Denny sleep in this morning?" Luke inquired, dumping cream in the steaming mug his sister placed in front of him. He felt irritated and let down by his family after the fiasco of Sunday afternoon, and if the kids hadn't been present, he had a feeling he might have leveled both barrels at Lorna.

"Yeah, I guess so," she said in a distracted way. Then she thumped down into a chair across from Luke and wailed, "Ever since Sunday I can hardly sleep at night. All I can think of is you and . . . and this Jessie. I think you're making a terrible mistake. Oh, Luke, there's so many women out there. Why can't you fall in love with somebody, well, somebody normal?"

Luke and Lorna had the ordinary growing-up quarrels that any siblings might have had, but they'd been few and far between, perhaps because the two were twins and each had an instinctive understanding of what the other felt.

Looking across at his sister's concerned features, Luke now felt the beginnings of an anger different and far more serious than anything he'd felt before for Lorna. Most of all, he felt betrayed by her total lack of understanding.

"Jessie's beautiful and intelligent and fun to be with," he said levelly, trying to subdue the murderous rage building inside him. "She's quick-witted and kind and generous. In fact, she's the woman I love and want to spend the rest of my life with. I plan to ask her to marry me the moment I think she'll agree. Now just what, exactly, do you consider abnormal about her?"

He'd kept his voice low, but he noticed the kids had all stopped eating and were staring at their mother and uncle wide-eyed.

"Don't be deliberately stupid about this, Luke." Lorna slammed a spoon down hard on the table. "You know very well what I'm talking about." Lorna's voice rose and her blue eyes, so much like Luke's own, spat fire at him with the passion of her convictions. "She's handicapped, she'll be in that chair for the rest of her life. If you marry her, you'll spend your entire life taking care of her, pulling her up and down steps just the way you had to here on Sunday. What kind of wife can she be? You couldn't even have children, you—"

"That's enough, Lorna."

The quiet command came from Denny, standing in the doorway behind them. His hair was wet from a shower, and his eyes were bloodshot, but his face wore a look of grim determination, and even through his anger Luke had to admire Denny's composure in the face of what obviously had to be one hell of a hangover.

"Boys, take Rob upstairs and get him dressed. Aren't you guys due at the park this morning for that trip to Dairy land? C'mon, Dave, Dan, hustle."

Reluctantly, knowing they were about to miss some fireworks, the rowdy crowd paid heed to their father and slowly trailed out.

"We never gets to stay with Unca Luke anymore," Robbie moaned soulfully, his pajama bottoms drooping dangerously as he trotted off after planting a huge, wet kiss on Luke's cheek.

"Yeah," Dave agreed with his younger brother, freckled face earnest as he related accusingly, "yeah, and 'member, you said you'd take us to the beach and we could get fish and chips and learn how to catch crabs, 'member you said we could when we got out of school, Uncle Luke?"

It was true, he had promised. Wishing all his problems could be solved as easily, Luke proposed, "How about doing it next Sunday, then? If it's okay with Dad and Mom, I'll come pick you up early, and we'll spend the whole day having fun."

"They're going on a sleep-over camp this weekend," Lorna said sullenly. "And the week after that there's a birthday party. It'll have to be several weeks before they can go with you."

Luke showed the boys a date on the calendar and marked it for them. "Right here, the end of July. We'll go then, I promise." The trio roared happily off.

Denny poured himself a mug of coffee and lit a cigarette with a less than steady hand. Lorna was still flushed and defiant, not looking at either her husband or her brother.

Luke was astonished to find his hands were trembling worse than Denny's were when he lifted his cup to his lips.

"Seems to me if Luke decides Jessie's the lady for him, Lorna, well, you and I oughta make it easier for them, not harder," he remarked mildly. But Lorna sat stubbornly silent, and Denny finally filled his thermos from the coffee-pot and said heavily, "C'mon, partner. Another day, another dollar. That retaining wall ain't gonna build it-self." He planted a kiss on Lorna's cheek similar to the one Robbie had given Luke, but she made no effort to recipro-cate or to say goodbye when they left.

"Ya gotta understand, she's never been around anybody like Jessie before," Denny apologized sheepishly when they were heading down the highway a few moments later, and it struck Luke how bizarre it was having his brother-in-law apologizing to him for his own sister's actions.

"Give her time, she'll come around," Denny advised. But seconds later he heaved a sigh and added bitterly, "If I could only say the same thing over that lousy business she's get-tin' into. It ain't even open yet, and the kids are farmed out at day camps every day, I get home and she's not there yet. Half the time we get hot dogs for dinner. With soup, of course." He snorted. "I never thought I'd get so sick of eating soup." He shook his head dejectedly. "I just never planned on a career woman for a wife, y'know?"

Any other time Luke would have reasoned with Denny, good-naturedly joshing him about his chauvinism until Denny talked out the real reasons for his resentment and felt better about it, but today buffering for his sister just wasn't on the agenda. He felt far too hostile toward Lorna today to try pouring oil on what were obviously becoming very troubled waters in the Mason's marriage.

How ironic that Lorna should worry about him having to care for Jessie, he mused, when the reality of the situation was exactly the opposite.

He and Denny worked and sweated silently in the heat that long day, each lost in his own thoughts, and for the rest of the week, Luke deliberately avoided going into the house when he called for Denny in the morning or retrieved his car at night. It was the first time he'd had a major disagree-ment with Lorna, and it bothered him deeply.

It was a problem he couldn't share with Jessie, either. He shuddered, thinking of the hurt his sister's comments would cause the woman he loved, and his anger with Lorna deepened and became a colder, harder schism that would be slower to heal.

CHAPTER TEN

DAYS PASSED, AND somehow most of Luke's clothing and many of his belongings ended up at Jessie's. There wasn't any special day when they decided to live together, and occasionally, impatiently, Luke wondered if the time was right to say simply, "Marry me, Jessie."

It was what he wanted, he was almost sure it was what Jessie wanted, but something held him back. There were problems between them that simply had to be solved before they took that final step, niggling but very real difficulties that often kept Luke restlessly awake long after Jessie tumbled deeply into exhausted slumber in his arms.

That exhaustion was part of the problem. Jessie was often worn out, although she'd never admit it. He suspected that she was pushing herself too hard at work, and he would hurry home each evening, anxious to be with her, eager to share the daily chores of two working people living together—only to find Jessie had done everything during the day: the marketing, the laundry, the dinner preparation, the vacuuming.

It was like living with room service, and it drove him crazy. The garden was weeded, the garbage taken out, the dishwasher emptied unless he managed to forestall her, and the effort of trying to do chores before she did was becoming a strain.

Could he help her with her workout, he'd suggest, maybe spot her with the weights?

No need, she'd inform him airily. She'd already finished her exercises for the day, thanks.

She flatly refused to allow him to pick her up at the station after work, insisting that he needed the several hours of sleep before she came home and woke him up, anyway.

"I've been doing the night show a long time. I don't need a caretaker, Luke." There was a dangerous set to her chin, and he didn't push.

It wasn't Jessie's ability to get herself home that concerned him, anyway. It was the lack of security at the radio station. Several times he'd come for her past midnight and found the building deserted and the door unlocked.

"It's the janitor," Jessie had explained. "He's an old guy, and he leaves it open when he goes to the diner for coffee." She'd teased him a little about his police mentality, and Luke thought sheepishly that maybe she was right.

But this prickly independence of hers began to stir a deep insecurity in Luke. The problem was hard to define because it concerned a nebulous and primal response that he had trouble pinpointing or explaining.

It had to do with the part of the male ego that urged a man to protect and nurture the person he loved. It was a very real need in him, this desire to cherish Jessie and to keep her safe. He was physically strong with boundless energy. Early in their relationship he'd tried repeatedly to help her in and out of cars, through doorways, up and over curbs, but he had soon learned such attention resulted in a scowl and a snapped, "I can do it myself."

He eventually stopped trying, but her rejection fueled the nagging doubts about himself that had lingered since his last months in the police force. It had to do with confidence in himself and in his ability to care for her.

If she didn't trust him enough to ask for assistance in these small everyday chores, how could she learn to trust and rely on him in other larger ways?

In the final analysis, would he be able to give Jessie what she needed in the years to come? How would he know what those needs even were, if she didn't ask?

The bottom line, ridiculous as it sounded, was simply that he needed Jessie to need him. And it seemed that with most things she didn't need him at all.

He tried to discuss his feelings with her the afternoon he came home after work and found her making trip after strenuous trip from the van to the kitchen, balancing a single bag of groceries each time. Her face was flushed, and tiny lines of strain marked the edges of her eyes.

Totally exasperated, he snatched the bag from her.

"Jess, for Pete's sake, why didn't you just give me a list of stuff you wanted? I could have picked it up on the way home. Or at least you could have left the bag out in the van for me to carry in for you."

"It's good exercise." She dismissed his concern airily, just as she'd done in numerous other situations when he'd wanted to help.

He gripped her chair firmly, holding her in one spot so that he could emphasize what he had to say, kneeling at her side to frown into her flushed face.

"I've worked out with you in that room you so aptly call the 'torture chamber.' We've run together every weekend, and I happen to know you do at least three miles a day by yourself. More exercise you simply don't need. Why the hell can't you let me do things for you, little things that don't take any effort for me but drain you until you're bloody well exhausted?"

Her face took on the stubborn, closed expression he was beginning to know so well, and her gaze slid obliquely past him to the wall behind, avoiding his intent, frustrated frown.

"I'm used to doing things for myself, Luke. It's important to do everything I can because there's lots of stuff I have to ask for help with, and I hate it. I despise having to ask people to do things for me, I always have." The passionate conviction in her tone made him sigh.

"I understand that, Jess, but every one of us has to ask for help along the way, in one form or another. Doing little things for you makes me feel happy, don't you know that?"

She did know, and the puzzled hurt on his face made her wretched, but she had no intention of falling into the habit of relying on him, regardless how tired she felt. How long would it take, she asked herself about a dozen times a week, before her demands became an annoyance, a burden, to him? How long before he would view her as a dependent instead of a partner?

She couldn't let that happen to them. She wouldn't. For all the growing openness between them in other ways, this was one area Jessie couldn't bring herself to discuss honestly with him. She was simply too afraid.

It was deep-seated, the fear, rooted in the scars of her past. And unfortunately, it also kept her from telling Luke about the scene she'd endured with her ex-husband in the restaurant. She'd been terrified that afternoon, and she'd promised herself that if Wayne tried to get in touch with her just one more time, she'd ask Luke for help.

But Wayne didn't. Days passed, the phone-in portion of "Heart Line" became more and more successful, ratings went up for both her show and the station, and the hoarse sound of Wayne's voice was blissfully absent.

It was Friday morning, the third week in July, when the phone rang and she was cheerily greeted by Kathleen. Jessie was doing her best to talk herself into getting out of bed and getting on with the millions of tasks she'd scheduled for the day.

"You sound sleepy, Jess. Did I wake you up?"

"I'm just being lazy this morning. Never mind me, what about that tummy of yours?" Jessie parried. "Is there a new little Dodd person yet?"

Kathleen's voice took on a note of proud accomplishment.

"That's why I'm calling. Oh, Jessie, I'm so happy. We have a red, wrinkled, supremely beautiful new son. He was born at eleven o'clock last night, easy as falling out of your chair. His name's Michael Joseph Nathaniel, so he'll have something to grow into. Joe's mother came all the way from Nova Scotia, and my mom's here from Prince George. With all these mums around just begging for things to do, we decided to have a little party next Saturday afternoon to show off Mikey." Kathleen's irrepressible giggle bubbled over the line. "This way the mums do all the work, but I get all the credit for production. Smart, huh? Can you come? And bring that hunk of a man you were planning on seducing the last time I saw you. I'd love to meet him. How'd that go, by the way? Are you two an item, or are you not?"

"We are, and I'm grateful to you." Jessie tugged Luke's pillow over and propped it beneath her head, reveling in the faint trace of his aroma lingering on the blue pillowcase. "As for the party, I wouldn't miss it for anything. We'll be there. What time? Do I get to hold Mikey?"

"For as long as you want. Come about two, and we can have a lovely long afternoon. The mothers have been cooking and baking since five seconds after they arrived, so bring your appetite."

Jessie felt delighted that at least she and Luke had an invitation to look forward to rather than dread. Both her mother and Lorna had been ominously silent since the ordeal of the dinners. How fantastic to help celebrate the birth of a baby with friends!

Feeling guilty about neglecting her workouts lately, Jessie turned the radio on and was grunting her way through a set of pull-downs when Cy appeared in the doorway.

"I hollered from the stairs, but there's no hope of you hearing with that music turned up and all the moaning and groaning. How about a cup of coffee when you're finished? I'll put a pot on."

Cy was staring morosely out at the rain, cup cradled in his hands, when Jessie joined him after her shower.

"Damn weather. Supposed to be summer and all it does is rain. Makes me feel like going to Arizona with every other over-the-hill pensioner and taking up golf." He snorted, and his heavy eyebrows beetled down over his nose. "If I didn't hate golf so much, I probably would go." He looked distinctly disgruntled and out of sorts, Jessie noted, and it surprised her. Cy was almost never down. She took the cup he offered and studied him, concerned.

"You have a fight with Amanda, or fail your last semester, or something? You always used to tell me the moisture in Vancouver was what kept you from aging. What's up, Cy?"

He tugged down the old purple jersey he was wearing and slumped back in the seat.

"What's up, my girl, is that you see before you a man hoisted on his own petard. All those pleasant years of dispensing advice the way I used to prescribe medicine, smugly enjoying the rewards of bachelorhood while having the pleasure of female companionship and no entanglements. And now I've gone and ruined it all by falling for Amanda." He smacked his cup down. "Falling hard, too. And the irony of it all is that although the lady professes to love me, she wants no part of a permanent arrangement of any sort. Her life, God help us, is neatly arranged. She writes, she travels, she has her own home, her own money, her own pension plan. She finds me unsettling although intellectually stimulating, more Bohemian than she'd prefer but a fine companion nonetheless and good in—Eh, well, let's just say compatible in other major ways. Despite my advancing years.'' Jessie would have teased him unmercifully, but she realized in time that Cy was absolutely in earnest.

"The central problem, as far as I can tell, is a fear of risk taking. Amanda's early life was difficult. She likes—no, more than that—she demands that her life be in scrupulous order. Her motto seems to be live by all the rules as neatly as possible. Mine, of course, is don't make any.''

Jessie was at a loss about what to say. Cy's assessment of his own situation was entirely apt.

"Don't you think if you just give it time...'' Jessie hesitated, thinking of her own romance and her reluctance to rush things. Cy shook his ginger head impatiently, and a trapped, sad expression came over his face.

"When you're sixty-one, time is a scarce commodity. Amanda's leaving for Greece next week, you see, to research her next book. She'll be gone until September, and that's when I'm leaving for Australia. The boat trip is confirmed, and I'll be away three months, maybe four. Doesn't leave much time for fooling around, does it?''

Jessie had to agree it didn't. They sat silently for a while, listening to the rain patter on the roof, and as much to distract Cy as to unburden herself she told him about Wayne's reappearance in her life, briefly describing the disastrous meeting she'd had with him, deliberately downplaying the traumatic series of phone calls that had preceded it.

"He's never called again, so I guess I'm rid of him,'' she summed up with an attempt at lightness.

Cy listened closely, appalled concern on his face.

"What does Luke say about all this?"

Jessie hesitated and then confessed, "I haven't told Luke, Cy. You're the only person I've mentioned this to." She described the difficult situation at the station, adding, "I didn't want to report it to Evan. He's already made it plain he's had to make concessions for me, not just because I'm a woman but also because of my chair. I know he'll resent it if he has to add extra security to the building at night just because of me." She shrugged helplessly and voiced the worry she was almost afraid to vocalize. "He's liable to decide I'm not worth the hassle."

Cy's expletive was pithy and short. "There's lots of radio stations out there, and you're too good to lose, Jess. Look how well 'Heart Line' is going. Report this nut right away to the station. And for cripes' sake, tell Luke." Cy spaced the command emphatically, narrowing his gaze sternly at Jessie. "He's an ex-cop, woman. He'll know what to do about this creep. I can't believe you haven't told him already."

Jessie flushed, knowing Cy was right. She ought to have told Luke about the calls weeks ago, but the longer she waited, the harder and more complicated telling him had become.

The real reason for not mentioning it—her own stiff pride in her ability to manage—niggled at her now, but she pushed it back where she wouldn't have to look at it.

She was doing just fine. They were doing just fine. *Don't rock the boat, Jessie.*

Cy was watching her sternly, waiting, she realized, for assurance that she would do as he ordered.

"I will tell him, first chance I get," she said, procrastinating.

Cy shook his head implacably. "You either tell him to-day when he gets home from work, or I'll have to break a confidence and tell him myself."

She gave him a shocked and angry look, but Cy was firm. "This isn't a matter for principle, Jess. You could be in danger, and I don't have the means or the muscle to protect you. But Luke does, and I won't relax until he knows, so make up your mind. You or me."

"I'm sorry I ever mentioned it now. I think you're over-reacting. I told you I haven't heard from Wayne now for some time. He's probably taken off back to the States and forgotten all about me."

Jessie heaved a huge sigh of frustration and impatience with Cy, but finally, when he simply went on giving her a level, questioning glance, she agreed irritably. "Oh, all right. Tonight. I never thought I'd accuse you, of all people, of treating me like a child, but that's exactly what you're doing right now over this, and I resent it."

Cy was completely unruffled by her accusation. Airily he dismissed the comment with, "Resent it all you like. I care far too much for you to let you bully me about a poten-tially dangerous situation. And as for treating you like a child, well, you're acting like one."

Jessie's temper flared dangerously, and she felt precar-iously close to quarreling with Cy for the first time in their long friendship.

He watched her color rise and an angry sparkle come into her dark eyes. Forcefully she suppressed the urge to say things she'd regret later, and after several long moments of studying her closely, he said slowly and thoughtfully, "Have you lost weight lately, Jessie? I haven't seen you for a few days, and it looks as if your face is thinner. You're not yourself. You look peaked. Are you feeling okay, my girl?"

The affectionate term, the old-fashioned word—peaked, as if she were a fainting Victorian maiden—and his honest and immediate concern quelled Jessie's sudden temper. She was deeply ashamed of herself. How could she be furious with him for caring about her?

"I'm great, Cy. Just feeling a bit tired after the Seafestival and all that hoopla." She'd helped with the station's mobile booth, working several afternoons in the hot trailer at English Bay to make the yearly festival a success.

"I'll maybe nap for a while this afternoon after I do some shopping for the baby."

The expression on Cy's face should have been photographed. He actually changed color, his ruddy complexion paling. He swallowed hard, and Jessie realized what she'd said. At the look on his face, she couldn't resist teasing him a little more.

Artlessly she cooed, "Oh, dear, I didn't tell you about the baby, did I?"

He shook his head slowly, his eyes riveted on her face.

Unfortunately, she couldn't hold herself back any longer. Her laughter exploded.

"You thought... Oh, Cy, that's priceless. I got you that time, good and proper. You figured I was pregnant, didn't you?"

He nodded weakly. "Go ahead and laugh, brat. See how funny you feel when you give an old man heart seizures. God. I naturally thought this was one more thing you hadn't found time to mention to Luke, and I could see myself saying, 'Oh, by the way, old chap...' So whose baby are we talking about?"

Between giggles Jessie told him about Kathleen's son, and the earlier strain disappeared in easy camaraderie.

They had more coffee, and she made a pan of scrambled eggs with toast. Cy didn't think to question her again about being thin. Jessie was profoundly relieved.

The fact was she'd lost seven pounds over the past month, and because of the strenuous training she'd recently completed for the marathon last May, this was once in her life when a weight loss wasn't something to celebrate. She'd been bone slender before, but she'd felt full of energy. Now she was beginning to look plain skinny, and her energy level was low.

Of course, Luke had noticed, and he kept nagging her to see her doctor, but he was away on holiday when Jessie phoned. She'd seen Dr. Braun at the beginning of the summer for the birth control pills Kathleen had suggested but not since.

Unwilling to go to a doctor over a matter she knew wasn't urgent, Jessie made an appointment for later in the month.

It was true she felt draggingly weary much of the time, and summoning the sparkling energy necessary to do her show each evening left her drained. And irritable, as Cy had undoubtedly noticed.

Jessie didn't need a doctor to tell her she was trying to cram too much into each day and she should slow down—she knew it very well. It was strange how often the teachings of her old dance instructor, Madame Nikova, popped into her mind these days.

"Ballet," Madame had lectured all those years before in her dry, accented English, "is the art of making everything you do look effortless, even when it seems impossible."

That described how Jessie felt about each new day. She did her best to make everything look effortless, and it was beginning to seem impossible to go on doing so.

The truth was, her firm determination to be totally self-reliant was costing her dearly. Before Luke there had been an easy relaxation to her days that allowed for periods when her job required more energy, leaving less time for herself. She really hadn't had an active social life.

It hadn't mattered before when things around the house got done, or even if they got done, and she'd hardly been aware of the extra time and effort everything took when one was in a wheelchair. Now she had a rigid schedule that had to be met, a self-imposed list of what tasks must be done each day before Luke arrived.

She wanted everything perfect for them during the few hours they could be with one another on weekday evenings and weekends, and that drive for perfection, with its resultant tiredness, was making her unreasonably short-tempered and irritable when Luke did come home. She recognized the ridiculous treadmill she'd created for herself.

She just couldn't seem to manage to get off it, and what was left of the day after Cy's morning visit was no different than all her days had been lately.

She emptied the dishwasher and ironed several blouses and one of Luke's shirts. He'd insisted he always sent them out, but Jessie reasoned if she had the iron out anyway... She defrosted meat for a stew for supper. She quickly freshened her makeup and drove to the central mall where she remembered there were several baby shops. She spent a pleasant hour and a half picking out things for Mikey and also a floppy doll and a toy truck for his sister. It would be hard on Kathleen's older child, having everyone make a fuss over the new baby.

It was absolutely teeming rain when she left the enclosed mall, and Jessie was soaked by the time she reached her van. She drove to the recording studio to do a dry run on commercials for a boutique and a large food chain, feeling a trifle nervous but hugely proud of having landed both contracts. After a preliminary few minutes of stiffness and an attack of nerves, she relaxed and enjoyed the experience.

Still, when she finally left the studio, a familiar dragging weariness overwhelmed her. She drove home, remembering she'd forgotten to put the stew on before she left.

Chilled from the wet afternoon, she had a hot bath, stretched out on the bed for a ten-minute nap and fell deeply asleep.

Luke came in quietly and found her sleeping when he arrived from work and gently tucked the downy comforter closer around her.

He frowned down at Jessie's still form. She didn't stir. She was lying on her back, head tipped to the side, hair tumbled over the pillow, and his eyes traced the delicate lines of her sleeping features. Her soft cheeks had deeper hollows than a week before, and in sleep the curved, full lips were slightly parted.

It was a relief to find her resting, but it worried him, as well. Knowing Jessie as he did, he knew she'd have to be exceptionally tired to sleep at this time of the day.

He tiptoed out, and glanced at the clock, calculated exactly how long he could let her sleep before he'd have to awaken her to get ready for work. He showered and set about making a salad and finding cheese and bread, arranging a simple meal on a tray to take to her when she awakened.

He found a perfect rosebud from the garden and put it in a water glass by her plate. It was wonderful to be able to do even something this simple for the woman he loved. He only wished she'd let him do more.

DRIVING HOME LATE the next day, Jessie reflected that the afternoon with the Dodds had been every bit as enjoyable as she'd anticipated, and she'd been able to hold the breathtakingly small bundle of baby for a long, enchanted time. She imagined she could smell the delicious aroma of clean new baby still clinging to her hands and dress.

She glanced over at Luke, maneuvering through the late-afternoon traffic. He was happy and relaxed. His lips were pursed under his mustache, and he was whistling along with the music pouring from the speakers of the radio. He'd obviously enjoyed the afternoon just as much as she had.

"Isn't Kathleen's mother a wonderful, funny lady, Luke? Imagine having the courage in a small town to go back to grade school at fifty-seven and graduate. I see now where Kathleen gets her spirit and her sense of humor from."

"I saw a lot more than that in both Joe and Kathleen, Jess," Luke said thoughtfully. "I don't believe I've ever met a happier married couple. And it's obvious that the closeness isn't a temporary high because of their new son, either."

"They've been married a long time," Jessie agreed. "I suppose they've had as many problems as anybody—Joe was out of work for a time, and they moved here without much money. But they're happy, all right."

There was an almost mystical bond of love and understanding between Joe and Kathleen, a partnership that epitomized the true meaning of the word marriage, Luke reflected. It was obvious from the modest farm and the well-worn, rather shabby furnishings of the house that the pair still didn't have a lot of money. But what they did have was everything he dreamed of someday having with Jessie.

Joe had come out to greet them as soon as they drove into the yard earlier that day. He was a quiet man with a wide smile and shy eyes. With a firm handshake and a sincere welcome for Luke, and after planting a warm kiss on Jessie's cheek, he'd led them into his home, a quiet dignity in his manner and speech.

His wife, Kathleen, was exactly Joe's opposite, a petite, flaming-haired dynamo with a grin like a pixie's. Words flowed from her mouth in a continuous stream of wit and mischief. She'd tipped her head to the side, studied Luke with twinkling eyes and pronounced, "Jessie, he really is a hunk, just like you told me," making Jessie blush rosily and Kathleen laugh with delight. But the teasing disappeared, replaced by bursting pride, when she and Joe introduced their small, shy daughter, Chrissie, and her new brother. Almost palpable love and fulfillment radiated between man and woman, and Luke felt a clenching envy grip him as he bent to make friends with the sober little girl.

There had been a constant stream of neighbors and friends arriving, until the house was too small to contain everyone. The party overflowed in a chattering, laughing throng onto the wide porch and out over the well-tended lawn.

Luke talked with farmers, carpenters, mill workers and the local minister, but over and over all afternoon he noticed the sweet exchanges between Joe and Kathleen Dodd.

Shared glances, a quiet word, and Joe would unobtrusively get some article Kathleen needed to change the baby, or give his daughter special attention, or simply run a fond hand over his wife's flaming hair in a gesture of caring.

What Luke noticed the most was that Kathleen asked freely, and Joe responded.

"She's got a hell of a temper, though," Joe confided to Luke at one point, tousling his wife's hair. "Prone to throwing things at me when she's mad, too," he added with a wink, and Kathleen aimed a playful poke at him. Luke glanced at the two of them curiously. It was hard to imagine Joe having an argument with anyone, much less the wife he obviously adored.

Joe intercepted the look and grinned roguishly. "We hassle just like anybody does who's been married a while. As you know, Luke, being somebody's legs isn't always easy or convenient. I do the things she'd like to do herself, but I don't always do them the way she would, so she gets bossy and I get irritated." He shrugged acceptingly, and Luke marveled at the security of a relationship that allowed such openness. Someone called to Kathleen, and she moved over to talk with him. Joe added quietly, "I'm really glad to meet you, Luke. It's great to talk to somebody who understands. It's hard on our women to have to ask, hard for them to lean on us. But after hearing a lot of guys at work complaining, a little problem like a wheelchair is nothing, right?" Luke was deeply touched at Joe's words.

"Our women," he'd called Kathleen and Jessie, unaware that he'd just described a difference between them instead of a similarity.

Kathleen might ask and lean. Jessie wouldn't. And technically, she wasn't his woman, either, unless she agreed to marry him. Perhaps that's what it would take to sort out their differences, he debated. Perhaps she felt insecure simply because they weren't married.

Luke tightened his hold on the wheel, made the decision and began, "Jessie, there's something—"

At the same moment Jessie blurted out, "Luke, there's something I have to—"

They both stopped, and Luke gave her a loving smile.

"You go first," he instructed.

She shifted restlessly beside him, and he noticed her hands were clenched into tight fists in her lap.

In a rapid, nervous voice she related the events involving Wayne Palmer and his reappearance in her life, and when she was done, Luke felt as if all the delicious food he'd eaten that afternoon was lodged in a solid mass deep in his stomach.

"Why couldn't you tell me this before, Jess?" His voice was tight and strained, and his hands on the wheel of the car were clenched, the knuckles standing out. "We've lived with one another for the last month, slept in the same bed, talked for hours about things far less important. And the whole time you've been under a strain because this guy is harassing you. You're probably also in physical danger, but you didn't say a word to me. For God's sake, Jess, haven't you ever heard of confiding in the person you claim to love? Can't you trust me with anything?"

His passionate, angry words stunned her. He was frowning darkly, and his eyes, when he turned to look at her, were blazing with frustration and something else. Disappointment? Anger?

Jessie had never seen him this way before, and she reacted by becoming defensive.

"Trust hasn't a thing to do with it, Luke. This situation with Wayne is my problem, not yours."

"Yeah, the same way your being in that chair is your problem because you insist on keeping it that way. You'll never allow anybody to share the load, really be a part of your life, will you, Jess? You'd go to any lengths to keep from having to ask me for help."

The bitter words made a mockery of the very thing she'd been trying so hard to accomplish. Her own anger and hurt surfaced, and she lashed out at him.

"If I asked you for all the things I needed, how long would it be before I became just a big fat inconvenience in your life?"

Luke sensed the fear in her, and his anger softened. "Why not try it for a day or two and see what happens? If it drives me nuts, you can bet I'll tell you." He deliberately took one hand from the wheel and slid it around her narrow shoulders.

"It would take a lot more than being asked to do the shopping or cook dinner once in a while to drive me away, Jess. As for being a fat inconvenience, you're going to have to gain a hell of a lot of weight first, lady."

Jessie knew, even as his embrace tightened around her and the argument seemed to dissolve, that the real issue was still unresolved between them. She knew, too, that Luke was hurt because she'd kept quiet about Wayne. But nothing more was said.

There were moments of strain that evening when each remembered accusations the other had made. There was also warmth and an illusion of closeness, but when they went to bed, there was no lovemaking.

Luke lay awake, staring up at the moonscape blankly, trying to figure out exactly what he was going to do about Wayne Palmer without ending up in court on a homicide charge.

Jessie lay awake beside him, remembering how Kathleen's face had looked when she gazed down at the nursing baby at her breast, how she'd looked up once to find Luke with little Chrissie on his arm, smiling trustingly into his eyes.

How infinite the amount of trust involved in the conception of another human life. Would she ever be lucky enough to have a child with Luke?

Tonight the possibility seemed even more remote than ever before.

THE NEXT MORNING Jessie suggested they use her van instead of Luke's Thunderbird to collect his nephews for the day's outing, and everything seemed back to normal between them as she drove through the quiet Sunday streets.

She felt hesitant about meeting Lorna again, however, so Jessie stayed in the van while Luke went to the door.

Denny followed the tumble of small excited bodies down the stairs, coming over to the driver's window to greet Jessie warmly.

"I hope you know what you're getting into, taking these guys for the day." Denny's heartiness seemed forced, however, as he added, "Lorna said to tell you hi and thanks. She's over at the Market trying to decide on what chairs and tables she wants to put in. Her big opening is a week from Monday."

"Why not come with us for the day, then, if Lorna's busy?" Luke urged, but Denny shook his head.

"I've got a million chores to do around here, and the yard's a mess, which isn't much of an advertisement for the business. You know what they say—the shoemaker's kids never have shoes," he joked feebly. Denny seemed depressed, Luke noted, feeling at a loss about what to do about it. Instead of fading, the strain between Lorna and Denny seemed to be increasing, and certainly the rift between Luke and Lorna remained. Luke even felt relief that Lorna wasn't home this morning. He'd never felt that way about his sister until now.

The boys scrambled into the van, immediately fascinated by the novelty of Jessie's hand controls. Luke made sure their seat belts were in place, and then took his seat up front again. Jessie smoothly maneuvered them back onto the highway and toward the main arterial road that led to Jericho Beach and the fishing pier.

"You drive good, Jessie," Dan complimented judiciously after watching her closely for several miles. "You drive just as good with hands as Mummy does with her feet. Do you use the brake with your hands?"

"I sure do. This lever here is the brake, and this is the clutch. Once you learn how, driving with hand controls isn't that difficult. Perhaps when you're bigger, I can teach you." Jessie smiled warmly at him through the rearview mirror and returned her attention to the road.

"What means handicap, Uncle Luke?" David piped next. The boys were examining Jessie's wheelchair with fascinated interest.

"I seen one of dose on *Sesame Street*," Rob announced importantly.

Luke leaned forward to turn on the radio and perhaps distract the boys from what he began to feel could turn into a troublesome conversation, but Jessie shook her head at him.

"Let them ask whatever they like," she suggested softly. "I really don't mind. It's better to answer their questions than to evade them."

Luke knew she was right, but he still felt on edge as Jessie did her best to explain the many variations of the term handicapped. All the boys paid close attention, and there was silence for a long while after she was done.

Then a small voice added, "I know what else it means. It means Uncle Luke got to take care of you, eh, Jessie?" David expanded importantly. "My mummy said Uncle Luke has to takes care of you for your whole life, and you never will get better, and you can't get kids like us, either. 'Member she said that, Uncle Luke?"

Jessie felt icy shock as the meaning of the child's words registered.

In an instant Jessie understood why Luke had been strangely silent about his sister lately. Obviously, there had been a quarrel between them that the little boy in the back had overheard and that he was now trying to understand.

"David, we'll talk about this later, okay?" Luke's face had flushed. "Now what tape would you like to hear?"

Luke recited several titles, and the boys argued and then chose. Luke fitted the tape into the deck, and rock music filled the van.

He reached across and clamped a reassuring hand on her shoulder.

"Jess," he said urgently, his voice tinged with concern, "it's not quite the way it sounds."

But Jessie could feel her eyes filling with tears at the hurt the child's innocent words and especially their import had caused. She was trembling by the time she'd parked the van in the crowded lot, and it was all she could do to pretend everything was fine as they set off in a noisy throng down the path leading to the dock.

"Uncle Luke has to take care of you for your whole life."

"You'll never get better."

"You can't get kids like us."

How much was truth and how much misconception? Jessie felt as if she were waking up again to the moment of waking nightmare that always followed the dream of dancing.

CHAPTER ELEVEN

"Show us how to bait the traps, Unca Luke."

The boys waved the basketlike crab traps that Luke had supplied for them, and Jessie was relieved to be able to roll along in their wake, trying to rebuild a semblance of composure. Luke kept turning to give her anxiously worried looks, but he had to stay with his exuberant nephews to make sure none of them tumbled off the open-sided pier.

David, blissfully unaware of her inner turmoil, came trotting back to get her.

"Jessie, hurry up," he ordered excitedly. "We're gonna put the fish heads in now and then let them down into the water. Go faster, Jessie, so's you can see us. You don't want to miss this."

She reached a hand to tousle the boy's soft ebony curls, thinking that this child was very like Denny. The youngest one, Rob, whom Luke was now balancing on his hip for safekeeping, was the most like Lorna and consequently could easily have been Luke's son with his dark curls and startling blue eyes. His rounded chin even had the same cleft Luke's had.

"Mummy said you can't get kids like us."

So Lorna believed disabled women couldn't have children, did she? Anger began to replace some of the hurt. Lorna should meet Kathleen, Jessie seethed. Kathleen would set her straight in a hurry about what women on wheels were all about.

Jessie stopped halfway along the old wooden structure.

"You go ahead, David. I'm going to just sit here for a minute. I can see from here how you do it. Don't worry, I'll be watching when you put them in the water."

She turned to the view of the inlet, the freighters waiting to be loaded, the sparkling white cruise ship moving in stately dignity out toward the open ocean. She could see the mass of green that was Stanley Park, the arch of a bridge against the canopy of blue sky.

Why, she asked herself, should Lorna's opinions bother her? After all, they weren't unusual attitudes, and it wasn't as if Luke shared them.

Hadn't she know from the beginning that she and Luke would be under scrutiny, open to criticism? Why did it bother her so much, now that it had happened?

It was hard to admit, but the harsh words exposed her own deepest anxieties about her ability to cope in a world in which she was a minority and Luke wasn't. Despite the happiness Luke had brought into her life, there were the corresponding difficulties over the details of daily living she did her best to hide or overcome—so many petty details she'd never made him aware of.

How long would she have the energy, the will, to go on making it all look easy? She'd never felt this tired before.

"Our traps are in the water, Jessie, and Uncle Luke gave us money for fish and chips. You want some, too?"

Dan regarded her seriously, an assortment of bills clutched importantly in his fist, his brothers waiting impatiently for him to lead the way down the beach to the concession stand. Luke was still at the end of the pier, securing the ropes from the traps.

"Just a coffee, Dan, black, please. You have enough money?"

"Sure. Uncle Luke gave us lots."

They charged off, dragging Robbie by the hand, just as Luke strode over. He looked endearingly handsome today, Jessie thought, wearing snug old bleached-out jeans and an armless T-shirt that revealed the smooth, tanned muscles of his body. He rested a lean hip against a piling and shook his head ruefully.

"Those crabs better want lunch, or my stock as a fisherman will drop out of sight."

His sunglasses obscured his eyes, but Jessie knew he was studying her. They were alone on this portion of the pier, and he dropped his bantering tone. "Look, the things Lorna said, I'm sure she didn't mean them the way they sound, Jess. She was just voicing a lot of stuff that morning. It wasn't anything personal about you." His words sounded weak even as he said them, and Luke silently cursed his blundering as he marveled at the beauty of the woman looking steadily up at him.

Jessie's hair was a shining halo around her face today. She tilted her head back to give him a lingering thoughtful look, her neck long and graceful and slender. He couldn't help but remember how the soft hollow at its base tasted when he pressed his lips there, a taste like honey and almonds. The taste of Jessie.

"Yesterday," she was saying reasonably, "you were upset because you felt I'd been less than honest with you about Wayne. Today I find out quite by accident that you and your sister had what sounds like a major argument about me weeks ago, and yet you never said a thing. I feel I had a right to know, simply to avoid any embarrassment it might have caused. What if Lorna had been there this morning when we picked the kids up?"

"I'm glad she wasn't," he growled, and Jessie felt worse than ever. Lorna was his twin sister. It was terrible to be the cause of a quarrel between them.

"I didn't want to hurt you, Jess." Luke sighed. He pulled the sunglasses off with an impatient gesture, and his earnest eyes met hers. "It's not the same thing at all, my having words with my sister and you being threatened by that...that..." He couldn't find an adequate noun and exploded impatiently, "God Almighty, I'm not in any danger from Lorna. Surely you can see the difference. Like it or not, you're vulnerable, you need someone to help you deal with this Palmer idiot."

"In other words, I really can't take care of myself." Jessie knew she was being childish, but the argument had suddenly become heated and her hurt and anger accelerated, needing release. She narrowed her eyes at him, half blinded by the sun on the water. "Better be careful, Luke, or you'll find you're spending your life taking care of me, just like Lorna said." She spat out the words contemptuously, wondering all the while how she could act this spiteful when her hurt over Lorna's words really wasn't Luke's fault at all. She was tired, on edge.

But her hasty words were the catalyst to all the frustrations between them, and Luke blew up. He reached out and grabbed the arms of her chair, viciously yanking her toward him, his jaw set, his face a mask of rage.

"I've had about all I can take of walking on eggs around you, trying not to interfere with your goddamn overdeveloped sense of independence. You'll never allow anybody close enough to take care of you because you're scared, you hear me? You're so bloody afraid of showing you're human, of trusting, of needing somebody. And that means you're afraid of love, Jessie. Love includes all those things."

The accusation was too close to the truth, and it left her naked, vulnerable, wanting to hurt him.

"Maybe it's just you I'm afraid of trusting, Luke. Have you considered that?"

All she was thinking of was his secrecy about Lorna, but the instant the words were out, she knew he'd given them a much deeper, more sinister meaning than she'd intended. He'd told her about the months of not trusting himself, of feeling fallible, unreliable at his work.

He couldn't think she was using that now against him, could he?

But she knew he did. His face flushed and then paled. He seemed to be unaware of holding her chair, imprisoning her between his arms, and Jessie felt trapped by the powerful, destructive emotions she'd unwittingly unleashed, by the naked pain in the clear blue eyes of the man she loved. Hurting him this deeply was enough to shatter the fragile control she had left.

She shot backward and veered sharply past his immobile form, pushing hard, sobbing as she headed up the pier away from him. She needed to be alone for a while, she thought, she needed time.

"Jessie, wait. Damn it all, woman, wait a minute." Luke's voice rumbled behind her, and in a moment of confused panic, she used all her strength to spin her wheels harder, faster....

The chair shot ahead, and then in a muddled instant her right wheel caught in the narrow space between the rough old planks that formed the pier. The force she'd applied to her forward motion made the chair veer sharply to the left, and too quickly for her to even realize what had happened, her body pitched up and out, catapulted as the chair tipped over.

Because she'd rolled herself carelessly close to the edge, Jessie went tumbling off the wooden platform, hitting her forehead on the edge an instant before she fell down, down, into the frothing waves formed by the incoming tide.

"Jessie..."

Luke's horrified roar came an instant after she'd disappeared, and utter terror of a sort he'd never experienced before enveloped him. In two strides he was at the place where she'd fallen, and dimly he could hear other voices shouting for help somewhere behind him.

He balanced on the edge, gauging the depth of the water below, and then he dove cleanly.

He couldn't see her at first with the force of the incoming tide making a cauldron of the water, and an awful fear enveloped him. He shot through the water, oblivious to the shock of it on his body, willing himself to find her.

Jessie was stunned by the blow to her head, and when the brine of icy-cold ocean water filled her nose and mouth, she took in a deep gulp, half strangling as it burned viciously in her nose and throat and chest, panicked and choking, unable to breathe.

Luke. Help me!

Time seemed suspended, a time when she was trapped alone in a dark nightmare, where breath and movement were impossible. She flailed weakly, and one hand struck a solid body close beside her. The relief she felt was indescribable.

She couldn't see, but she knew who it was.

Luke. Luke would save her if she could only...

There. She was just below him, and he saw her face, eyes wide open and full of terror, pale hair floating like seaweed.

For Luke, in that one dreadful instant, her face was the face of the girl in his nightmares, the girl he'd pulled from waves like these, with her eyes staring and her hair tugged by the sea as he pulled her over the side of the boat.

Too late. Dead. The girl he'd been sent to rescue—the girl he'd failed.

But this was Jessie, his love, his very life, and the moment he lunged toward her, he knew she was alive, and the relief of it sent adrenaline charging through him.

Her flailing arms found him, wrapped around him with panicked strength, circling his neck and pulling them both deeper into the water with the mindless terror of one beyond reasoning.

This he could deal with. In one well-practiced motion he was able to break that dangerous stranglehold and turn her body away so that he could control her, at the same time using his formidable strength to send them both shooting up toward the surface, her body clamped against his own, limp now, giving itself up to him.

Jessie.

Once he had her head free of the water, she tried to drag air into her lungs, choked again and gagged, half fainting but no longer struggling because she knew Luke held her safe. Trusting him finally.

"Give her here, mate, that's the way."

But Luke ignored the command, staggering to his feet when he reached shallow water and lurching out with Jessie still clinging to him as if she'd never let go again.

Lifeguards were swarming all over the pier, and she was swiftly and competently taken from him. They helped her expel the generous quantity of seawater she'd swallowed, gently cleaned the ugly gash on her forehead and bundled her shuddering body like a mummy into warm blankets. Through it all Luke was right beside her.

Two of the guards supplied Luke with dry shorts and a shirt, holding a blanket around him as he swiftly stripped and pulled on the dry clothing. With quivering fingers Luke rescued a quarter from his dripping wallet and raced for the pay phone at the end of the pier, feeling relief flood over him when Cy answered.

In short, explicit sentences Luke described what had happened to Jessie and explained that his nephews needed supervision while he went with Jessie in the ambulance. Cy's voice was professionally calm and unruffled, and Luke felt a little of his own tension ease.

"Take it easy, son. Amanda's here with me. We'll be down there in ten minutes."

An ambulance finally appeared, lights and sirens flashing, and seconds later Cy and Amanda came running from the parking lot.

Dan and his brothers were located, still waiting patiently in line at the concession.

It was unbelievable to Luke that no more time had passed than a few minutes. It seemed like a lifetime. Luke explained to the boys as calmly as he could what had happened, adding that Jessie was fine, but she'd swallowed half the ocean and had to go and have a doctor check her over, so he was putting Cy in charge of them until he returned. The three small faces turned suspiciously to study the older man.

"I'll help you check those crab traps you've set, and then we can build a sand castle. I used to be an expert at building sand castles," Cy volunteered. He'd spent the first few moments assuring himself that Jessie was in capable hands and really was going to be fine, and now he grinned widely down at the three upturned faces. "We'll need ice cream to keep us cool, of course."

The boys relaxed.

Luke explained carefully that he'd be back to take them home, and as the doors closed and the ambulance pulled away, he caught a glimpse of Amanda distributing ice-cream cones to them, oblivious to the damage the dripping treats had already done to her white skirt.

Jessie's teeth were chattering, and all that showed out of the blanket cocoon was the bleached triangle of her face. The white gauze pad covering the wound on her head hardly contrasted with the whiteness of her skin. Her dark eyes were still glazed with shock, and they centered on Luke's face. The attendant moved slightly, allowing Luke to crouch more easily at Jessie's side.

"Where's my chair?" Her voice was weak, more husky than ever.

"Right here beside me. I told them you'd throw a fit if they left it behind," he assured her gently, and she closed her eyes.

"She's a bit shocky, her blood pressure is low," the attendant murmured, inflating the band attached to her upper arm.

Luke felt as if he must be in some sort of shock himself. He felt numb and totally removed from his surroundings, his whole being centered on the slight blanket-wrapped figure on the stretcher beside him. His muscles twitched uncontrollably every few seconds, and he felt nauseated. All he could think of was that endless moment under the water when he couldn't find her, when the familiar empty sickness of failure had stripped him of courage and filled him with the knowledge of his helplessness in times of need.

Jessie was alive, but Luke could only think of how close she'd come to drowning. She was alive, but the reason she'd fallen in the first place was because he'd lost his temper and shouted at her out there on the dock.

Every lingering doubt he'd had about his ability to cherish and protect Jessie was reinforced and verified as his brain replayed the incident like an endless video in his head.

"SHE'S FINE as far as I can tell," the young resident assured Luke an hour later. "A slight concussion from the blow on the head, nothing serious. However, I'd like her own doctor to have a look at her. He'll be here in a few minutes. She's still pretty white, and she's also light-headed when she tries to sit up. You can go in and talk to her until

Dr. Braun arrives. She's making noises like she wants to go home, but I'd rather you convinced her she stick around a bit longer.''

Jessie argued but not with any degree of conviction. Rotund Dr. Braun bustled into the curtained section of the emergency room a short time later, and after asking a long list of questions, he ordered a battery of tests that seemed to have little to do with the day's accident. Then he briskly informed Jessie that, like it or not, he was keeping her in the hospital overnight for observation.

"Observation of what?" Jessie was thoroughly sick of the whole procedure by now. "For heaven's sake, all I did was fall into the ocean. I'm warm again, I feel fine, I want to go home.''

"Your blood pressure's lower than normal, and I want to run some blood tests." Dr Braun was firm, and when Luke followed him anxiously into the hallway, he was reassuring.

"There's nothing seriously wrong with her, young man, but I'd feel better if she stayed at least overnight after that bang on the head. I want her to rest, and if I know Jessie, that's the last thing she'll do if I let her go home.''

Jessie was moved to a private room, still resisting her hospitalization, but by the time Luke left in a cab to collect his nephews from the beach forty minutes later, she'd fallen into an exhausted sleep.

After giving the adults a detailed account of the accident while sidestepping the reasons it had occurred, Luke answered all the millions of anxious questions his nephews had for him about Jessie and the hospital and drowning in general. He listened to their enthusiastic recital of how they'd built the biggest sand castle the beach had ever seen. He marveled over the bucket of crabs they'd managed to catch, and finally, he tried to express his gratitude to a slightly wilted-looking Cy and a disheveled Amanda as they headed wearily for their car. Surprisingly, the older couple seemed to have thoroughly enjoyed the boys and even suggested they all visit the zoo together sometime in the near future.

After Amanda had driven away, Luke realized with something less than enthusiasm that he was going to have to drive his nephews home in Jessie's hand-controlled van.

"You jerks a lot, don't you, Unca Luke?" Rob commented when he finally had them headed in the right direction down the highway. There was no point in denying it. Driving Jessie's van was a lot more complicated than it looked, and Luke had to apply every ounce of his concentration to the tricky knack of hand brake and clutch.

"Coming in for a beer? Where's Jessie?"

Denny ambled over to the van when they finally arrived in the yard. He helped his sons tumble out, and the boys gave him an erratic but accurate version of what had occurred.

Luke elaborated, and Denny was both shocked and concerned. "Come on in and stay for supper," he invited Luke. "Lorna'll be back any minute now. She phoned half an hour ago." He gave his brother-in-law a pleading look. "It's time you two talked this thing out between you, Luke. God, it's enough that her and I are on the warpath lately, never mind you and her at loggerheads, as well. I can tell she feels miserable about it. C'mon in, you look pretty bushed yourself."

"Thanks, Den, but I'm going home. Bye, kids." Luke's emotions were in a turmoil, and he simply couldn't face confronting Lorna today. What had occurred on the pier was too wrapped up with all the things Lorna had said, and a hard knot of hurt anger remained toward his sister, mixed with all the other emotions churning inside him.

He got the van turned around finally, cursing his inepti-
tude, and drove back to Jessie's house. With every clumsy
mistake he made using the unfamiliar controls, his sense of
desolation and failure grew more pronounced.

The house was silent when he let himself in, and re-
minders of Jessie were everywhere: a cake on the kitchen
counter that she'd made—chocolate because she knew he
loved it—her makeup in the bathroom, the formidable
chrome and steel of her machines in the "torture chamber," her frothy pink underwear on a chair in the bedroom. And most poignant of all, the silent gray moonscape
on the ceiling.

Jessie.

Because of his blundering she'd come close to death today.

Was it any wonder she couldn't trust him?

Luke shuddered, the coldness in his soul reaching every
pore, the well-remembered sense of inadequacy and fear
coursing through him, making it impossible to relax.

Especially in this place, Jessie's place. With feverish haste
he gathered some clothing, then scribbled a garbled note
thanking Cy again and promising to call in the morning. He
tacked it to the door at the top of the stairs.

Back in the West End, in the musty, impersonal apartment he'd hardly visited for weeks, he considered going out
and getting drunk. That had been his escape the other time
this kind of agony had twisted inside him.

But even in his present frame of mind, he couldn't quite
convince himself it had helped at all.

Luke stripped off the borrowed clothes the lifeguards had
loaned him, yanked on his well-worn running shorts and
singlet, laced up his Adidas.

It was early evening when he left the building, and Sunday crowds thronged the streets in the West End, shopping

in the open markets and wandering through the boutiques, discussing which ethnic restaurant they'd choose for their evening meal.

He threaded his way past them unseeingly, legs and feet automatically choosing a route that would lead eventually to the beach, the park, farther and farther away. But from what?

He began to run.

The boutique owners took in the racks of clothing set out on the sidewalks to attract passersby, then closed and locked their shops. The dinner patrons lingered over café au lait, arguing over which foreign film they wanted to see.

Luke found a rhythm after a while that mirrored the procession of words passing through his head. He ran steadily, not fast or slow but always away.

The sun set in spectacular brilliance over the western water, and the silhouette of a Japanese tanker was outlined like a cameo against the horizon.

He ran, and late movies ended. Crowds thickened, enjoying Italian ice cream, or steamers, or pizza.

His jagged thoughts faded into images, short, painful scenes he couldn't seem to blank out. His legs moved like pistons.

The street people and the police officers became visible as night deepened, greeting one another in friendly fashion now that the dark city belonged rightfully to them.

Winding along the dimly lit streets, up and down with only the barest attention to where he was going, Luke ran, and the dusky city took on the murky undertones of water, and his breathing was heavy and strenuous.

Surfacing from the nightmarish images of Jessie's face, drowning, that other face, lost long ago—he was able at last to move away from them, discard them, leave them behind him in the darkness as the beginnings of physical exhaustion forced him to slow his pace.

He looked around, trying to get his bearings, stopping for the first time to check a street sign on the corner.

He was somewhere in Kerrisdale, miles away from the apartment. He bent, hands on his knees, panting, aware of the depth of darkness around him, the hushed quiet of a residential neighborhood late at night. There was a bus stop up ahead, its covered awning lit eerily by a fluorescent lamp, and he went over and collapsed on the bench. He was soaking wet, sweat running in rivulets down his nose, off his chin, dripping from his arms.

The last time he'd sweat like this was the marathon.

In perfect detail he saw Jessie on the hill, felt again the poignant agony of her effort, saw himself taking hold of her chair, pushing, forcing her to accept help she didn't need or want. Was it simply the same thing he'd been doing all along?

He heard her velvet-tinged voice saying when first he knew her, "My life is full now, and I'm happy."

He loved her as he'd never loved anyone or anything before.

He knew beyond a doubt that she loved him. But sometimes love wasn't enough. Or maybe, he thought with profound weariness, love was sometimes too much. It seemed that way for him and Jessie.

She wasn't the same sparkling woman she'd been in the beginning. She often looked tired, drawn now, worn down—with love?

The best thing he could do for her now was retreat, he admitted at last. That was the truth he'd been running from all evening. Now he'd have to go back and face it.

If he could figure out a way to get home. He didn't have any money. He'd come away without even enough for a phone call.

A police car drove slowly past, and Luke got unsteadily to his feet. He waved an arm and the car pulled to a stop, backed up until it was beside him. A young, trim constable got out and eyed Luke warily.

"I've been running," he explained redundantly, too drained to even feel like a fool, "and I've come too far. I didn't bring bus fare. Could I borrow enough from you to get me home?"

After a few questions the officer drove him home instead, making casual conversation. The radio blurted fuzzy reports now and then of speeding cars, domestic battles, a motorcycle accident, and Luke remembered poignantly how it felt, patrolling the streets while most of the world slept.

This policeman had an air of anticipation about him, a muted excitement and relish for what his shift would hold, the kind of invulnerable, world-beating confidence Luke himself had once felt as a young constable.

Luke watched and listened to his companion and felt a million years old.

When the car stopped near the apartment, he said thanks and got out with a silent prayer for the eager, young officer. Police work was notorious for driving men to their breaking point, and the ones in the most danger were the ones who felt they could deal with anything.

"Everything was going great," Luke heard another young man, Sergeant Luke Chadwick, saying in confusion. "Everything was fine, I was in control and then I heard the gun go off."

Behind his eyes an endless scene played out, the way it had done for years.

Stress burnout, the experts called the thing that had done its best to destroy him.

The last time Luke had talked to Graham Marshall, the psychologist had suggested that Luke eventually consider becoming a counselor for other police officers suffering through the same trauma.

Luke hadn't been ready then to give what the job would require—the daily exposure of his own wounded soul.

Maybe it was time to go back and talk to Graham again.

He stood under the shower until his shivering body was warm, and then he set the clock radio and collapsed into bed. His last waking thought before exhaustion overtook him was of something Jessie had said about recovery after spinal injury.

"It's hard to figure out," she'd told him once, "what parts of your life you can put back together and what parts are gone forever. But eventually, you find there are pieces you can salvage and reuse."

He'd learned a lot from Jessie.

CHAPTER TWELVE

WHEN THE BLOOD TESTS came back, Dr. Braun insisted on keeping Jessie in the hospital for three full days. She objected vehemently, but he waved the computer sheets at her the morning after her accident.

"Your hemoglobin count is way below the normal range, which means you're severely anemic, young woman. This sheet here—" he waved the paper under Jessie's nose "—tells me that your iron stores are low. What that indicates is that you need extra iron for an extended period of time. We'll begin with three days of complete rest here in the hospital with some shots so that we can keep a close eye on you and see which form of iron your body accepts easily."

He gave her a quizzical glance. "You've obviously been overdoing it, Jess. You must have been feeling pretty tired and light-headed with an iron count as low as this. You've successfully drained your resources, and it'll take a while to build them up again."

Jessie slumped against the pillows after he'd gone. At least there was a physical reason for the way she'd been feeling lately, and that was something of a relief.

Dr. Braun had explained that heavy exercise, like the running and weight training Jessie did, often resulted in female iron deficiency. He'd explained, as well, that anemia affected the emotions, making its victims cry easily or suffer fluctuations in temperament. Jessie was sorely tempted to blame all her emotional turmoil on her condition and convince herself that by having the shots and taking the magic pills the doctor prescribed, her life with Luke would be perfect.

Honesty forbade it.

Anemia didn't account for her deep insecurities or the lack of trust Luke had accurately accused her of yesterday. It didn't erase the weight of censure from Lorna and from Chandra.

Well, she'd certainly proven Lorna right on one score. Luke had been forced to take care of her on a grand scale yesterday. She remembered the blessed strength, the safety of his arms holding her in the water, and the love she felt for him welled up in a painful rush inside her.

If only she could feel free to borrow his strength when she needed it with no fear of consequences. If only she could trust that his love would always outweigh her fear of dependency.

But she couldn't. Common sense told her that sooner or later he'd hate that dependency just as strongly as she did.

She phoned Evan at the station to tell him she wouldn't be at work for several days only to find that Luke had already been in touch with him. Her boss didn't sound as annoyed as Jessie had expected him to be, considering the short notice he had to find a stand-in for her.

A full hour before visiting hours officially started Cy breezed into her room carrying two paperback novels, a radio-tape player with a selection of her favorite tapes and a bag containing hamburgers and french fries for each of them. Jessie was sitting listlessly by the window, and she felt better just having Cy in the room. She remembered vaguely that he'd also appeared as if by magic when she was lying on the pier waiting for the ambulance.

He explained how that had happened and then added, ''I talked to Jack Braun this morning. He was an intern when

I was on staff in this joint. So we've allowed you to suc-
cumb to the 'disease of pale ears,' as it used to be called.''
He spread out the food on a towel on her washstand and
nonchalantly produced two bottles of his homemade beer to
accompany it. ''This is made with hops and yeast, full of
iron. An ancient treatment for anemia was to stick rusty
nails into a sour apple, allow it to stand overnight, remove
the nails and eat the apple. Or was it the other way round?
Well, no matter, apparently Jack's using modern methods,
anyway.'' He scowled accusingly at her. ''Damn it all, why
didn't you elaborate on how you were feeling? I should have
realized what was up the other day. I figured you looked
pale. Too damn involved in my own affairs, that's what's
the matter.''

''You're my friend, Cy, not my physician,'' Jessie reminded him tartly. ''And if apples with nails in them are
your usual cure, I'll happily stick with Dr. Braun, thanks.''

Jessie wasn't feeling hungry at all, but she made an effort with the hamburger and had her mouth full when he
calmly announced, ''I talked with Luke again this morning, and then I phoned your mother. She'll be here during
visiting hours, which is why I pulled rank with the head
nurse and arrived early.''

Jessie glared at him and sputtered, ''Why did you go and
do that? The last thing I need around here is my mother.
Damn it all, Cy, what possessed you to call her? You phone
my mother, Luke calls my boss. Don't you two think I'm
capable of making any decisions of my own? I'll only be in
here two more days, and it's not as if I've got a life-
threatening condition.''

''From what I saw down on the beach yesterday, you sure
had one hell of a life-threatening condition going for yourself, so don't get on your high horse with us.'' Cy had had a
long talk with Luke. He studied her intently. ''You gave that

young man of yours quite a scare, Jess. I told him about the test results. He said to tell you he'd be in to see you after work this afternoon. Now tell me, exactly how did you manage to throw yourself into the drink like that? Luke was a bit short on details.''

Jessie turned her head toward the window, remembering, hearing all too clearly Luke's angry words, her own cruel rejoinder.

''I, we . . . we were . . . having an argument.''

''Must have been a real dilly to make you jump off the bridge, as it were. I trust you made up afterward?''

Cy already knew from Luke that they hadn't, but he wanted to hear Jessie's version of the incident. To hear Luke tell it, the entire episode had been all his fault, and Cy simply didn't accept that conclusion. This pale blond angel in front of him had both a stubborn streak and a formidable temper.

Jessie shook her head, and then her face crumbled. ''It's just not easy, Cy.'' She mopped her tears with the Kleenex he handed her and found herself pouring out the whole garbled story into his sympathetic ears.

''He says I don't trust him enough, and he's right. My situation involves very real problems, and he refuses to see the effect they could have on us. Plus, all the pressure from other people has to affect him sooner or later. I'm scared, Cy. Wanting this relationship to work just isn't enough, and I couldn't stand it if I started to believe it would, just to have it all collapse around my useless legs a couple of years down the road.''

She blew her nose and gave him a halfhearted, watery smile. ''I learned to get along without my legs, but I don't think I can survive without my heart. If I should come to rely on Luke too much and if he resents it and ends up leaving me, I don't think I'd be able to stand it.''

Cy gave a snort, balled up the remains of the forgotten lunch and tossed them into the garbage.

"Rubbish. Everybody leans on their partner in some way or other, and most of the time it evens itself out. One partner needs more this way, the other that. You're taking the coward's way out and not trying just in case you should fail. I never saw you as a coward, Jess." A pensive look came and went on his face, and he looked at his watch.

"I'm a great one to lecture about cowardice. I'm taking Amanda out this afternoon, and I've been trying to convince myself to give her an ultimatum. Me or Greece, take your pick. The more I mull it over, the more certain I am that Greece will win. I hate losing, so maybe I just won't get into it with her. Now that's guts for you." He shook his head in disgust and looked at his watch. "I'll have to be going. My advice, for what it's worth, is just to give yourself lots of time to get feeling better before you make any major decisions." He planted a hearty kiss on her cheek. "Anemia is known to cause mental confusion." His faded eyes twinkled. "Maybe I ought to have my own blood tested. I hand out fine-sounding advice, but when it comes to Amanda, I have to admit I'm stumped."

Cy must have passed Chandra in the hallway, Jessica figured, because her mother swept in bare seconds after Cy had disappeared. She brought a bag imprinted with the name of an exclusive boutique. It contained two ruffled, shirt-style cotton nighties, one emerald, one dusky rose, each with a matching wrapper, and an assortment of makeup.

"There's no need to look so pale, Jessica, it doesn't suit your coloring. Here, let's use this blusher."

Jessie had to smile in spite of her dragging spirits. Die if you must, but look your best doing it was Chandra's motto.

She waved away Jessie's thanks, plunked the bag down on the bed and insisted that Jessie trade her hospital garb for the new finery.

She opened the windows wider and complained about the smell of junk food in the room. She lectured her daughter about the importance of a good diet and then stated she was taking Jessie home with her for at least a week after she was released from hospital.

"Your father insists, so don't argue. He's very concerned about you, dear."

Jessie felt trapped, tired and browbeaten, as well as too weary to argue. After an uncomfortable half hour Chandra left for a tennis game, and Jessie finally fell sound asleep.

When she awoke, it was early afternoon, and Luke was sitting quietly beside her, still wearing his dusty work clothes. She was startled at the lines of strain around his eyes and mouth, and remorse almost choked her.

"Hi, Jess. How you feeling?"

He didn't kiss her, and there was a new remoteness about him. For the first time since she'd known him, Luke seemed almost unapproachable, and she realized with a sinking sensation that the damaging words they'd each uttered the day before were as fresh in his memory as they were in hers. Nothing had really changed. Nothing could change because what he'd said was the truth.

"You're afraid of love," he'd accused, and she knew it was so, but knowing didn't stop the fear, or magically bring trust.

It wasn't even Luke she didn't trust.

Her world had all but ended once, and all she was left with was a mirage, a vision of an imaginary dancer on the moon. What guarantee was there for happiness?

Haltingly, the words hurting her throat, she said, "It's not going to work for us, is it, Luke?"

He looked at her, the achingly beautiful face, the body he adored not in spite of but because of its vulnerability.

Everything about her drew him, made him long to cherish and protect her. And that very response, so elemental, so natural, was the reason it wouldn't work between them. The pain of what was happening choked him for a moment, and his face felt frozen when he answered as truthfully as he could, "It's not working at the moment, that's for sure, and I'm damned if I know what to do about it. But I'm far too stubborn to see this as anything but a temporary problem." His tone was harsh, but the words he'd spent all day planning were unnecessary because she understood as well as he did. He said them, anyway.

"Right now I just want you to rest, get feeling well, and I think it would be easier for you without me around." His hurt showed on his face for an instant before he hid it again, and Jessie felt trapped between her love for him and her fear. She wanted to reach out and smooth her fingertips over his face, smooth away the stern lines, tell him she was his entirely, with no reservations.

But she couldn't break through the barrier that held her captive, the brittle, protective shell that kept her from trusting.

He seemed to understand intuitively what she was feeling, and he gently offered her the space she needed.

"The next couple of weeks are going to be really busy for me, so I'm staying at the apartment for a while. I want you to have time by yourself, to think about us and most of all to get feeling well again."

His blue eyes were infinitely sad. "I love you, Jessie. I want you for my wife—you must know that by now. But I want you to be happy, as well, more than I've ever wanted anything." She recognized the finality in his tone when he said, "The next move has to be yours, Jess. Decide what you

want. This is my number at the apartment. Call me if..."
He'd been about to say "if you need me," but of course she
wouldn't. And that was really what this separation was all
about.

"Call me when you make up your mind." He choked the
words out, brushed her lips with a fleeting kiss and turned
blindly toward the door.

The awful irony of it all, he thought viciously as he hurried unseeingly toward the elevators, was that it was his own
need and her independence that had driven them apart.
Shouldn't it be the other way around?

At least, with Jessie safe in the hospital he had several
days to find Wayne Palmer. Luke concentrated on that goal
as if it were a lifeline, doing his best to block the torturous
ache that threatened to consume him each time he thought
of Jessie and the wordless agony reflected in her dark gaze
when he had walked out of the hospital room. But she
hadn't called him back, he reminded himself.

He found a pay phone in the lobby and dialed the Mason's number.

Lorna answered, knowing instantly who it was, not giving him time to ask for Denny before she hesitantly began,
"Luke, the boys told me what happened to Jessie. How is
she? I feel terrible about the things I said. I want you to
know that if she's the woman you choose, well, I'll do my
best to understand. I just don't want trouble between us,
Luke. You're—" Lorna choked up, and she cleared her
throat hoarsely "—you're my favorite brother."

He shut his eyes tight as a welter of conflicting emotions
tore at him. It would have meant so much if Lorna had
adopted her present attitude in the beginning, shown Jessie
warmth and welcome. There was no point in telling her that
now. Lorna was obviously doing the best she could.

"That could be because I'm your only brother," he managed to joke feebly, and he could hear the deep sigh of relief from the other end of the line.

"Are you coming over tonight?" Lorna's voice was hopeful, and Luke knew she was disappointed when he said no.

"I'll come over soon, though," he promised, and then he asked for Denny.

When his brother-in-law came on the line, Luke quickly explained that he'd arranged for a young man they'd often hired as casual labor to work in his place for the next week or maybe two.

Luke was grateful when Denny didn't press for an explanation. "Our next job is that rockery, anyhow. And all that takes is a strong back. Lorna's hollering for you to come for dinner Sunday. And bring Jessie, she says."

Luke swallowed. "Tell Lorna we've got plans this week. We'll take a rain check. Tell the kids hi from me, wouldya, Denny?" Then he hung up.

Early the next morning, for the first time since leaving the RCMP, Luke visited the General Investigation Section. Frank Mahoney, one of the men he'd been in training with, was assigned there, and Luke recognized several other members of the force, as well, as he walked into the large office.

They came over, and there were the usual handshakes and questions about what he was doing now, along with the familiar embarrassed evasiveness about why he'd left the force in the first place.

They all knew about Luke's story, of course, but they'd never admit it to his face. Stress burnout just wasn't a macho ailment, Luke thought sardonically. It didn't mesh with the whole police image, so dangerous to the individual who believed in it, of toughness, invulnerability, infallibility. There would be no admission of weakness, or of need. . . .

With a sudden shock of recognition, Luke realized how much that analysis fit Jessie.

Or himself, for that matter. Even now he never came right out and admitted the real reasons behind his leaving. What made him, what made anyone, so afraid of revealing weakness?

Deliberately, for the first time, Luke referred casually to the psychological problems he'd encountered as a result of his work with the force, and to his surprise, the admission seemed to unlock a closed door among the small group gathered at Frank's desk.

"Same thing happened to Thomas, remember him? Big guy, like yourself. Working undercover narcotics. And Simpson, God, he was the kind of guy nothing seemed to bother. Then one day he started crying, couldn't stop, after that kid was shot."

Hesitantly they asked questions, and Luke did his best to be open and honest. A full hour of heated discussion passed before he could finally ask the favor he'd come to ask, and then the men were all eager to help, as if he'd helped them and they wanted to return the favor.

"Wayne Palmer? Western singer. Any other info on the guy, Luke?"

Luke related every last detail he'd drawn from Jessie and from his conversation with Cy. He explained, without going into a lot of detail, the way in which Wayne was causing trouble for a woman he cared about. They nodded understandingly.

"We'll run a check on him through the computer, get a photo if we can. If he's a bad apple, you can bet he'll show. Hey, Jack, you know your friend Amherst on city force, is he still working the streets down around Gastown? Good, we'll get a make on our pal here and put out the word for you, Luke. Give us a call in a couple hours. We'll probably have something by then.''

It was nearly lunchtime. On impulse, Luke phoned Graham Marshall at the Justice Institute, and half an hour later Graham was taking the seat across from Luke in a small neighborhood pub.

Luke had no conscious intention of telling his friend about Jessie, but once he'd started, he couldn't seem to stop. It took a long time, and when he finished, Graham's suggestions were unusual. Luke listened carefully.

When lunch was over, he realized what else he'd wanted to say, and in a way it, too, was about Jessie.

She'd helped him find the answer.

''If the offer's still open by the time I find somebody to take my place in the landscaping business, I'd like to try that position you offered me as a one-on-one counselor, Graham. I'm going to register for the psych courses I'll need.''

Graham's bony face broke into a wide, delighted smile, and he said heartily, ''Anytime you're ready, Luke. I think you'll find it satisfying work, and the institute will be damn lucky to get you. Books never teach as well as experience does.''

The agreement was confirmed with a solid handshake.

''PALMER, WAYNE JASON. Fair-sized rap sheet on this dude, Luke. Driving offenses old and new, Eastern Canada and all over the U.S.A., assault, once with a weapon, did time for that down in Iowa, got an ex-wife in Washington charged him for nonsupport, drunk and disorderly here in Vancouver. He's a loner, traveled with a band for a while, but they dropped him for missing performances or turning up too soused to sing. No current address on him, but the word's out on the street. Somebody will know where he's at.

Last address was the Union Hotel over on the East Side. He left there two weeks ago. Give us a couple days. We'll locate him.''

Luke took the brown envelope his friend handed him.

"Thanks, fellows, thanks a lot. I think I'll drive over now and visit some of the old guys in the lobby of the Union Hotel see what they might have heard. I'd like to have a heart-to-heart talk with this Palmer, soon as possible.''

ENDLESS, EMPTY DAYS had passed since she'd last seen Luke. Jessie was released from the hospital on the third morning after her near drowning, physically stronger but emotionally dazed, not even caring when Chandra made all the arrangements for Jessie to come home with her.

It didn't seem to matter where she went without Luke.

Her father's delight in having Jessie home for a few days more than made up for Chandra's slightly martyred attitude when she mentioned missing a tennis tournament because of visiting the hospital.

Chandra responded with a smug "I told you so, it couldn't possibly last, it's all for the best" when Jessie admitted she and Luke were no longer together.

Well, Jessie asked herself cynically, what had she expected from her mother, anyway?

By Sunday afternoon Jessie had had enough.

"Will you drive me home, Dad?" she asked at lunchtime, and after a token amount of argument, her parents finally agreed.

Jessie knew that it had satisfied some obscure parental need in Chandra to fuss over her for the past few days, but she could also see that her parents' lives were busy and complete without the awkward presence of an adult daughter.

A "differently abled" daughter, as Jessie had heard Chandra describe her over the phone to one of her friends. The usually acceptable euphemism had made Jessie smile bitterly. How like Chandra to search for a socially "acceptable" label for what she would always find unacceptable.

Late in the afternoon Jessie rolled up to her own red front door, feeling absurdly relieved to be back in her own home.

Chandra had brought bags of groceries—a great deal of liver, which Jessie hated—and she swept through, putting the packages away quickly. Jessie knew her parents were invited out to dinner that evening, and she hurried them away, reassuring them both that she felt perfectly capable of being on her own again.

Finally, the door closed behind them, and she was alone. She waited for the quiet sense of peace and stability that being in her own house had always provided, but it didn't come.

She rolled through all the rooms on the main floor of her house slowly, puzzled, looking around as if she'd been away far longer than a week, and everywhere she looked, she remembered Luke.

He was there in the kitchen, the bedroom, the shower. Especially he was there in the garden, which was resplendent with multicolored blossoms, full of scent and bees and midsummer lushness.

As if she were seeing it for the first time, she gazed in awe at the garden he'd created for her.

The somnolent heat of the afternoon was gentled here, shaded by the trees he'd cleverly incorporated into the finished design.

She could hear his voice, full of enthusiasm, explaining the groupings of flowers to her when the earth was still a muddy mess in the beginning.

"There we'll put rhododendrons—they'll flower in the early spring—wilburts here—they're pink—red hummingbirds there, white cunninghams mixed with salangia stellar, the star-shaped kind, over there where the soil is more acid." He'd waited for her to follow him, protectively close but scrupulously not touching her chair.

Oh, Luke, how careful you were with me.

"Here, we'll have periwinkle, night-scented jasmine, when summer comes. There'll be honeysuckle, lavender, clematis."

And there was. Her garden was a palette of colors and scents. More than that, Luke had managed to make it seem uncontrived, wild and passionate and free just the way she'd wanted, with the sliding glass doors he'd installed by her eating area standing open to invite the delicious scents and shades inside through the screen.

The indefinable soreness inside her found a focus, and she admitted how much she missed him.

She'd have to fight it, that was all there was to it. Better now than later.

In the garden she found some measure of peace, tugging on the light nylon coveralls he'd bought her and slipping from her chair down into the raised bed of vegetables, already showing signs of neglect after only a week without weeding.

Lettuce, butter, romaine, iceberg.

Tomatoes, broad beans, squash.

The seeds he'd planted for her.

Ferociously she set to work, cleaning the rows meticulously, and it seemed appropriate that soon every muscle in her body ached in direct proportion to the awful ache growing in her heart, the ache she'd done her best to subdue ever since the last time she'd seen Luke.

Cy arrived home from taking Amanda to the airport for her flight to Greece. He was subdued, sinking into long periods of silence, and Jessie thought wryly that the two of them made a dismal pair.

He insisted on ordering in a Chinese dinner for them, which neither of them ate.

Jessie was helping him scrape the uneaten moo goo guy pan into containers for the fridge when the phone rang.

"Hello?"

Her voice had a peculiar breathless quality, and Jessie felt a hurtful expectancy stretch as she waited for the caller to answer.

She wanted it to be Luke, but a female voice said hello.

It was Lorna Mason, and after the first awful pang of disappointment, Jessie was astonished at Lorna's friendly words.

"How are you, Jessie?" Lorna actually sounded sincerely concerned, and it was hard for Jessie to reply without sounding resentful. She did her best, though, reminding herself that this was Luke's sister. There was an uncomfortable pause, and then Lorna said, "I have an apology to make to you. My son Dan explained what went on in the van, about Dave repeating the things I'd said, and I want you to know I'm sorry if I've hurt you, Jessie. I wanted Luke to bring you here for dinner today so I could do this in person. I even got Denny to build a ramp up those steps." She sounded forlorn. "Luke refused, he said the two of you were busy. I guess he's still pretty upset with me. Anyway, I thought maybe both of you might like to come to the opening of The Soup Kitchen on Tuesday at noon."

Now there was both pride and defiance in her voice, and also gratitude when she added, "I took your advice and called the local radio station here, and they're sending out a mobile crew. I'm pretty nervous about it all, to tell you the truth.''

''I'm sure it's going to be a huge success. It's innovative, and I think it's a great idea,'' Jessie reassured her truthfully.

An anxious note crept into Lorna's voice. ''Is Luke there now, Jessie? I haven't seen him this week at all. He's on holiday, Denny said, but I . . . I need to talk to him.''

As steadily as she could Jessie said, ''Luke's not here, Lorna, and I don't expect him. I haven't seen him this week, either. We...we both decided we needed time to think things over.''

There, gloat over that, Jessie thought maliciously as the seconds of silence lengthened. Finally, Lorna said earnestly, ''Jessie, I'm truly sorry. If this is a result of my stupidity, I'll never forgive myself.'' She drew in an audible breath and then continued hesitantly, ''I'd like the chance to get to know you, one woman to another. Why not come to the opening, anyway? I seem to be at the store most of the time lately, and perhaps we could find time for a quiet lunch?''

Jessie thanked her politely and hung up, not committing herself.

''I take it that was Luke's sister?'' Cy made no polite pretense of not having heard the conversation.

''Yes, it was,'' Jessie confirmed and stubbornly changed the subject. She didn't want to explain the call. She wasn't sure she ever wanted to see Lorna Mason again, and certainly she didn't want to engineer an accidental meeting with Luke.

Or did she? And where was Luke? He hadn't mentioned holidays. She couldn't help but think of the blissful week they'd had together and feel a stab of jealous pain at the idea of his having holidays now without her.

"The next move has to be yours," he'd stated.

She could call the number he'd given her.

But nothing had really changed, and before long the same old problems would resurface between them.

Wasn't it fortunate, she reminded herself stoutly, staring vacantly out at the garden he'd made for her, that she'd never really come to rely on him?

Unexpectedly, as Cy was explaining a new technique for beer-making to her, Jessie burst into stormy tears.

Cy was no help at all. "For God's sweet sake, phone that man and tell him you need him. That's all he wants to hear from you, you boneheaded, stubborn woman. You're cutting off your nose to spite your face."

It wasn't that easy at all.

"I can't, Cy." She blew her nose and leveled a baleful stare at him. "And before you even begin to consider the idea, I absolutely forbid you to interfere. This is private."

Cy lost his temper then, swearing foully and stomping away up the stairs without saying good-night.

IT SEEMED THAT even the weather conspired against Jessie. Rain sluiced down in great dismal sheets the following day, and a fuzzy blanket of grayness that all but obscured the city contributed to her deepening loneliness when she drove through the bedraggled, wet streets to work that evening.

"Evening, everybody. This is 'Night Shift,' and I'm Jessie, delighted to be back with you again. With all that rain out there, it's a fine evening to build a fire in the fireplace, dim the lights and pour a glass of wine while we cast a magic spell with music and conversation. I'll be taking your calls on 'Heart Line' a little later on, and if you're having problems with your love life, why not drop me a line? I'll read your letter on the air, and all you amateur love experts listening out there can phone in solutions. Address your letters to Jessie, care of 'Night Shift.'"

What effort it cost her to sound carefree that night. How nice it would be to have someone to solve her own heartache.

In an effort at distraction, Jessie riffled through the stack of messages left on her table by the young announcer who'd stood in for her while she was away.

One scrawled page caught her attention, and a shiver of apprehension went through her.

Unidentified male caller, mystery man (no name) insistent and finally abusive, wanting to know exactly when you'd be back. Persistent, too—called at least twice each shift. Mentioned this to Evan. It's that bedroom voice that gets 'em, Jess.

She waited apprehensively all evening, forcing lightness and gaiety into her voice by sheer will, tensing each time the phone blinked a summons. It could be Wayne. But then again, it might be Luke.

But Wayne didn't call and Luke didn't, either.

Jessie found herself glancing over her shoulder when she left the station after work that night, peering through the hazy gloom of the streetlights, hurrying into her van and then cursing herself for being paranoid. How pleased Wayne would be to think he had her this spooked. Besides, she didn't have any real way of knowing whether the calls had been from him, or whether she'd attracted yet another weirdo. She dragged herself home and into bed, locking all the doors and windows first.

She woke after a restless night and groaned when she heard the rain still pattering determinedly against the windows. It was cold, wet, gloomy. How was she going to make it through another day? Jessie thought numbly. How was she going to make it through the rest of her life?

You were alone before, she lectured herself sternly. *You'll learn how to be alone again. It'll just take time.*

But the emptiness she felt was nearly unbearable. She turned her head and stared at the telephone.

"Call me," he'd said. Surely it wouldn't hurt just to talk to him, like civilized, normal adults?

Before she could change her mind, she reached for the phone, dialing the number of his apartment, not even aware that she knew it by heart.

He wasn't there. The phone rang and rang, and after the twelfth ring, she slowly hung up, feeling as bereft as she ever had in her life and irrationally angry at Luke. Where was he, if he wasn't working and he wasn't at home?

The date on the clock radio reminded her it was Tuesday, the day of Lorna's opening. Luke was sure to be there, at least. There'd be a huge crowd of people around. Just seeing him again for a short while would be enough to get her over this mad compulsion she had. She hated going alone, though, and she wasn't about to ask Cy to come along after his temper fit the evening before.

She reached for the phone again and impulsively called Kathleen.

"I'd love to come," her friend responded. "Mom's still here to stay with Chrissie, but I'll have to bring Mike. I'm his only source of nourishment at the moment."

Jessie remembered all too clearly Lorna's comment about disabled women not being able to have children, and she assured Kathleen that Mikey could only add to the festivities. They agreed to meet at the entrance to the Market just before noon, and as soon as she hung up, Jessie began to mentally choose and discard outfit after outfit, visualizing the clothes on hangers in her closet and carefully plotting what she would wear.

She might as well look as if being alone wasn't bothering her. As if she wasn't missing him at all.

Jessie groaned and crawled out of bed. It was going to take her all the rest of the morning to create such a major illusion.

She swallowed her iron pills with the huge glass of milk the dietician had ordered, shuddered and set to work.

CHAPTER THIRTEEN

WHEN SHE WAS READY, Jessie concluded that the effort had probably been worth it. That opinion was confirmed when she rolled up to the Market entrance and greeted Kathleen.

"You're disgustingly gorgeous, you know that? It's a good thing we're old friends because meeting you now looking like that would just make me hate you on sight."

Having delivered this compliment, Kathleen studied Jessie's outfit.

She was wearing a rich shade of plum silk that emphasized the pale glory of her hair. Her long top was cut like a man's collarless shirt, with outrageously padded shoulders and sleeves that Jessie had rolled casually to the elbow. She'd left the front buttons undone enough so that a lavish amount of peach lace camisole was exposed. A narrow belt nipped the shirttails in at the waist above matching straight-cut trousers, but her dainty heeled sandals were peach. The combination of unlikely colors was echoed by rings of bangles on her arms. Bangles Luke had bought her on her birthday.

"Simple, elegant and wildly sexy, as they say in *Vogue*," Kathleen commented, but Jessie motioned to Mike, who was sound asleep in his baby carrier, which was strapped to Kathleen's chest.

"As far as accessories go, nothing comes close to that for originality and charm." Kathleen's proud smile was still in place when they rolled into the huge open-area shopping mall.

The casual, open market system of merchandising had taken the Lower Mainland area by storm over the past several years, and this pleasant, noisy mixture of booths and stalls gathered under one immense roof was closely patterned on the wildly successful Granville Market on False Creek in the heart of the city.

There was a considerable amount of hoopla going on there today, Jessie noted, with curious onlookers and serious shoppers milling around, jugglers and street musicians performing impromptu acts in the crowded aisles and the merchants themselves conducting noisy and good-natured business.

The Soup Kitchen and two other new businesses shared a block of space in a sunny corner overlooking the river, and the area was roped off for the official opening. When Jessie and Kathleen arrived, there was a traffic jam blocking the area. A mobile TV crew was covering the opening as well as a radio announcer Jessie recognized, and it took some time before they were done interviewing a flushed and excited-looking Lorna.

Jessie's eyes roved over the assembled group, locating an unsmiling Denny and the three well-scrubbed boys sitting stiffly at one of the tables. There was no sign of Luke, and her heart plummeted. It was only then that Jessie realized how much she'd counted on seeing him there, how much she longed to see him.

"Jessie, I'm so delighted you came." Lorna had spotted them and hurried over, and Jessie noted the way Lorna's eyes lingered on the baby strapped to Kathleen's front. Jessie made introductions.

"How, um, how old is the baby?" Lorna asked. Kathleen said, "Oh, he's six weeks now. Still too new to make me want to have a third one quite yet."

Lorna's face was a study.

The gregarious deejay Jessie knew ambled along beside her, gossiping about the industry and asking about "Night Shift." In the confusion of introductions and greetings and congratulations, the two women were taken to a table and glasses of wine appeared, as well as steaming bowls of soup and rounds of homemade bread, served by the smiling, competent older women Lorna had hired to assist her.

"Hi, Jessie, mind if the gang and I join you guys?" Denny seemed uncomfortable in what was so obviously his wife's arena, and soon two tables were pushed together to accommodate them all.

"Is that baby a new one? He sure is little." David's wide eyes were riveted on tiny Mike, and Kathleen chatted to the boys, casually letting each hold Mike for a few minutes. Soon she was giving them an animated account of life in the country.

"Why not get your parents to bring you out to visit us, and you can feed the pigs and ride the neighbor's pony?" she suggested blithely. When Mike began to fuss, she asked the boys to help her find a washroom where she could feed him, and they trooped off proudly, feeling important, surrounding her chair like an honor guard.

The bustle in the area gradually quieted. Jessie and Denny had mutually avoided any mention of Luke. The deejay finished his third glass of wine and left reluctantly, and Lorna came over and sat down in the chair he'd vacated.

"Looks like your Soup Kitchen's going to be a smashing success, Lorna," Jessie said. Lorna's features relaxed into a smile so much like Luke's that Jessie caught her breath.

But Jessie also noticed that Lorna glanced anxiously at Denny and that he wasn't smiling at all.

"I should get back to work, Lorna," he said abruptly. "I'll take the kids and drop them off at the baby-sitter's."

Lorna frowned at him. "For heaven's sake, Denny, I promised them they could stay at least until two. Do you have to—" She bit off the rest of her words, and Denny stubbornly got to his feet.

"They're off with Kathleen, and I'm afraid I overheard her promising them ice cream," Jessie said, uncomfortably aware of the palpable tension between the other two. Glancing from husband to wife, she suggested tentatively, "I could drive them home a little later, if that's all right with both of you." Lorna looked relieved. Denny agreed, thanked Jessie and left without another word to his wife.

Lorna slumped back in her seat dejectedly.

"Thanks, Jessie. The kids would have been disappointed to have to leave so soon." She swallowed hard and then cursed softly, "Damn it, why does he have to be this way? You'd think he'd be proud of me, and instead, he's acting like a spoiled, sulky kid." Lorna's voice was full of unshed tears, and it took her a moment to regain her composure. Then she turned to Jessie and met her eyes in a level, honest exchange.

"It was generous of you to come here today after the awful things I said. I'm pleased you brought Kathleen, too. I have a lot to learn, Jessie." She fumbled with a spoon on the tablecloth. "Seeing your friend with her baby, well, it completely threw me. I hope it didn't show."

Jessie had to laugh. "Kathleen has that effect on me every now and then, too. She's quite a lady."

Lorna reached across and lightly touched Jessie's hand. "I suspect you're quite a lady yourself. My brother certainly thinks so."

It was Jessie's turn to swallow and look away. Then, in a voice she tried and failed to make sound absolutely normal, she said, "I thought Luke might be here today."

Lorna shook her head impatiently. "I phoned and phoned him, but he's never home, and he hasn't called by the house. He didn't say a word to me about going away, either. And if Denny knows where he is, he sure isn't saying anything." She caught Jessie's glance and said succinctly, "Men."

A tentative bond was formed between them, which given the chance, Jessie mused, might just develop into friendship.

It TOOK MUCH LONGER than Luke had anticipated to find out where Wayne Palmer hung out, where he was currently staying and where he'd disappeared to in the past week. The trail, after numerous false leads, brought him to the dingy, urine-smelling basement parking garage of the El May Apartments about the time of Lorna's grand opening on Tuesday afternoon.

The license number of the black Buick checked out with the one GI section had unearthed. Luke ran a finger over the car's surface and left a clean path in the thick covering of dust. So Palmer hadn't used the vehicle for at least a week. Luke headed for the stairwell in search of the manager.

"You the fuzz? What's he done, this guy? This is a respectable place, I don't want no shooting or nothin' like that around here," the sleazy, fat man whined when Luke located him. His cigarette dangled from the corner of his mouth, and he coughed and spat. Luke decided to keep right on jogging if this was what smoking looked like.

"I'm not police," Luke assured him. "I just want to talk with Mr. Palmer, and a mutual friend told me this is where he was staying." About fourteen mutual friends, Luke thought wearily, thinking of all the informants he'd courted in the past forty-eight hours, all the lunches and dinners and drinks he'd bought as bribes to try to find his man. Vancouver's underworld was a closed shop, and without the help of the street cops, he'd never have even come this far.

Luke slipped a twenty-dollar bill from his pocket and silently handed it over.

"Palmer's in 405," the fat man volunteered as the money disappeared. "But there's no use going banging on the door—he's out of town. Vegas, he said, but who knows? All those leftover singers'll tell you they're goin' to Vegas, as if anybody gives a damn. His stuff is here, and he's paid up for a week, so guess he'll be back before too long."

Another twenty passed from hand to hand.

"Call me and leave a message at this number when he shows up, and there'll be a fifty in it for you." After a moment's thought Luke scribbled his number on a scrap of paper. He wasn't home much, but he planned to invest in an answering machine that afternoon for the apartment telephone.

True to his plan, Luke bought the machine and then headed for the rental address he'd located in the phone book.

There was nothing to do about Palmer now except wait, and he had time for the experiment Graham Marshall had suggested. Dialing the number, he remembered Graham's words: "The reason you'll be invaluable as a counselor for victims of stress burnout is because you've experienced it, Luke. You've been there, and all the classes in the world won't give you what that personal experience teaches. Maybe it's hard to understand where Jessie's coming from because you've never really found out what it's like to live in a wheelchair."

Luke had frowned impatiently. "I've been with her, watched, wanted to help. As for experiencing disability, there's not a hell of a lot I can do about that, short of going out and breaking my back."

"There is if you've got guts enough to try it. You could always rent a wheelchair and commit yourself to two, three days of using it, no time off. That wouldn't come close to the real thing, but it's a damn sight better than nothing."

Hours later Luke unloaded the wheelchair and took it and the answering machine up in the elevator to his apartment. He hooked the machine up in five minutes and then spent forty more staring at the wheelchair. It was strangely frightening to finally sit down in the thing, knowing he wouldn't be using his legs for the next two days.

Two whole days. It seemed like an eternity as he tentatively rolled around the small rooms, bumping into furniture and accidentally pulling the electric kettle off the counter when the cord caught on a wheel. It crashed down on the tile, spilling water all over the floor and destroying the metal bottom.

Luke stared down at the mess. How did you wipe up water from a sitting position, anyhow? Clumsily he retrieved the long-handled mop and swabbed at it.

The kitchen sink forced him to stretch up uncomfortably high to wring the water from the sponge, and too late he realized all his dishes and glassware were now inaccessible in upper cabinets, along with the bread and most of his canned food and cereal.

He swatted at the high shelves with the mop handle and broke two plates and spilled the sugar.

Swearing, he stood up, angry with himself, and slammed a hurried assortment of foodstuffs on the table where he could reach them, then flopped back into the chair. Four minutes and he'd already broken his contract with himself by standing.

Well, that would be the last time. No matter what, he wouldn't stand again for anything. He glanced at his watch.

Forty-seven hours and fifty minutes of this left. And Jessie had done it for—he swiftly added it up. Ten years. With a lifetime left to go.

He'd honestly thought he understood.

The first thing that became evident was how much more time was required to do even the simplest things, like making a pot of coffee.

Mentally Luke listed the steps as he went along. *Empty the dregs—garbage bag full, needs to be taken downstairs. Tie top of the bag, prop it on knees—whew, it stinks like hell up this close—roll to the door. Forgot the apartment keys. Roll back, locate them, roll back to the door. Heave it open—that's harder to do sitting down—roll out. Ouch, skinned my knuckles on the doorjamb. Reach up to close the door and the garbage falls on hall rug. The bag splits.*

Luke stared down at the mess, stymied. A blue-haired matron got off the elevator, peered in disgust at him and the mess and hurried to a door far down the hall. At last Luke got his long-handled broom and the plastic container from the kitchen, swept the bottles and empty carton into it as best he could, glanced around to be sure he was alone and then scrubbed the coffee grounds into a larger area of the rug. What the hell did he pay a caretaker fee on this dump for, anyhow?

Back inside, he got a huge garbage bag this time, good and strong, and took it out to the elevator. He was too slow getting in, and the door closed on his chair, bumped open, then closed again. Eventually he got down to the basement dumpster, bumped his way out of the elevator and when it almost shut on him, he ended up feeling compacted.

The bin looked eight feet tall from where he sat. He lobbed the bag up and in, and unbelievably, his arms were starting to ache.

To hell with coffee, Luke decided. He'd go out for an early dinner. He took a shower, positioning a kitchen chair in the stall to sit on as Jessie had, then shot across the bathroom and rammed the far wall when he attempted his transfer before he remembered to set the brake.

Trying to wash thoroughly sitting down was a royal pain, and his skin was still wet when he finally, and with difficulty, dragged fresh clothes on. He concluded Jessie must be a lot more lithe than he was, too, when he tried to get his shoes on.

He was out the door before he thought about driving his car. He realized he'd have to call a cab and went back to the telephone.

"Sorry, sir, that will be about three-quarters of an hour. Our special cabs are all booked at the moment," the dispatcher announced.

In the lobby a bodybuilder Luke had talked to several times on the elevator glanced at him, did a double take and said as he edged past, "Hey, man, what happened? Slipped disk? Jeez, rotten luck, anything I can do, just holler." He edged away nervously, as if Luke had leprosy.

The cabdriver in the special taxi with the raised roof, which advertised itself as accommodating wheelchairs, showed him how to mount the movable platform in his chair and roll in and out without crashing to the sidewalk.

"Accident?" he inquired solicitously, and Luke nodded, a trifle grim.

"Motorcycle? Car?"

Luke sighed. "Flying." *By the seat of my pants,* he added silently.

"Guess you're lucky to be alive, then," Chatty Charlie observed. "Musta changed your life, though. Most people tell me it really changed their life for them." There was a pregnant pause, then he asked, "You married when it happened? How'd your old lady take it? She still around?"

It took a second before Luke realized he was probably being questioned about his sex life.

"She's in the hospital having our sixth kid," Luke drawled laconically and then felt mildly ashamed of himself.

The driver shot him a respectful glance in the rearview mirror. "That a fact," he said wonderingly. "Never changed things a bit, huh?"

"Not a bit," Luke assured him. They pulled to the curb before the driver had a chance to ask him to elaborate.

From the moment he rolled into the steak house, Luke felt as if every eye was on him. People stared, looked away and looked again, pity etched clearly on their faces.

"Such a shame, a good-looking man like that," he overheard a buxom woman whisper.

The busboy ostentatiously swept away a chair to make room for his wheels at a table, leaving Luke conspicuously seated in the aisle.

"Hello, dear, I'm Julia, your waitress this evening. Now any little thing I can do..." She treated him like a feeble-minded invalid. "Sure you can manage that, honey?" The woman offered to cut his steak. The salad bar was impossible to reach, but Luke vowed he's starve to death before he asked Julia to fill a plate for him. He had two double scotches in lieu of dessert and rolled thankfully out.

Everyone in the restaurant had stared, but out on the busy downtown Vancouver street Luke became invisible. It was because he was below eye level, Luke deduced at last. People all but tripped over him without saying a word or even seeming to see him. One other man rolled toward him through the sea of midriffs and pant legs, and when his tired gaze met Luke's, he smiled. His nod was one of comradeship, one alien being acknowledging another, both survivors in an alien land.

Seeing a phone booth ahead, Luke hurried toward it, only to find he couldn't reach the coin slot on the older style phone once he finally was able to cram his chair inside the booth. It was difficult to subdue the frustrated rage that unexpectedly boiled in white-hot fury inside him, but he choked it down and called as calmly as he could to a teenager pushing a bike.

"Could you please shove this quarter in for me after I dial?"

It was one of the hardest requests Luke had ever had to make because it involved such a ridiculously simple, everyday gesture, a thing he'd done countless times without a conscious thought.

No wonder Jessie hated asking for anything.

How many million other traps were out there waiting when you were on wheels?

There was one more, for certain. Luke found his chair was well and truly stuck in the damn booth when he tried to leave. He was sweating profusely by the time he extricated himself, and two young women were strolling back and forth watching the performance and listening to his colorful language with fascinated interest.

The cab came, and this time the driver was blessedly silent. Luke slunk back to the apartment, childishly grateful to shut the door after himself and turn on the TV to a football game. He hardly knew which team was which, however, because his mind was on Jessie.

He resisted turning the radio on. He knew if he heard her voice, he'd have to go to her, and he'd told her the next move was up to her.

He wanted the Palmer business over with, he needed to complete this experiment with the wheelchair, he had to give her time alone. He had to wait for her to reach a decision.

Jessie. How did she do it, how did she survive? How could she be so cheerful all the time? He'd watched her, smugly positive that he understood the difficulties she faced.

He found an old bottle of scotch, fortunately misplaced in a bottom cupboard, and drank a quarter of it.

He forgot the brake again at eleven-thirty when he groggily tried getting into bed, and the crash of his body hitting the floor brought a pounding on the wall from the apartment beside his. The chair had struck his night table and sent it toppling in a wild mass of books and broken glass.

"Hey, we're trying to sleep, we have to work in the morning!"

Without thinking, Luke scrambled to his feet and shouted a string of demented obscenities at the invisible protestor, pounding like a madman on the wall using both his fists.

Breathing hard, he finally stopped and listened to appalled silence. For God's sake, what was he doing? He knew these people, had borrowed coffee from them once.

With a groan of shame, feeling utterly defeated, Luke collapsed into bed.

He knew he'd be safe, for ten good hours. If he were a cowardly man, he'd stay right in this bed for the next day and a half.

Luke spent the next twenty minutes trying to pretend he really didn't have to get up again and visit the bathroom. Then at twelve-forty-five Lorna phoned.

"Luke, oh, Luke. Thank heaven you're home." Her voice bordered on hysteria, and Luke steeled himself for the worst. One of his nephews—it had to be. His heart hammered as if it were going to burst from his chest.

"You've got to go and get Denny. The manager of Murphy's Pub phoned me a few minutes ago. Denny's drunk and he's starting fights with everybody, and the manager doesn't want to call the police. He knows us because Denny did some landscaping for him." Lorna sniffed wetly into the receiver. "Oh, Luke, Denny's been acting awful all day. He didn't even come home after work, and I don't know what to do anymore." The forlorn litany ended on a sob, and Luke said soothingly, "Calm down, sis. I'll go get him, so stop worrying."

Denny was quite capable of taking care of himself in any brawl. In an effort to distract her, he said, "Wasn't today your big opening? How'd it go?"

"It was great, but I really missed you. Denny took time off work to come to my opening and then sat around with a long face. If it hadn't been for Jessie driving the kids home—"

"Jessie was there?" His voice sharpened.

"Yes, she certainly was. And Luke, I don't know for sure what's wrong between you two, but couldn't you give it another try? She's kind of...unique, I guess. I like her." There was a pregnant pause, and then Lorna added, "She's also strikingly beautiful. One of the radio men covering the opening sure thought so, too."

A welter of conflicting emotions raced through Luke, with jealousy winning out. He felt like strangling his sister to start with for her about-face concerning Jessie. Did any man ever begin to understand women?

He hung up, reassuring Lorna again about Denny, and started to swing his legs over the edge of the bed. Then he stopped short.

What now? Did he give up the wheelchair just because it wasn't convenient? It was utter insanity to go through the extra problems it entailed to use it.

He started up once more and paused. Jessie just couldn't change her mind and give it up. How many thousands of times each week would she choose not to use her chair if she only could?

"Commit yourself to a definite block of time," Graham had suggested, "and don't let anything interfere with that commitment. Otherwise, what you learn about Jessie isn't valid."

Luke called the cab first and then got dressed lying on the bed. He was getting better at it, better at planning every move before he made it.

Damn lucky thing he'd gone to the bank yesterday. Besides everything else, this being disabled was an expensive proposition when you had to take cabs everywhere, he reflected.

Murphy's Pub was in Gastown, the oldest part of Vancouver, which had been restored and promoted as the hub of downtown nightlife.

Luke rolled into the huge smoke-filled, noisy bar, which was part of a restored warehouse. He had no trouble at all locating Denny. His brother-in-law was the center of attention.

The volatile landscaper was being held down in a chair firmly, noisily and very much against his will by two large bouncers, and several others were restraining a struggling giant with muscles bulging from a checkered shirt.

"Lemme go, I'll kill him, you heard the little creep," the giant was saying in a rumbling voice to a frazzled older man in the midst of the melee, obviously the manager. "You can't throw me out and let this dago stay. I got rights, you heard what he said to me." He took several lurching steps toward Denny, dragging his retainers, hissing, "Ya little puke."

No one paid any attention to Luke. All eyes were on the action.

Luke shoved several chairs roughly aside to make room for his wheelchair and rolled close beside Denny.

"I'll talk to these guys, Den, but I want your word you'll come quietly with me," he murmured into his brother-in-law's ear.

Denny was drunker than Luke had ever seen him. He peered at Luke with bloodshot eyes that were obviously having trouble focusing. He frowned in a puzzled fashion and studied the wheelchair.

"That you, Luke? What ya doin' in that contraption, you kiddin' me? Luke?" His voice went from a wheedle to a snarl as he turned back to the bouncers, "Let go 'a me, you stupid clowns. This here's my friend, my family. Now take your filthy mitts offa me so's I can buy him a drink. For Pete's sake, what you doin' in that wheelchair, Luke?"

This extrication wasn't going to be easy. "I'll explain it all later, Den. Now let's just get you out of here. Before the cops come." He turned his attention to the bouncers, who were studying him curiously and paying no attention at all to Denny's renewed writhing.

"I think he'll be okay," Luke assured the two men. "Let him up, and I'll get him out of here."

Obligingly, they shrugged and let go. Denny brushed off his shirt in an aggrieved manner and started to get up with exaggerated dignity.

"Be a good little boy and let Daddy take you home now," taunted his adversary, and like a spring, Denny catapulted across the space separating them, roaring wordlessly, intent on mayhem.

Luke leaped up, dived for Denny and threw a professional headlock on him, dragging him, still bellowing, toward the exit. Remembering his wheelchair, he detoured while onlookers swiftly cleared out of his way, grabbing the chair with one hand and trying to shove it ahead of him with his foot. The chair wouldn't track straight. After the initial shock Denny quieted.

Luke shoved him roughly into the chair and held him down with an iron grip on his throat.

"Shut up, and stay put," Luke warned, and knocking several chairs out of his way, he wheeled Denny toward the door.

It wasn't exactly a dignified exit, but it was the best he could manage under the circumstances, Luke decided.

The patrons of Murphy's Pub cleared a wide and silent path for him, and Luke felt a little like Moses parting the Red Sea. The illusion was reinforced by one wide-eyed man who intoned breathlessly as they passed, "It's a healing. It's a miracle, he's been cured. Praise the Lord. It's a sign for all of us in these troubled times."

That sentiment was ruined by a cynic at his side who grunted, "I always said they could walk if they tried hard enough."

Walk was exactly what they did. Luke was so furious with Denny he insisted they march back to his apartment through the ocean-cool night air. Denny staggered and complained loudly at first, then retreated into an alley where Luke could hear him being noisily sick.

By the time they'd crossed the Burrard Street Bridge and covered twenty or so blocks, however, Denny was considerably more sober. He listened without commenting to Luke's explanation for the wheelchair, which by now Luke was occupying once more.

Denny walked beside his brother-in-law in silence for some time. Then he said morosely, "You know what, Luke? I hate this goddamn business Lorna's got herself into." They stopped at an intersection, waiting for the light to change, and there was reluctant pride in his voice when he went on, "You shoulda seen her today, talking on the radio, showing off her soup stocks on TV. I heard one guy asking her about his chances for a franchise operation. Can you believe it? She's only been open one day. She's gonna be a big success." His grimace under the yellow streetlight was intended as a laugh. "Hell, she'll probably earn more than I do this year."

"Is that it, Den? You just can't handle Lorna maybe earning more money than you?"

Denny shook his head after a minute of thought. "No, that's not what's got me going. We been together a long time, Lorna and me. We went together for must have been four years, and we been married eleven this November. Fifteen years, and in all that time, we never did things apart from each other, know what I'm saying? Even when she was working before, it was for us, to get enough to start the landscaping business. Then she ran the paper part of it, you remember. We were always working toward the same goal before."

There was a long pause while he gathered his thoughts.

"Now with this Soup Kitchen, it's got nothing to do with me. It's all hers."

They were heading through back streets now, close to the bay, taking short cuts down silent boulevards with the sound of the waves on English Bay sliding up on the sand and retreating.

"You may have worked together, but it was basically to attain your goal, Denny," Luke reminded. "Not Lorna's."

"The hell you say. It's our livelihood, it's what's earned us a good living for years." Denny was defensive.

"Sure, but it's still your business. Lorna helped, but now she wants to try a business of her own. And instead of helping her, like she did for you, you're being a real—" Luke swallowed the epithet. It wouldn't help a damn bit to call Denny names.

There was silence. Denny strode faster. Then he halted suddenly between one step and the next. "I'm scared, Luke. I'm scared spitless of losing her. I watched her today, she's one hell of a woman, good-looking, smart, capable. Give her six months, she'll go places. And then what will she see in a middle-aged Wop with dirt under his fingernails? So I get scared, see, and then I get mad. And then I get drunk."

"That's a great way to convince a woman you're irresistible, all right, Den." Luke's tone was sarcastic. "What happened to the big Italian lover routine, hotshot?"

"I talk too much, you know that. Hell, I looked in the mirror one morning, Luke, and you know I'm starting to go bald?" Silence again for half a block. "So what you figure I should do about this whole mess?"

Luke gave the wheelchair a vicious shove, almost steering it into a fountain. He couldn't even manage his own love life, for cripes' sake.

"Why don't you use that silver tongue of yours to talk the whole thing over with your wife honestly, the way you ought to have done months ago? Try telling her exactly what you've just told me, and see you don't leave out the good parts. And if I were you, I'd stop on the way home at some all-night market and buy them out of flowers." He eyed Denny dubiously in the bright glare of his apartment's lobby. "You'd better come up and phone her, then have a shower and borrow a shirt before you go home. You look like you've been in a fight."

"Yeah, thanks, Luke. You're a great guy, you know that?" Denny grasped the handholds on the wheelchair. "I'll shove you upstairs. Relax. This is some crazy experiment you got going here, huh? Putting yourself in the other guy's shoes probably ain't such a bad idea, now I think about it."

They were in the elevator when Denny said thoughtfully, "You know what else I think I'd better do before I head home?"

Luke shook his head. It was heaven just to sit in the wheelchair and have somebody push him around. Somehow he had to get Jessie to let him just push her sometimes.

"What else, Den?"

"I think I'd better try and remember just where the hell I left the company truck tonight. How much do those tow companies charge, anyway?"

CHAPTER FOURTEEN

JESSIE WAS SITTING on her patio, staring listlessly at the garden. August was ending, and the weather had been spectacular for several weeks, sunny and warm, but already there were traces of fall in the air. The lettuce in the raised vegetable bed was going to seed, and several ripe and juicy tomatoes had fallen from the overloaded vines.

Jessie couldn't have cared less. Gardening had lost its appeal.

Everything had, actually. She'd done her workout this morning, gone for a run and still had energy to spare when she was finished. The iron supplements were working amazingly well.

Why couldn't there be a pill for heartbreak? She felt lonelier than she'd ever felt in her life, and instead of lessening, her longing for Luke grew alarmingly with each hour that passed without him.

She heard the crunching of Cy's bike tires coming down the path at the side of the house, and in a moment he appeared, wearing an electrically gaudy Hawaiian shirt and Bermuda shorts that clashed dramatically with the shirt. He had a baseball cap on his head to keep off the sun. He was sweating freely, and he leaned the bike against the house and collapsed exhausted into a chair, tossing his cap to the tiles and stretching his legs out.

"Exercise is supposed to release endorphins, the internal opiates of the body, which produce relaxed euphoria. I have just ridden that infernal machine at top speed for what felt like eighty-seven miles, and all I feel is sore. Modern research leaves immense credibility gaps, if you ask me.'' He eyed Jessie's downcast face.

''Your endorphins aren't up to much either, huh? Who'd have ever dreamed that the two of us, clever and competent, would be wasting away because of unrequited love?'' Cy got to his feet, winced and said, ''I need a shower and a stint in that hot tub of yours. Join me for a soak, and then I'll take us out somewhere lavish for a farewell lunch.''

Cy was leaving the following week, to fulfill his dream of being one of the crew on a sailboat heading for Australia.

His phone was ringing urgently, and he squinted up at his open window, scowling. ''I'm not breaking a hip rushing up to answer that, either. It's probably Maryanne, upset about having a fight with her husband again.''

He winked at her lewdly in an attempt at his old spunk. ''After my body, as usual.''

The ringing stopped, and Jessie heard it begin again a few minutes later, but she decided that Cy must be in the shower. The phone rang repeatedly and stopped. He came down in his trunks, looking refreshed, and Jessie and he soaked in the hot tub for a half hour, not saying much.

Cy's phone rang twice more during that time, and he ignored it grandly.

They went out for a long, leisurely lunch at an open-air Greek Taverna on Broadway, and Jessie did her best to pretend she was having fun and not thinking of Luke, and she suspected Cy did exactly the same about Amanda. He talked enthusiastically about the boat he'd be on, the other members of the crew, the amount of time it would take to get to Australia, but he didn't once mention his lady.

They didn't get back until after five that afternoon because Cy insisted they go to an afternoon matinee.

Once again Cy's phone was ringing when they opened the front door, and with a martyred sigh he slowly climbed the steps, and Jessie heard him answer it.

"Jessie." His bellow brought her quickly from her bedroom moments later, and she gaped in amazement as Cy all but tumbled down the stairs toward her, hair on end and eyes shining.

"That was Amanda on the line. She's in the hospital in Athens—she's fallen and broken her wrist. I'm going to try and get a flight out this evening. I told her I'd be there as fast as I could."

"But, Cy, what about your trip to Australia? You'll have to give up your berth on the sailboat."

He was totally unconcerned.

"I'll cancel it. Australia will wait. Amanda probably won't."

Through some mysterious network of female travel agents he'd met, Cy secured a seat on a flight leaving at eight that evening, and Jessie drove him out to the airport on her way to work.

"I don't think I've ever seen you in a suit, Cy," she commented, feeling oddly shy with the smartly dressed, distinguished image he presented in his silver-gray finery.

"I'm planning on marrying Amanda within an hour of getting off the plane," he said firmly. "I proposed over the phone, she accepted, and I promptly phoned the hospital back and got them to arrange for a justice of the peace, so I thought I'd dress for the occasion at this end. She'll still be fuzzy from the anesthetic. There's no point in letting her think anything over."

She pulled into the unloading zone for foreign departures, and Cy wrapped his arms around Jessie, giving her a long, unhurried hug while car horns protested behind them.

"Go phone that man of yours, Jess, and tell him how much you're missing him. If he's still not home, he's probably got an answering machine. Life's far too short to waste time on indecision."

Jessie drove back into the city thoughtfully. She'd spent the past weeks proving to herself that she could manage perfectly well alone, just as she had for years, and yet her sense of well-being was nonexistent.

Undoubtedly Amanda was also a woman who could take perfectly good care of herself, by herself, Jessie suddenly realized. A woman who'd traveled the world alone for years wasn't about to be demoralized by a simple broken wrist, and yet Cy was this moment speeding to her side, certain that she needed him. And actually, Jessie mused wryly, she must or she'd never have been so persistent about phoning.

Dependence.

There were so many faces to dependence. She remembered the blazing pride on Cy's face when he said, "Amanda needs me."

Jessie had never considered before that by accepting help occasionally a person permitted others to feel good.

Didn't she feel good herself when she was needed?

Hadn't she felt full of pride when Luke admitted that talking things over with her helped him resolve them?

And what about all the calls that came in to "Heart Line?" All those people wanted to help, they needed to share what they'd learned with someone else. And the ones who wrote in with problems—was their need less than her own because their problems weren't physical?

Jessie was still mulling the problem over when she found a parking space near the station and rolled into work her usual forty-five minutes ahead of airtime.

She waved to the announcer in the control room and checked the message bunk. There were two invitations to

attend new restaurant openings and one to participate in the
Squamish Lumberman's Festival. In an axe-throwing contest? she thought, almost laughing out loud.

Swiftly she tucked the notes into her pocket and concentrated intently on getting set up.

Would she ever be able to get through one single hour
without automatically thinking of Luke? Quite suddenly she
decided that before the night was over, she'd phone him.
And if Luke were out, she'd leave a message on his machine.

A simple message, after all.

Should she say, "I love you, I need you? I'm ready to
trust you implicitly and accept your help when necessary
and even sometimes when it's not?" The idea was scary, but
the decision lifted a little of the heavy weight inside her, gave
the evening ahead a goal and a purpose. She'd tell him how
she felt and then leave all the rest up to him. If he'd thought
over what he was letting himself in for and changed his
mind, she'd just have to find the strength to accept that.

But, oh, she hoped he hadn't.

She popped her head into the newsroom. Barry was sitting with his back toward her, his head propped in his hands
on the narrow slice of desk not covered with machinery and
paper and coffee cups.

"You asleep in here?" she queried brightly, and he turned
and gave her a wan smile.

"Hi, Jess. I feel as if I ought to be sleeping, all right. My
head's splitting. I must have picked up a flu bug. This shift
can't go too fast for me."

He did look rough. "You want some coffee, or water, or
anything?" she inquired sympathetically, but he shook his
head no.

"My stomach's not so hot."

"If it gets too bad, let me know. You can tape the weather report for me and leave early, and I'll do the news for once."

"Thanks, Jess. I might just take you up on that."

She rolled into the control booth, and moments later began her show.

"Evening, everybody. It's a glorious summer night out there, and this is Jessie with 'Night Shift.' If you're tuning in from the beach, or just from your own backyard, take a look at that sunset sky. Spectacular, isn't it?"

Tonight she could sound cheerful and bright without feeling as if she deserved an Oscar for the effort it took.

The early announcer waved goodbye at her, and she waved back through the glass. The station emptied as it always did after the bustle of daytime, and an hour into her show, Barry came into the cubicle.

"I'm feeling rotten, Jess. Here's a tape with the weather update. I phoned for a replacement, but it'll take a while for him to get here. I'll let the janitor know so he can let him in."

Ten minutes later, before the "Heart Line" lead-in, Jessie mustered her courage and rang Luke's number. It rang three times, and then his recorded voice asked for a message, and her heart sank. Damn you, Luke, where are you hiding these days?

Disappointment at not being able to talk to him in person overwhelmed her at first, but she made up her mind that she wouldn't just hang up. She'd leave a message, ask boldly and rawly for what she desperately needed this once in her life.

The beep came, and she shut her eyes tightly. "Luke, it's me, Jessie. I phoned to say I love you, I—"

The control room door opened softly behind her. She turned with a frown, annoyed at the interruption, and everything in her seemed to freeze.

Wayne Palmer had entered the glass-enclosed booth and shut the door softly behind him. His eyes were bloodshot, his smile cunning. His unsteady movements and flushed face indicated that he'd been drinking, and what shocked Jessie into numb terror was the hunting knife with an evil-looking six-inch blade held almost casually in his right hand.

"Hi, Jessie. Remember me? Quiet in here at night, isn't it?" His speech was slurred. "I saw your friend leave a while ago, and I checked every last one of these cubbyhole rooms. Not another soul around, you know that?"

Her shock and then the quick, immobilizing terror he inspired in her made her throat nearly close.

"Wayne. What are you doing...how did you..."

He crossed the narrow distance between them and took the telephone receiver from her nerveless hand, pressed it to his ear for a moment and listened. Then he shrugged and hung it up, making two attempts at cradling the receiver properly before he managed.

"You musta scared him off, sweetie, telling him you loved him that way. He's gone and hung up on you."

She couldn't seem to get enough breath into her lungs. From the corner of her eye, she saw the light flash, indicating the song she was playing was nearly over and it was time to go back on the air.

Wayne was smiling, an evil, taunting smile. He gestured at the light, raising his eyebrows at her teasingly, and she saw that he was getting pleasure from frightening her. He had power over her, and he was enjoying it. The realization made her angry, made her struggle harder to control her outward signs of fear, but inside she had to fight the whirling dizziness that filled her. Had he come here to kill her? Against her will her eyes went to the knife.

"Better change that tape, Jess. Just put on continuous music for a while. Nobody will know the difference. You and me need to talk some."

With fingers that trembled she changed the cassette. Would anyone notice the absence of conversation between medleys and think it strange? In four minutes she was due to lead in for "Heart Line." Surely someone would suspect something then—wouldn't they?

"How...how did you get in here, Wayne?" Her voice was calm, but she still hardly recognized its thin, wobbly tone. If she kept him talking, if Barry's relief turned up, if...

Shudders ran uncontrollably over her. Too many ifs, and most of them unlikely. Or simply too late.

"The janitor was just leaving for his lunch break. Real nice old guy. He said something about me being the relief man and I nodded, and that was it."

Luke's lecture about careless security at the station came back to her. He'd been right, she saw that now. Luke. He was right about so many things....

"What do you want from me, Wayne? Money, is that it?"

He laughed, and the mirthless sound was horrible, filling the small room. Jessie felt again as if she didn't have enough oxygen. She was almost panting. She tried to control her erratic breathing, gain some semblance of control over her emotions.

"You figure you can just give me money, and I'll take it and go away, don't you, Jess? People like you think money will buy anything." He came closer to where she sat, and she felt herself shrinking away from him, trying desperately not to breathe in the foul odor of his whiskey breath, smell the dank sweat on his body. He still had the twisted smile on his face, the crooked facsimile of the grin she'd fallen in love with so long ago.

He held the knife up and brought it close to her throat in a sly, experimental kind of fashion. She heard herself utter a tiny, thin squeak of fear, and he laughed.

"Money's not enough anymore, rich girl. When I needed it, your snooty family wouldn't give me a cent. If I'd never met you, Jess, I'd be a star today, you know that? I'd be famous, have my own TV show maybe." He shook his head sadly. "Instead nobody who was anybody would hire me for years after that crash. All over the papers, right across the country, that headline: Country-and-Western Singer Palmer Cripples Prima Ballerina While Driving Impaired. And big pictures of you in that skimpy little costume, taking your sweet little bows after a performance. And right beside them ones of me, Jess. Being led away by the cops from the scene, blubbering and ugly, getting shoved into a police car." His voice had become progressively louder, and he was almost shouting. He glared at her furiously, breathing as hard as she had been seconds before. It took long moments before he calmed slightly. "Doesn't do much for a guy's professional image, you know?"

He was sweating. Huge drops of perspiration rolled down his forehead and off his chin. He rubbed his face clumsily with the hand not holding the knife, and he gestured toward the cassette player.

"Hot in here, isn't it? How long to go on that thing? Don't want to have people wondering where their favorite nighttime disc jockey is, now, do we? So fix it up with plenty of music, Jessie. And don't try calling for help over the air. Nobody could make it here in time, anyway, you know that." She hesitated, and like a snake he slithered closer, running the blade along the back of one of her hands this time, leaving a thin red line and making her gasp aloud with utter mindless panic.

She fumbled with the discs. *The weather report, I can't do "Heart Line."* Almost panicking, Jessie stacked the ones she'd played earlier. She'd play them again, the same songs over and over. *Please, someone. Anyone out there—notice. Wonder. Please, oh, please, call the police, you people waiting to help.*

Help me.

The telephone lines were blinking madly.

"I...I have to answer them," she stammered, "they'll wonder..."

Wayne shook his head warningly. "Music, Jess. No telephones. I do the talkin' around here now. Say, you got any of my singles around? This'd be a really fine time to play them, you know. How about it? Play some good music on this show for a change."

"They're not in here. They're down the hall in the record library." Maybe out in the corridor, she'd have more of a chance. Surely the janitor would be back before too much longer. He'd notice—but would he? Her heart sank. The careless old man seldom came near the announcers' booths.

"Well, get them, you hear me? I want my songs playing for us, Jessie. My music."

"In the library, just down the hall," she repeated.

He studied her closely and then seemed to decide it was the truth. He pulled the door open and gestured her through in a hideous parody of courtesy, stumbling a little.

As she rolled swiftly past him, he grabbed the back of her chair. "Not so fast, Jess. Wouldn't want to lose me in this place, would you? We'll go together."

Jessie stifled the overwhelming urge to scream and fight with him, to end it any way at all. Just to end it.

Luke, she pleaded wordlessly. *My love, if ever I needed you, I need you now.*

LUKE NOTICED THE LIGHT flashing on his machine the moment he entered the apartment. There'd been no messages when he'd awakened late that morning. He'd gone for a run, marveling at the power in his legs, at the joy of movement. He'd never noticed before the wheelchair experiment how good it felt to move one leg after the other, to feel the muscles responding smoothly.

The hours in the chair had taught him many things. Using it, the simplest of tasks was on a par with running two marathons, back-to-back. The entire world was designed for giants with working legs, he'd concluded long before he returned the chair to the rental agency.

He strode across to the machine and punched the buttons that would replay his messages.

Cy's was the first.

"Sorry to let you down this way, but I won't be able to keep an eye on Jess after six o'clock today. I'm flying to Greece to marry Amanda. Jessie's missing you, Luke. See you when I get back."

The second message brought Luke to attention.

"The party you was wanting to talk to is back in town, came back late Thursday night. Hope you remember our deal, mister."

Luke hurried into the bedroom and hastily grabbed his car keys and a jacket. He was striding toward the door when the next message began to play, and he stopped between one step and the next.

"...Jessie. I phoned to say I love you, I—"

Jessie. His heart seemed to constrict, just hearing her musical voice saying the words he longed to hear. With luck he could put the fear of God into Palmer and then be there when she finished work. He hurried toward the door, forgetting the machine, yanked it open, and then the next words on the tape hit him like a blow to the stomach.

"Remember me? Quiet in here at night, isn't it? I saw your friend—"

The tape ended. He wasn't aware of crossing the room to punch the replay button. Breathing as if he'd run miles, he concentrated as the message played again, listening as hard as he could for background noises. Where had Jessie been calling from?

He heard soft music, then the whoosh of what could have been a hydraulic door closing an instant before the man's voice began.

She was at the station. He listened again. His eyes flew to the clock. It was nearly ten. God, how long ago had that call been made? Luke felt as if he were crawling in slow motion through a nightmare.

He knew the voice had to be Palmer's because of the slurred speech and the sly undertones. Then there was that heartrending soft gasp of fright from Jessie, the fearful sound that had first caught his attention.

Fear, sharp and copper tasting, filled his throat as he dialed the general investigation section, cursing under his breath as the phone rang and rang twice more. He almost bellowed when a man's voice growled, "General Investigations, Conahan here."

Luke identified himself. "I need to speak to Sergeant Frank Mahoney, it's urgent. Can you contact him and get him to call me at—"

"I remember you from the other day, Chadwick. Frank's working tonight, he's over at the Ovaltine Café having coffee. Here's the number."

Feeling as if he were swimming in a sea of molasses, Luke finally convinced the Chinese waiter at the Ovaltine to call Frank to the phone.

"It's Luke," he said tersely when the questioning male voice finally answered. "Frank, I've got a hell of a problem and I need your help. You remember Palmer? I've got good reason to believe he's holding my woman hostage at the radio station on Fourth.''

When Luke drove his car onto Fourth Avenue, abandoning it more or less at the curb a half block from the station, an unmarked car and two police cruisers were already there, roof lights flashing. Another car screeched to a halt as Luke sprinted toward the scene. Frank hadn't lost any time.

WAYNE SAW THE flashing lights reflecting from the front reception area as they left the record library, and he cursed viciously, slamming Jessie's chair against one side of the narrow corridor in frustration, then dragging it along as he inched forward in an effort to see out the wide front window.

"Cops," he confirmed, his voice a thin, frightened snarl. He flipped all the light switches off. The only illumination in the room now was the streetlight outside the building and the eerie blue-shadowed flash from the police cars. Wayne struggled to pull a heavy desk over to barricade the doorway, but he couldn't budge it. He abandoned the effort and all but leaped at Jessie, catching her neck under his arm and brandishing the knife not four inches from her face in a hand that visibly shook.

"How'd you notify the cops, bitch? Tell me, just tell me. How'd you get the cops here so fast?"

"Please, Wayne, I didn't. Please..." Jessie could hear herself begging, but she felt as if she were a long distance away. Mist seemed to swirl in her head, and she thought gratefully that she was fainting, that it would all be over soon. She willed the fog to envelop her, to help her sink into oblivion quickly, easily.

And then, out of nowhere Luke was there in her mind.

She could see his face, feel the searing intensity of his blue eyes.

Trust me, Jess, he was telling her silently, over and over again. *If you love me, trust me. Believe in me.*

For an interminable instant she resisted. It was terribly hard, what he asked of her.

It meant trusting in the intangible. It meant believing in happy endings. It meant finding a way to stay alive a little longer, with the certainty that Luke could come for her.

She loved him that much. She'd try.

It really wasn't all that hard to commit herself.

"Wayne," she said, and her voice was low and cajoling instead of terrified, "there's a lock on the door of the control room. It's safe in there. They can't get in, anyway, you locked the entrance door from the inside, remember? Let's go put your tape on. You'll be able to think better listening to it. And everyone else will get to hear it, too."

"WHAT'S TAKING SO LONG?" Luke knew now why the relatives of hostages came close to insanity during negotiation. After the first dramatic arrival of police, everything seemed to just stop. It appeared as though nothing was being attempted or resolved, and it was enough to drive the bystander berserk.

Frank Mahoney gave Luke a long, curious look. "The mobile telephone unit will be along directly, and we'll try to make contact. You know the routine better than anyone, Chadwick." He held a portable radio tuned to "Night Shift," and the uninterrupted stream of popular ballads seemed incongruous in this atmosphere of charged tension. Curious people from neighboring apartments were beginning to collect, and their voices carried through the night, loud and excited, although the street was now barricaded at either end.

Luke did know the routine, remembered it, in fact, as if he'd done negotiations yesterday instead of years before.

It was the knowledge that it was Jessie inside, Jessie's life that was in danger, that appalled Luke, horrified him, paralyzed his reasoning ability. He could barely restrain himself from rushing forward, smashing the door in, roaring like a demented maddened animal through the building until...

Only he knew that when he reached her, it would already be too late.

Mahoney was talking to him.

"Lucky thing you're here, Chadwick. It would take us an extra hour to locate one of the guys trained for this and get him over here."

It took long seconds for his meaning to sift into Luke's consciousness, and then his heartbeat increased until he thought his chest would explode.

"But you know I'm out of the force," he began.

Frank shrugged. "In or out, I remember you were the best around at this sort of thing. This one's probably just a false alarm, anyhow. This Palmer's a small-time troublemaker, not a political activist. Still we can't afford to take any chances. The guys out in Surrey took a chance and rushed a house two months back, same scene as this, thinking the guy was harmless, and the woman and kid got shot. Andy's never been back to work since, you remember Sergeant Andy Sloane? He was the officer in charge, friend of mine, you must remember him, too, Luke. I don't want one of those on my conscience."

Luke could feel himself tearing in two, the old, carefully healed scars ripping open inside to allow the ugly blood of indecision, of guilt, of inadequacy, of failure and shame to gush out.

He couldn't do this, didn't this man understand that? He'd vowed never to attempt this again, this carefully orchestrated dance that could end in death, that had ended in death.

This time it would be Jessie's death, and with it the death of all that had meaning in Luke's heart.

If he failed.

When he failed.

It was too much to ask of him ... wasn't it?

"Here it comes now." The van with its intricate electronic equipment rolled quietly to a stop. The double doors on the side slid open to reveal two men wearing headsets working calmly at a board in the rear.

"We're trying all the incoming lines the station has, ringing them in sequence to see if we get an answer anywhere," one of them explained. "There're four lines into the control room. They're the most likely, so we're trying them constantly."

Without warning there was an ominous silence, dead air on "Night Shift's" radio band, and Luke stopped breathing. It went on and on, and then a new ballad began abruptly, a male singer crooning a song of love and betrayal. Almost simultaneously the technician lifted a warning arm.

"Contact," he said briefly. And at a frantic signal from the officer in charge, he handed the headset to Luke. "Male," he whispered.

There was nothing for Luke to do but accept the phone. As if in slow motion, he reached for it. And into his tormented brain came the image of a pockmarked, gray and lonely landscape far from earth and a young, exquisitely lovely woman who convinced herself that all things were possible.

Jessie.

Surely if she were brave enough for moon-dancing, he could be, too.

The receiver was at his ear, and a cool, deliberate self-assurance flooded over him, a sensation he'd lost and thought never to regain.

Confidence was returning. And belief in his ability, in himself and his training and his wits.

His voice was strong, and his love for Jessie filled him, fortifying him.

He could do this for her.

He initiated the first stylized movements of the opening duet.

CHAPTER FIFTEEN

THE CONSTANT, RELENTLESS flashing of the phone lines irritated Wayne, and he waved at them angrily.

"Why don't they just give up? It's the cops, anyhow, I know it is."

"Do you want me to answer, Wayne?" Jessie asked reasonably.

"You just keep away from that phone, you hear me? Any talking that's done here, I do it. This isn't your show anymore, Jessie, you do what I say now." For all the tough talk, Jessie could see indecision flicker over his face. Part of him wanted to answer, wanted the importance of letting people know he had power.

Jessie assessed both him and her situation.

Wayne was a performer with an ego that demanded feeding. She was sure he wouldn't be able to resist a larger audience for long, and she was right. When the telephone kept insistently blinking, he finally reached for it, a mixture of apprehension and cockiness in his expression.

"Yeah?" he barked into the receiver. "Who's this, anyhow?" The knife was still close to her, and Wayne's foul smell pervaded the cramped studio. But the moment he spoke to whoever was on the line, Jessie felt an easing within her.

There was another person involved now, and it had to be someone from the police, someone who knew what to do, who would try to help. The realization that she wasn't in this entirely alone any longer brought the sting of tears to her eyes.

Wayne inclined his head to the side, squinting his eyes at her, moving the knife in a menacing arc back and forth in front of her, but his next words made Jessie forget the knife, the danger, the precariousness of her situation. A light went on inside her, a blinding, beautiful illumination, and she struggled to keep it from reflecting on her features.

"Luke, huh?" Wayne sneered. "Well, Luke, baby, what you callin' me for? I've got nothin' to say to you."

OUTSIDE, LUKE DELIBERATELY blocked out all thoughts of Jessie, the terror he felt for her and, most of all, his murderous rage against the man whose voice now echoed in his ear.

This was a job, a delicate, tricky performance that sent the adrenaline coursing through his veins. Once the action had begun, there was no room for hesitation. The dance must proceed to the final curtain.

Luke became an actor, assuming his role, becoming the negotiator. Confidence filled him. He was good at this. He would win.

His tone was soothing, his speech slow and deliberate. His goal was to calm, to stall for time, to force sobriety, hunger and tiredness on the deranged man inside. Time was a potent weapon in Luke's favor. Wayne's mood would change, his reasons would blur, the liquor in his system aggravating his rage would oxidize, Luke reminded himself.

"I'm a representative of the Vancouver City Police," Luke identified in a nonaggressive way. Pleasantly he added, "Who am I talking to?"

Wayne's answer would reveal whether or not Jessie had given away her relationship with Luke, and the rest of the action he took depended on that. Luke prayed she hadn't, and Wayne's answer confirmed it.

"Just call me Wayne."

The sergeant handed Luke a hastily scribbled note, and Luke nodded, matching the voice tones in his ear with the western singer Jessie was playing over and over on "Night Shift."

"Your voice sounds just like the tape I'm hearing on the radio. You wouldn't be Wayne Palmer, the country-and-western singer, would you?"

"You heard of me, huh?" The drunken slurring of the words told Luke that Wayne still had a dangerous amount of liquor in his system.

"Sure, I was a big fan of yours." Would flattery work?

"That's me, all right. The late great Wayne Palmer." Self-pity and anger. It was time to get down to basics, find out what there was to bargain with.

Conspiratorially Luke said, "What's going down here, Wayne? You feel like talking about it?"

"Talk about it? Why the hell should I talk about it?" The words rose to a near scream, and Luke felt drops of apprehensive sweat form on his head and roll down his face.

Danger, danger. What weapons did he have?

"This is private, you hear?" Wayne was shrieking into his ear. "Between me and my wife. She used to be my wife, anyhow." Viciousness oozed from the phone. "We nearly died together once before, you know. This time—don't you try anything, cop. This time, Jessie and I are going out together. Don't try and rush me, I can stab her five times before you get anywhere near."

Dismissing his panic and loathing, Luke concentrated only on information. So Palmer had a knife, at least. The conversation was on a speaker phone now, and Frank nodded at Luke.

Ever so soothingly Luke cajoled, "Take it easy there, Wayne, let's just be calm. It's a hot night out here. You hot in there? Is there anything you need? What do you want, Wayne? Why don't you come out into the reception area? It's cooler there, we could talk comfortably."

"The action's in here, wise guy. I want forty ounces of the best scotch around, and I'm not coming out. I call the shots here, remember?"

Give nothing harmful, no booze, no drugs.

Luke sounded regretful. "No, Wayne, sorry. If you want booze, you'll have to come into the reception area and talk to me there."

Time. Time is on our side, Luke reminded himself again. Soon now he'll start to sober up, grow more rational. Won't he?

Bargain. Luke forced a note of concern into his query. "How you fixed for other things, there, Wayne? You comfortable, you need coffee, or something to eat maybe?"

Wayne snarled back at him, menace in his ugly voice. "You get me a bottle of scotch, or so help me, I'll end this whole thing." A sound came over the line that made Luke's insides cringe, made him long for an instant alone with this animal, for the chance to kill Palmer with his bare hands.

There was a low gasp of fear and Jessie's voice pleading, "No, Wayne, please don't..."

What was happening? What was that animal...? Luke was sweating copiously, although the air was cooling as the evening darkened. He was shaking again, and nausea rose to choke him. Steadfastly he willed himself not to feel.

Play for time, bargain. Don't think of what he might be doing to her.

It was horrible to have to say gently, "Sorry, Wayne, no trading until we get Jessie back."

A string of oaths, and then with awful finality the line went dead in Luke's ear. He looked around, dazed. He'd forgotten the presence of all these policemen.

"The SWAT team's arrived, Luke." Frank had relinquished command of the operation the instant Luke had agreed to negotiation. From here on, Luke was in full charge.

"You want them to try to get in the back?"

Luke thought carefully and shook his head. "Not yet. She's still okay. He's only threatening. I've seen the back of the building. There's no way in. We won't try it just yet, not unless..."

He didn't have to finish. Frank knew he meant not unless Jessie was hurt. Or dead.

THE CLOCK ON THE WALL seemed to stand still, and the knife felt as if it were slicing into her throat.

Jessie flattened her body against the back of the chair. She was beyond fear, frightened too much and too long now to react each time a new crisis arose. The phone went crashing down, and Wayne cursed in a steady monotone. When he seemed calmer, Jessie began to talk. She talked as she'd never talked before, coaxing, flattering, working on the goal of getting Wayne to leave the station, using every subtle facet of his character she could remember to convince him.

"They'll give you a car, Wayne, and you can leave. My checkbook's here in my purse. I'll write you a check for all I have, and there's some cash and gas in the van."

At first he spilled out vitriol at her, screamed for her to shut up, but she could see him growing more uncertain, more sober, as time passed.

The phones had started their remorseless signal an instant after he hung up. They flashed and flashed in endless beckoning. Wayne grew less certain, more undecided, as the endless moments lengthened.

"You got wheels?" he demanded suddenly. Jessie nodded. "A van, with hand controls, parked just up the street from here. But it's hard to drive it unless you're—" She stopped and felt the tension in her body ease slightly when he turned away.

He'd snatched up the phone again.

"Okay, you, I want Jessie's van up on the sidewalk by the door, running with both doors open. She's going to drive us away from here, and you know what'll happen if you touch me. Now you listen good. You get all those cop cars off this street, everybody way back. No tricks, or I use this knife on her, understand me?"

Even as the words were broadcast, Luke's brain was forming a plan, coldly and methodically, while he agreed. "We'll do that for you, Wayne. What about keys? Are the keys in the van?"

Luke knew the van's interior. There was a space behind the seats.

Hearing Jessie's voice answering Wayne was almost Luke's undoing. The ragged edges to the husky tones signaled clearly to him of fear she was doing her best to subdue.

He steeled himself, forcing impassivity, forcing his mind to the task and nothing else.

He heard Wayne's voice again. "She says there's a spare set hidden under the back bumper. Ten minutes, and we're coming out. No tricks, or she's dead."

The connection broke, and Luke ordered curtly, "I want the smallest guy on the SWAT team, completely in black, hidden behind the back seat in the van. No weapons." It was too risky with Jessie near. For an awful moment he considered exactly how risky it was, and he shuddered.

"The wheelchair lift on that van is slow. There'll be a minute when she's halfway up when Palmer will be farthest away from her—hopefully inside while she's still out." Luke squinted up at the streetlight near the front doorway.

"Get the power on those streetlights reduced fast before he gets out here. Frank, you and I will be there." He motioned at a narrow black space between the buildings, gauging how many steps it would take to cross the sidewalk. Four, five maybe?

Timing. Milliseconds. Luck.

Luke prayed silently, passionately.

Six minutes.

Four.

There was frantic activity as cars pulled away, and policemen took up vantage points wherever they could. A wiry, short shadow totally in black, face darkened, appeared at Luke's side, and together they set off at a run for Jessie's van.

Luke maneuvered the van into place, positioning it as far as he dared from the door, leaving it running as he stepped out to take his place in the shadowed space to the right of the entrance.

The streetlights suddenly dimmed to half power.

There was utter silence. Luke's brain raced. Had he done enough? Too much? What were the chances?

Nothing happened, for what seemed like hours, and then the front door of the station opened enough to allow a wheelchair to be shoved roughly through. The wild-eyed man behind it pushed with one hand, loping unsteadily, holding a glinting knife far too near Jessie's slender throat with the other.

Luke's fists clenched, and every muscle hurt with the effort of being still. He caught a glimpse of her pale hair, gleaming in the darkness, and he imagined her eyes, wide and brimming with horror.

She rolled onto the lift, activated the mechanism. Wayne hovered nervously nearby. He obviously hadn't given much thought to how she'd get in because he hesitated, and Luke held his breath.

Then it was over between one instant and the next. Jessie's chair rose slowly, Wayne clumsily put one foot up, reaching for the frame to pull himself inside, and a lethal black hurricane hit him like a projectile, knocking him flat on the cement, sending his knife flying through the air to land with a splintering crash on the cement, and policemen were instantly everywhere.

Luke never remembered exactly how Jessie came to be in his arms. He knew only that he had the sweet weight of her clamped against him and that tears were running unashamedly from his eyes and from hers. She was trembling so violently that it frightened him, and he demanded roughly, "Are you hurt? If he hurt you, I'll kill him." She shook her head, struggling for control, arms locked around his neck. He sat down, cradling her on his knees, allowing the sweet night air to cleanse them both, aware of the moon high above the buildings.

"Nice work, Luke." Frank grinned down at them, shook his head and said, "I'll call you tomorrow. There's still as much paper to fill in as there ever was, and I'll need you for it." He gave Luke a half salute and was gone.

A dog barked, and more police arrived and drove off. Time passed. Onlookers wandered home, talking in high tones and laughing from the excitement of the experience.

A car drew hastily up to the curb, and two relief announcers went bounding into the station. CKCQ would be back on the airwaves in a few minutes.

Luke savored every instant, knowing he would remember in minute detail as long as he lived the feel of Jessie's slight body, safe, trustfully resting on his knees, and the taste of her salty tears like nectar on his lips each time he kissed her.

"I'll get your chair for you," he promised after a long while, knowing how she hated to be separated from it, helpless in this way. But he waited, not quite able to release her yet.

Her arms tightened around his neck. "I don't want my chair just yet. There's something else I need."

"Anything, Jess. Just tell me, I'll see you get it."

She drew her breath in slowly and tilted her head up to where the moon seemed to race across the sky. When she expelled her breath, she said softly and all at once, "I need you to marry me, Luke."

She felt the hard chest supporting her body become absolutely still, and a new fear took the place of the night's terror. What if . . . ?

But then, as casually as if she'd asked for a drink of water, he said, "You got it. But it better be soon, lady. It took you an awfully long time to get around to asking."

It also took a long time after they returned to Jessie's house to talk through the nightmare events of the past hours. It was necessary to review every detail before they were finally able to discard the horror, store it in its rightful place in the past as something evil, shared and over.

"What will happen to him, Luke?"

They were in Jessie's bed, and the savageness of their first loving had left them spent, floating in exhausted peace, their bodies linked.

Luke moved restlessly, a blazing anger rising and then retreating. It was still hard to separate what he'd like to have happen to Palmer from the probable course the law would have to follow.

"He'll get a thirty-day psychiatric remand to see if he's fit to stand trial, then at least a couple years behind bars."

"In a strange way, I feel sorry for him. That accident long ago left him far more crippled than it left me."

Jessie forgave more easily than Luke could. He wanted to curse Palmer, tear him apart with his bare hands for all the scars he'd caused Jessie, both old and recent.

"I haven't thanked you, either," she added softly. "For being there, for being strong when I needed you. It's taken me so long to learn about weakness and strength between two people. It's the sharing that really matters, isn't it, Luke?"

He nodded. "I'll make plenty of mistakes, but I'll always be there for you, Jessie."

Maybe he owed Palmer something, after all, Luke mused thoughtfully. His old confidence in himself had been restored tonight, and a deep, self-doubting wound had been healed at last.

He felt her fingers roam down his chest, and her lips followed, igniting a tempestuous blaze where Luke would have sworn there were only exhausted embers.

She touched him intimately, and his blood pounded in his loins, in every inch of his body. He groaned and tumbled her beneath him, reveling in the instant response her mouth afforded when he claimed it. The intensity increased, and a wildness drove him.

His mouth demanded and then withdrew, plundering her throat, her shoulders, the bend of her elbow, the racing pulse at the nape of her neck, returning over and over to her breasts and the engorged nipples that pulsed and throbbed between his lips until her cry rose and rose and his control was gone. He drove himself into her soft, wet heat, and the world shattered and reformed with love at its center.

LUKE KISSED JESSIE awake far too early the next forenoon and determinedly drove them to city hall for a marriage license. He would happily have whisked her off to a justice of the peace immediately afterward, except that she grew stubborn and insisted on having a lovely, small, intimate wedding.

"I'm only doing this once, Luke. I want pictures of us cutting a cake to show our kids someday."

The argument was taking place in the parking lot at city hall. He thought it over and finally agreed, but reluctantly.

"Okay, have it any way you want, but make it quick," he insisted.

Jessie laughed, the happy bubbling laughter that Luke adored, twisting her chair so that she blocked his way, her face tilted beguilingly up to his, her hazel eyes dancing.

"You sound as if there's a shotgun held at your head," she teased. Looking around to be sure they wouldn't be overheard, she hissed, "I'm not even pregnant."

That was a mistake. Grabbing her chair, Luke whisked her into a shaded corner under some trees and scooped her, giggling helplessly, out of the chair and into his arms, raining enthusiastic kisses randomly over her face.

"We'll fix that right now," he growled, ignoring the amused attention of city employees strolling back to work.

During the next two weeks Jessie wished heartily that she'd agreed to the justice of the peace routine as the entire wedding got more and more out of hand.

Chandra, so quick to express her doubts about Jessie's marrying at all, did a total about-face concerning the wedding.

"Every mother should have the right to plan a special day for her daughter," she kept repeating in an aggrieved tone each time Jessie objected to ever-escalating guest lists. Chandra insisted on the rental—which horrified Jessie so that she almost suggested to Luke that they elope—of the Stanley Park Restaurant and Pavilion for the ceremony and the reception to follow.

Worst of all, Jessie confided morosely to Kathleen one afternoon, her mother had now joined forces with Lorna, and between the two of them, Jessie felt borne along by a whirlwind.

Kathleen was in town to order a new wheelchair, and Jessie had taken advantage of the trip by inviting her friend over to her house for lunch and sympathy.

Mike was asleep on Jessie's bed, and the women were keeping an eye on Chrissie, who was happily splashing in the hot tub.

"How's Lorna's Soup Kitchen going?" Kathleen sipped her iced tea, obviously reveling in the relaxed peace of Jessie's garden.

"Fantastic. Lorna had to hire another employee, and Luke and I are going to borrow the nephews on Saturdays after we're married so Denny can work with her that day."

"Super. Why not bring them out to visit us? Chrissie loves having kids visit." She waved to her daughter, who was jumping into the tub, sending waves of water splashing. "Denny must have changed his mind about Lorna's business. He didn't seem very pleased about the whole thing the day I met him," Kathleen observed.

Luke had given Jessie a hilarious, detailed account of the events surrounding Denny's rebellion. "I think he felt threatened at having such a successful businesswoman for a wife," Jessie summarized diplomatically, and Kathleen nodded.

"Men and women work out certain balances in a marriage, and almost regularly things come along that upset the scales and force change. It's happened several times to us. The first big upset, of course, was my accident, but it sure wasn't the last." She thought for a moment. "Change is necessary for growth, I guess. Each change we went through caused us lots of problems, individually and together, but after we bungled through each one, our marriage was stronger and so were we." She grinned and gave Jessie a mock bow. "And there you have Advice for Newlyweds by Professor Dodd."

"Now if you could just tell me how I can get my mother and Lorna to be reasonable about this damn wedding," Jessie moaned. "Luke's parents are coming, and I'm terrified about meeting them. My mother's invited the entire golf and country club. You're going to have to live through this as my attendant. Don't you mind that it's sounding more and more like a three-ring circus?"

Kathleen shook her head emphatically. "I get to wear that heavenly emerald silk dress your mother insisted on buying for me, and my new chair will be in by then and Joe will be overcome all over again by my beauty and my charm. And Mike is now on two bottles a day, which means we get to stay in town that night while a neighbor baby-sits for us." She winked lewdly before becoming practical again. "Besides, Jess, they're right, you know. Being married on the lawns in the park at sunset is absolutely romantic. If it doesn't rain," she added, like a true Vancouverite.

"It won't dare. Mother and Lorna have the poor guys at the weather bureau totally intimidated. They phone them every day for an updated forecast." There was a comfortable silence between them, and then Jessie confessed, "You know the only part I absolutely dread, Kath? It's selfish and childish, as well, but I wish there wasn't going to be a band or any dancing at my wedding.'' She stared moodily at the late blooming flowers in the lush garden without seeing them. The thought of not being able to waltz on her wedding eve, held close in her beloved's embrace, was bothering Jessie more than anything else, and there was no one who could fully understand. Except Kathleen.

"When you're on wheels,'' her friend said with soft nostalgia in her voice, "you and I both know there are situations up with which we simply have to put.''

Jessie met Kathleen's eyes, and a wealth of rueful understanding passed between them in a glance, a knowledge of all that was possible and an acceptance of much that wasn't.

"Thank you, Dr. Dodd. Is that your son I hear demanding his midafternoon snack?''

THE FOLLOWING SATURDAY evening Jessie and Luke were married. All the female guests wept copiously, insisting it was the most beautiful wedding they'd ever attended.

Jessie agreed wholeheartedly.

The verdant lawns in Stanley Park surrounding the stately Pavilion rolled fragrantly down to the manicured splendor of the rose gardens, and heady perfume from acres of roses in every hue floated in the warm air.

Everyone had forgotten that a twilight service outdoors in the park would necessarily be accompanied by the exotic and amusing noises of the animals and birds that occupied the zoo only a few hundred yards away. The ceremony was punctuated by the screams of peacocks, the chattering of monkeys, and at one crucial point the strange squeal and splash of Skana, the white whale, leaping for his dinner at the aquarium pool, followed by the clapping of all the strangers who celebrated his feat.

Jessie, in a simple long silk dress the exact shade of Luke's eyes, with satin slippers dyed to match, felt strangely blessed by the sounds, as if all of nature's creatures were approving their union, and the sun timed its splendorous disappearance beyond the far mountains exactly to the simple profundity of the minister's last words.

Crimson and gold spilled up from the rim of the world, bathing the last of the day in shades of glory as Jessie and Luke were bonded in the holiest of man's ceremonies.

The feast that followed was sumptuous, orchestrated by a proudly beaming Lorna.

John and Nellie Chadwick, Jessie's new in-laws, had swiftly welcomed her into their family, and it was obvious Lorna had done much groundwork in helping them adjust to a daughter-in-law in a wheelchair. They were warm and loving parents, and if Jessie was to be Luke's wife, then she was included unconditionally in that circle of love.

Luke was calmly confident through the entire day, but each smoldering glance he sent his bride hinted at magical hours alone, later, when they would celebrate their marriage in quite a different manner. Each glance sent a thrill of anticipation coursing through her.

The only discordant note came after dinner. Jessie determinedly ignored the arrival of the band, refusing to allow anything to interfere with the joy she felt, even as the tables were cleared away and the music began.

The first notes made Jessie's hands clench in sudden pain. She'd lost sight of Luke in the past few moments, and she steeled herself, trying to control her expression so that the longing inside didn't show on her features. She forced a smile, and Kathleen, Joe's arm fondly looped across her shoulders, caught her eye and sent her a thumbs-up signal from across the room.

Then, without warning, Luke Chadwick grasped the back of Jessie Chadwick's wheelchair and pushed her swiftly across the width of the hall and out the door, taking everyone by surprise. He left the startled wedding guests behind with a flourish and a wave of his arm.

Outside, night had fallen, and the air smelled of damp, freshly cut grass and evergreens. Jessie could just see the outline of the red Thunderbird, pulled close to the exit, its motor running.

"What's going on? Luke, you madman, what are you doing?"

Without a word he scooped her up and deposited her in the passenger's seat. With the deftness of long practice, he folded her chair and stowed it in the trunk.

When Luke had taken his place behind the wheel, he bent across and took a long silk scarf from the glove box. He pressed his lips to hers, lingering and sweet, and asked, "Trust me, Jess?"

Breathlessly, not even needing to consider it, she nodded. "Of course."

He fumblingly wound the scarf around her head, covering her eyes and knotting it, dislodging the simple circlet of dainty flowers and baby's breath she'd worn as a headpiece. He laid it gently on the seat beside her.

"Sit tight then, Mrs. Chadwick. We'll be there in fifteen minutes." He grasped her hand and rested it on his leg, as if he couldn't bear to be beside her without that small contact.

It was a unique sensation, sitting close beside him and relying on senses other than sight. She could feel his thigh beneath her hand, feel the iron-hard muscles tensing and releasing as he stopped at traffic lights, then accelerated again. Jessie smelled his special smell, after-shave and some particular heady scent that was strictly Luke, and she savored the thoughts that flitted through her mind of the miracle of being his love, his wife.

She avoided questions about where they were going, chatting instead about the day's occurrences.

"Doesn't Cy look happy?" Her old friend and his radiant new wife had arrived home for Jessie's wedding.

She could hear the smile in Luke's voice. "Cy looks tidier, and Amanda looks more disheveled. Did you hear him say they're taking a bike tour of Europe next spring?"

Jessie giggled. "I heard Amanda say that it would have to be a tandem bike so he could do all the pedaling." She was quiet for a time, and then she giggled again in fond reminiscence. "Luke, Denny was so funny when he made that speech. He's naturally amusing, and Lorna looked so proud of him."

Luke chuckled. "Your mother wasn't at all amused. I think Denny's a bit too much of a rough diamond for her."

"Dad likes him." Jessie remembered vividly the proud pleasure on her father's face today as he conducted her to where Luke and the minister waited.

"We want you to be happy, Jess," he'd whispered to her. "Your mother loves you dearly, and so do I." And Jessie believed him. In spite of everything, she understood that Chandra did love her.

Jessie imagined she could taste the night now slipping invisibly past her.

Her wedding night.

Luke lifted her fingers now and then and kissed them. He was feeling a tiny bit anxious about the scheme he'd concocted, but there was no turning back at this point. He followed an arterial path southeast of the city, through New Westminster, across the Queensborough Bridge. A sign indicated the secondary road to Annacis Island, and the car bumped across the neglected wooden bridge.

The island was a stretch of windswept sand in the middle of the south arm of the mighty Fraser River. The RCMP had used it for tactical training purposes occasionally, but mostly it was forgotten and deserted.

An autumn moon was rising, full and round and heavy in the night dark sky. Luke pulled to a stop.

Jessie listened curiously as the car's motor faded.

At first the silence was profound. Where was the traffic noise, the constant busy hum always under the surface of a city? Her heart drummed in anticipation. Of what? she wondered breathlessly. Luke's lips closed over her own for an instant in a kiss that made stars dance inside the darkness of her blindfold.

She heard his indrawn breath when he drew reluctantly away, felt him move to insert a tape in the car's tape deck, and then the soft overture began.

It was Beethoven's *Moonlight Sonata*.

The music dripped into the warm air and rose like incense on the breeze to fill her senses.

At last, when she thought she couldn't bear the suspense a heartbeat longer, he tugged at her blindfold.

Jessie blinked, her eyes adjusting first to darkness, then to the spill of light drifting like dust from the heavens as the autumn moon cast shadows on a vista of gray sand, rolling dunes, mystical secret hollows and hills. Far off the lights of the city twinkled like distant planets and in the sky were their star reflections, stretching to eternity.

She understood instantly. Luke had brought her to the moon, where all things were possible. Her eyes filled, making the scene shimmer, and she turned toward him. He was already out and around the car, opening the door.

Tenderly, reverently, he slid his arms around her and lifted her into his embrace, holding her slender length easily upright against him. She could feel his heart and her own, pounding in matching cadence. The breeze lifted her hair, depositing strands like silver ribbons on the shoulders of his dark suit.

Her arms rose, encircling his neck, and she floated, dancing, graceful and weightless and free as the music surged.

It was Jessie's wedding waltz.

IT'S NEVER TOO LATE FOR LOVE....

A SEASON FOR ROSES

A VERY SPECIAL SUPERROMANCE
BY A VERY SPECIAL AUTHOR

Ashley Harte is an elegant fifty-year-old widow whose fondest desire is someday to have grandchildren. But from the moment the handsome and distinguished Ryan McKay sets eyes on Ashley, he courts her with the fervor and determination of a man half his age. Ashley had always thought that romantic love was for her children's generation. Ryan McKay is about to prove her wrong....

A SEASON FOR ROSES is a heartwarming story, filled with the intensity that well-loved Superromance author Barbara Kaye always brings to romance.

Coming in April 1987

ROSES-1 BPA

Harlequin Superromance

COMING NEXT MONTH

#254 DRIVE THE NIGHT AWAY • Jocelyn Haley
Sara Deane thinks she's found love at last in the
arms of Cal Mathieson. But she's a teacher, he's a
woodworker, and Cal is adamant their relationship
won't work. Sensing that Cal's hiding the real
reason for his reluctance, Sara devises a plan to
uncover the truth. . . .

#255 TANGLED DREAMS • Lynn Erickson
When financial consultant Margery Lundstrom
meets Dr. Warren Yeager, a brilliant scientist, she
finds her emotions soaring. But she soon decides
he's beyond help in matters of romance. It's up to
him to prove her wrong. . . .

#256 CHANCES • Janice Kaiser
Blaine Kidwell is a professional poker player.
Caleb Rutledge is a man of the cloth. They've got
as much in common as a church and a gambling hall.
So why are they falling in love?

#257 A SEASON FOR ROSES • Barbara Kaye
Fifty-year-old widow Ashley Harte thinks romantic
love is for her children's generation. But the
handsome and distinguished Ryan McKay sets out
to change her mind.

PATRICIA MATTHEWS

America's First Lady of Romance upholds her long standing reputation as a bestselling romance novelist with...

Enchanted

Caught in the steamy heat of America's New South, Rebecca Trenton finds herself torn between two brothers—she yearns for one but a dark secret binds her to the other.

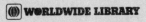

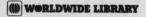

Can you keep a secret?

You can keep this one plus 4 free novels